Praise for the Mac McClellan Mysteries

DEADLY DUNES

"This story is addictive and an easy one to get lost in as the reader continues to turn pages. The characters are well-drawn, the even pace builds tension, and the ending satisfies. The author is adept at creating settings and has an eye for detail giving one the feeling they are a part of the landscape."
—Edie Dykeman, BellaOnline mystery reviewer

"Another deftly crafted mystery/suspense masterpiece from author E. Michael Helms, *Deadly Dunes* is the third title in his outstanding Mac McClellan Mystery series. Very highly recommended reading for action/adventure mystery buffs."
—The Midwest Book Review

"An apparent suicide, a missing map, a dead client—Mac's latest case takes him from the earliest history of modern Florida to a present day murder in his own backyard. The story grabs you on page one and the twists and turns don't let go until the do-or-die conclusion."
—Kait Carson, author of the Hayden Kent Mystery series

"Michael Helms has done it again! In this engrossing, nonstop action adventure, Mac McClellan investigates treasure hunters, greedy developers, and even greedier heirs."
—Connie di Marco, author of the Zodiac Mysteries and (as Connie Archer) author of the national bestselling Soup Lover's Mysteries

DEADLY RUSE

"An entertaining sequel.... Helms expertly steers the elaborate plot even as the stolen identities, suspicious missionaries, and diamond smuggling stretch credulity."
—Publishers Weekly

"Studly Mac and the bevy of available beauties who swarm around him should provide red meat for fans who still miss Travis McGee."
—Kirkus Reviews

Top Pick: "A wonderfully paced mystery that is filled with all the deceitful things a reader can find good when reading a book.... This was a great-high stakes mystery for any mystery or suspense lover."
—Bemiown, for Night Owl Reviews

"Roll on further McClellan adventures in the future!"
—Col's Criminal Library

"I loved the first novel in this series but absolutely adored this one. I couldn't put it down. It's a fast paced, easy, enjoyable read that was a delight."
—Pure Jonel: Confessions of a Bibliophile

"I love the fact that [Mac] is just a regular guy. He stumbles onto clues, follows leads, and does his best to fit the pieces together, though he sometimes makes mistakes."
—WiLoveBooks

"Full of familiar characters, as well as some colorful new ones, *Deadly Ruse* is a fast-paced mystery that will keep you on your toes. Highly recommended!"
—Epic Book Quest

I love a good mystery and this one is a real doozy! *Deadly Ruse* is fast-paced, full of drama, with a side of romance."
—Mary's Cup of Tea

DEADLY CATCH

"Read this tale and soak up single malt, inhale Mac's grilled potatoes and roasted onions, learn how to make marijuana brownies (first heat the canola oil ….), and join Mac in a really fine set piece toward the end. In fins and mask and carrying a camera, he goes under the dark water to document the villainy at dock's end. It's a scene reminiscent of Fleming, and it's the Mac we want to see if we meet again: a man of action, working alone."
—Don Crinklaw, Booklist

Starred Review/Debut of the Month: "This debut will resonate with retired military, boomers, and crime fiction fans. Helms's love of setting and engaging first-person narrative suggests a winning new series is underway."
—Library Journal

"*Deadly Catch*'s fast paced narrative is clear and concise. The main character is a likable guy whose involvement in this murder-mystery creates a tense situation."
—RT Book Reviews

"Readers will find themselves rooting for Mac and Kate as they read this extremely well-written mystery."
—*Suspense* Magazine

"This book has something for everyone with mystery, suspense and even a little bit of romance.
—Terry Ambrose, *The Snitch*

Pick of the Month: "A story you won't want to put down until the last page."
—Bookviews by Alan Caruba (charter member, the National Book Critics Circle)

"*Deadly Catch* gifts the reader with quirky characters and an intriguing plot."
—Fran Byram, Portland Book Review

"Helms avoids cliché and propaganda to create a three-dimensional hero who will appeal to a wide spectrum of readers."
—Eric Petersen, The Internet Review of Books

"*Deadly Catch* is a superb mystery thriller and a great first offering for a new series."
—Edie Dykeman, Bella Online Mystery Books Editor

"This fast-paced story starts off with a bang and doesn't let up until the last page turns!"
—Janna Shay, InD'tale Magazine

"Strong characters and an interesting setting make for a most satisfying read."
—Mysterious Reviews

"*Deadly Catch* is a firm foundation to a new series and great way to escape into a good mystery that will find you riding the twists and turns while trying to figure out who-dun-it!"
—Dianne Bylo, Tome Tender Book Reviews

"Mystery at its finest. I couldn't unravel it until the very end, and even then, I was stunned."
—Pure Jonel: Confessions of a Bibliophile

DEADLY
DUNES

DEADLY DUNES

A Mac McClellan Mystery

E. MICHAEL HELMS

CAMEL
PRESS

Seattle, WA

Camel Press
PO Box 70515
Seattle, WA 98127

For more information go to: www.camelpress.com
www.emichaelhelms.com

Cover design by Sabrina Sun

Deadly Dunes
Copyright © 2016 by E. Michael Helms

ISBN: 978-1-60381-347-1 (Trade Paper)
ISBN: 978-1-60381-348-8 (eBook)

Library of Congress Control Number: 2015955689

Printed in the United States of America

To Karen, my wife, lover, and best friend. Your belief, input, and dedication to my work has, and always will be, an inspiration that mere words can never convey.

———•———

Many thanks to Leslie McFarlane, whose early Hardy Boys mysteries (written under the nom de plume Franklin W. Dixon) provided me with countless hours of adventure, entertainment, and escape during a sometimes challenging boyhood; and to Ross Macdonald, Raymond Chandler, Robert B. Parker, John D. MacDonald, Jeremiah Healy, and Robert J. Ray, whose brilliant work inspired a novice to undertake the challenge of tossing his effort into the shark-infested genre of mystery. Gentlemen, one and all, I am honored to be counted among your tribe.

Chapter 1

———•———

MY GIRLFRIEND, KATE BELL, and I were sitting on her living room sofa waiting for the Final Jeopardy answer. The category was Major League Baseball. "That's a no-brainer," I said with supreme assurance. I'd been a baseball fanatic since I could walk. "You might as well concede."

"I beg to differ," Kate shot back.

"Pfft."

"Rib eye steaks here tomorrow after work," she said. "Loser buys."

"But tomorrow's my birthday. You're sup—"

She gave my bearded cheek a playful pinch. "Ooh, is the big bad Marine afraid he'll lose?"

"You're on!"

Kate and I met a little over a year ago when I rented a boat from her at Gillman's Marina. I had recently arrived in St. George—a quaint fishing/artsy village on the "Forgotten Coast" of Florida's panhandle—shortly after retiring from the Marine Corps. I don't believe in love at first sight, but with Kate's auburn hair, green eyes, and pretty face sprinkled with freckles, it was close. And she had moxie—another trait I admired from the get-go.

My visit to the panhandle began as a fishing vacation while I decided what to do with my post-Corps life. While fishing one morning I hooked the badly decomposed body of Maddie Harper, a popular young local woman. Further plans were put on hold when the local sheriff warned me not to leave Dodge. Maddie was only twenty when she died, the same age as my daughter, Megan. During the funeral I decided to find out who had snatched away her life and future. By hook and crook I solved her murder. Afterward, I decided to stay in St. George a while, thinking it might be time to put down roots. Meeting Kate had a little something to do with my decision, also. She'd been a big help in solving the case, and we'd been an item ever since.

The commercial ended. Alex Trebek repeated the category just as my phone rang with the opening refrain of "The Marines' Hymn." "Pause it," I said, fishing the phone from the cargo pocket of my shorts. Kate raised an eyebrow and frowned. *Oops.* "Please," I added. After twenty-four years, old habits are hard to break. I still sometimes relapsed into my commanding First Sergeant's voice.

I swiped the talk icon. "This is Mac."

"Mr. McClellan?"

"Speaking."

"My name is Jessie Lofton," a young woman said in a flat voice. "Mr. Frank Hightower suggested I call you. I'd like to retain your services."

"How can I help you, Ms. Lofton?"

"Someone murdered my brother. I want you to find out who did it, and why."

———————

WE AGREED TO MEET at ten thirty the next morning at Panama Joe's, a café near the city marina in downtown Panama City.

My prospective client's drive was a little longer than mine, but it would save her several miles. On the way to PC, I rehashed our conversation of the evening before. Long story short, Jessie Lofton taught nursing at Northwest Florida State College in Niceville. Normally that was the territory of my boss, Frank Hightower. However, Jessie's older brother, Jacob Lofton, was found dead in his car along an isolated stretch of Highway 71, a few miles south of Marianna. A gunshot wound. The incident occurred two months ago. Somehow I hadn't heard about it, probably because I was neck-deep in a case at the time. According to Jessie, her brother—an associate professor of archaeology at Florida State University—was headed to Palmetto County to conduct preliminary research on a possible archaeological site. He never made it. Palmetto County was my territory. Hence Frank's referral of the case to me.

I'd been a licensed private investigator for all of six weeks now. Frank, a retired Okaloosa County deputy sheriff and close family friend of the Bells, operated Hightower Investigations out of Destin, another beautiful coastal town seventy miles west. Destin is Frank and Kate's hometown. Frank was looking to extend his business eastward. When a ghost from Kate's past made an unexpected appearance a few months back, her world was turned upside down. Frank offered me on-the-job training as a PI in exchange for Kate's fee. The case ended—semi-successfully—shortly before I'd completed the necessary studies and requirements to satisfy the state of Florida. Looking into the death of Jacob Lofton would be my first official case as a bona fide private eye.

Jessie described herself as trim with long red hair. She'd be wearing a short-sleeved white blouse and blue jeans. During my previous case, another redhead had almost been my undoing, so I didn't take her hair color as a particularly good omen. It was a blazing hot August morning, and I was glad to get out of the heat and into the air-conditioned café.

As soon as I entered Panama Joe's, the aroma of ground

gourmet coffee beans and fresh-baked bread and pastries made my mouth water. I glanced around at the few customers scattered about and spotted Jessie seated in a secluded corner booth. I caught her eye and gave a quick wave so she'd know it was me, and then ordered a cup of dark roast coffee from the young lady working the counter.

It took effort to resist the glazed cinnamon-raisin buns beckoning from the glass case filled with baked goodies. The health kick Kate had dragged me into was taking a mental toll, although I'd lost a couple of pounds in the past few weeks. Another five and I'd be down to my fighting weight of one ninety. The slice of dry wheat toast I ate for breakfast would have to hold me for now, despite my protesting stomach.

Steaming mug in hand, I headed for the back of the room. Acoustic folk music flowed from surround-sound speakers. When I got a closer look at Jessie I almost dropped the mug. She was damn near the spitting image of Sissy Spacek in her heyday.

Jessie must've read my face. She held out her hand. "You were going to say I look like Sissy Spacek, weren't you?" she said as we shook hands.

I set the mug on the table and slid onto the bench opposite her. Jessie's fair skin was lightly freckled, and she had the prettiest shade of blue eyes I'd ever seen. Cornflower blue, I think it's called. Straight, strawberry-blonde hair and a pert nose. "Actually no, because I bet people say it all the time. But since you mentioned it, you could be her twin if you were the same age, which you're obviously not."

She flashed a friendly smile, something I never would've expected given the tone of her voice last evening. "Thank you. Sissy has thirty years on me, and no, I wouldn't have been offended if you had."

I returned the smile. "What, mentioned you look like Sissy Spacek, or asked your age?"

Jessie held the smile and my eyes. "Either."

"Since we're confessing, today happens to be my birthday."

"Well, happy birthday, Mr. McClellan."

I ran a hand through my sandy-blond hair, which now that I was in my early forties was beginning to show a little frost along the sides. "Thanks, I think. Please, call me Mac."

She laughed at my gesture. "If you'll call me Jessie."

"Done." A few seconds of awkward silence followed. It was time to put my PI license to work. "I'm sorry about your brother."

She took a sip of herbal tea and carefully placed the cup on a matching saucer beside a half-eaten croissant. Her nail polish matched her eyes, and I noticed she wasn't wearing a wedding ring. "Thank you. It was a terrible shock. Jake and I were very close."

I nodded and sipped the strong dark roast. "I took the liberty of looking up the incident in the online Marianna and Tallahassee newspapers last night. Both papers said Jacob's death was ruled a suicide."

Jessie sighed and looked away for a moment. "There's no way Jake would have shot himself," she said when our eyes met again. "He enjoyed life too much. He loved his job, and he was absolutely crazy about his two boys. He would never have done such an awful thing to hurt them."

Maybe, maybe not. "One of the articles mentioned a recent separation. Could be your brother was despondent over his marriage falling apart."

Jessie frowned. "It's true Laurel had been having an affair for several months, with a coach from the middle school where she works as school nurse." She idly stirred her tea. "I feel partly responsible because I encouraged Jake to go out with Laurel when she and I were student nurses. They had known each other in high school, just as friends. Jake was shy, and he wasn't seeing anyone at the time. I thought it would be good for him to get out for a change instead of spending all his time cooped up in his room studying. Laurel was always the hot-blooded type, but she seemed to settle down once she and Jake began dating seriously.

"Anyway, Jake was upset over the affair, but he certainly wasn't suicidal. When he found out about it he begged Laurel to break it off and go to counseling with him. She refused, so he went by himself to deal with the situation as best he could. He kept hoping Laurel would change her mind, but she didn't. About three months ago she moved in with the guy and took the twins with her. Jake was devastated, but at least Laurel was decent enough to let him spend as much time with the boys as he could."

"Twins? How old?"

My daughter Megan and son Mike were twins. Mike was attending UNC Wilmington on a baseball scholarship. Megan was at North Carolina State studying to become a veterinarian.

"Almost five. Clark and Kent. Cute, huh?" Jessie wasn't smiling.

"I take it Jake was a big Superman fan?"

"No, it was Laurel's idea. She had the absolute hots for Brandon Routh, the actor who starred in *Superman Returns*. Jake was more into the Hardy Boys and Indiana Jones. He probably would have named the boys Frank and Joe if he'd had his way. He absolutely loved the Hardy Boys. He read every one of their mysteries when we were kids. I think he collected most of the books in the series. Jake would read them to the boys for their bedtime story, even though he knew they couldn't understand most of what was going on yet." She gave a little laugh. "I think he wanted to relive the experience through sharing the books with his sons."

I waved to a waitress working tables and held up my mug. There was a small teapot near the napkin holder. I picked it up and topped off Jessie's cup.

"Thanks, Mac."

"You're welcome. Speaking of Indiana Jones, you mentioned Jake was an archaeologist. You said he was on his way to Palmetto County to research something?"

Jessie added an opened half-packet of sweetener to her tea.

"Yes. It was supposed to be another quick trip to St. George to conduct a preliminary visual survey of the area. Jake had been there twice before that I know of, but he wanted to be certain he had enough evidence before he took it to the department head to present his case for a possible site excavation. If it turned out to be what Jake believed it was, it could have been his ticket to a full professorship." She exhaled slowly, as if weary of relating the story.

"About a year ago Jake was researching at the State Library in Tallahassee, and accidentally discovered an old document buried in the Spanish Land Grants collection. Somehow it got misplaced there, because the land grants date from the late 1700s. That's about a hundred and fifty years later than Jake dated the document he found. Jake thought it might have been a missing entry written by Rodrigo Rangel that had somehow gotten lost from a copy of his original logs."

The waitress walked up with a decanter and refilled my cup with dark roast. I thanked her and turned my attention back to Jessie. "Who was this Rangel?"

"He was de Soto's personal secretary."

"DeSoto?" I hated to show my ignorance, but it had been a long time since I'd studied anything other than military tactics and more recently, private investigator lessons. The only DeSoto I remembered was an out-of-production automobile.

Jessie eyed me over the rim of her cup. "Hernando de Soto was a sixteenth-century Spanish explorer. He and his men landed in Florida and spent the winter of 1539 to 40 in Tallahassee. At the time it was the capital of the Apalachee Indian Nation."

She placed her cup on the saucer. "Jake believed a party of around fifty of de Soto's men might have traveled south to the coast that winter. The document stated they traveled thirty-eight leagues to reach their winter quarters. A league is about 2.6 miles. It works out to roughly a hundred miles, considering the route they would've most likely taken. The distance would be the same if you drove the same route today. From the description, Jake believed they spent the winter somewhere on or near Five Mile Island. At the time it was a peninsula rather than a true island."

Five Mile Island. That's where I'd discovered the body of Maddie Harper. This story was getting more interesting by the minute. "You seem to know your history."

Jessie smiled. "Not so much. I told you Jake and I were always close. Our parents died in an accident several years ago, and the only other family we have is our paternal grandmother, Jake's boys, and my daughter."

"You have a daughter?"

Jessie's brilliant blue eyes brightened. "Yes, Sydni just turned fourteen. I was still in high school and convinced I was in love, like so many other foolish girls with stars in their eyes. When her father found out I was pregnant, he wanted nothing more to do with me or the baby."

"Did you at least nail the SOB for child support?"

Jessie shook her head. "Since he chose to abandon us, I wanted no part of him in our lives. So I've been a single mom all these years."

I wondered why she hadn't met someone decent and gotten married during the course of fourteen years. She was damn sure attractive enough, but it was none of my business so I didn't go there. "What about your grandmother?"

"She's in assisted living suffering from dementia, so there's not much support there. I suppose losing our parents drew Jake and me even closer. Anyway, we kept up with each other's lives regularly, including our careers."

I hesitated a moment. The subject I was about to bring up wasn't a pleasant one, but it was part of the job and had to be addressed. "I don't want to upset you, but I need to ask. What about the weapon Jake supposedly used?"

Jessie finished a bite of the croissant, pulled a fresh napkin from the holder, and lightly wiped her lips. "Jake didn't own a gun. He hated them. When he was twelve, his best friend was killed in a hunting accident. After that, he had nothing to do with guns of any kind."

I hated playing devil's advocate, but it came with the territory. "Then how did the weapon wind up in your brother's car with his fingerprints all over it?"

Jessie locked her big blue eyes on mine and frowned. "I don't know. The police called it a Saturday night special. The serial numbers were filed off so it couldn't be traced. They said Jake probably bought it illegally from someone on the streets. But I don't believe he had anything to do with it. I know he didn't."

When we'd first introduced ourselves, I'd noticed a large manila envelope on the bench between Jessie and the wall. I'd been waiting for her to mention it, but I guess she needed a little prodding. "Any other information you can give me about Jake's death or the research he was doing?"

She reached for the envelope and laid it on the table. "I have a copy of a map Jake was using in his research. I don't know whether it was part of the Rangel document or not. He didn't say." She opened the flap, pulled out a sheet of paper, and handed it to me. It showed a narrow peninsula jutting from the mainland a good distance and turning about ninety degrees to the west where it gradually widened. If you laid it on its eastern coastline, it roughly resembled South America. "Jake believed this was Five Mile Island as it appeared at the time of de Soto's expedition. I made this copy for you, hoping it might help with the investigation. Please don't let anyone else see it."

I gave the map a quick once-over. Today Five Mile Island resembles a pork chop running east to west from the small end to the big. With a little imagination, and knowing what damage over half a millennium of tropical storms and hurricanes might do, it was conceivable I was looking at Five Mile Island before it became an island. I tapped a finger on some letters and numbers inside a block. "Do you know what this writing means?"

"It's a scale, but in leagues," Jessie said. "According to the scale, the main body of the peninsula would lie approximately five miles from the mainland, and would be about seven miles in length from where it makes the westerly turn."

The locals said Five Mile Island got its name from being located about five miles off the mainland, and about five miles in length from stem to stern. Storms could account for the lost distance in length. I pointed to what I figured was the map's title. "What does this say?"

"*La Península de los Médanos Grande.* I'm no Spanish scholar, but roughly it means 'The Peninsula of the Great Sand Dunes.'"

That fit. Even after all these years the undeveloped areas of the island were loaded with impressive sand dunes on the gulf side, especially the last two miles of the western end, now a state park. "And this?" I tapped my index finger on what looked like a drawing of a small rectangular enclosure. It was located about three-quarters down the western end of the peninsula where a thumb-shaped spit of land jutted into the bay.

"*El fuerte invierno.* The winter fort."

"Looks to me like your brother might've been on to something. But I'm betting it would take more than an unproven log entry and a copy of an old map to verify de Soto's men ever set foot on Five Mile Island."

Jessie glanced around and then pinned me with those big blues again. "You can't breathe a word of this to anyone," she said as she slid her hand inside the envelope. Her knuckles bent the top upward as she dragged something onto the table with her fingertips, making sure whatever it was stayed hidden behind her cup and saucer. She looked around again, and then pushed a rusted elongated object and a tarnished coin to me.

I cupped my hand over the objects and took a close look. The rusted piece of iron was about three-and-a-half inches long with a broken or worn-away hollow end. It gradually slimmed toward the other end and then formed a definite triangular point similar to a small arrowhead. "What is it?"

"The iron tip of a crossbow bolt," Jessie said, "identical to ones found at de Soto's winter encampment in Tallahassee."

"Bolt?"

"It's what they called the arrows for the crossbows."

I looked up and studied her eyes. "Looks like Jake was doing more than a visual survey."

She nodded. "The copper coin is also identical to at least one found at the Tallahassee site. It was minted in Spain in the early 1500s."

The coin was notched irregularly in several places around the edge, and whatever was imprinted on the front and back had been scoured by five-hundred years of shifting sand. I slid the coin and bolt-tip back to Jessie. "Where did he find these?"

She slipped the two objects back inside the envelope, took a deep breath, and let it out slowly. "On the island near the bay overlooking what Jake described as a dead forest sticking out of the water."

"The Stumps?" It was a popular fishing spot not far from the eastern border of the state park.

Jessie shrugged. "I'm not familiar with the name, but it sounds like it could be the place."

"How did you get these?"

She glanced around the room again. "Jake knew he'd be risking his career if he showed the relics to the department head, so he gave them to me to keep in my safe deposit box. If permission was eventually granted for a dig, he planned to slip them back among the artifacts found at the site."

"Are there any others?"

"A few."

"What are they?"

She pressed her lips together. "I'd rather not say right now. They're all in the safe deposit box."

"Are you the only one who has access to the box?"

"No. I have a friend who's a co-signer."

"This friend … is he or she trustworthy?"

Jessie flashed me a stern look. "Absolutely. I'd rather not say who it is, though."

"I understand. Do you know who owns the land where Jake found these?" To my knowledge there wasn't a square inch of Five Mile Island not privately owned except for the state park. That meant Jake was trespassing and illegally took the artifacts, unless he'd contacted the owner for permission.

She shook her head. "He didn't say."

"Do you have a copy of the Rangel document?"

Jessie lifted a hand to her forehead and pinched the bridge of her nose as if she had a headache. "It's missing. Jake snapped photos of the original copy with his cellphone when he came across it in the library. It was such a potentially huge discovery he didn't even share what he'd found with the library staff. That's why he didn't have them make copies. He wanted to keep it hush-hush, at least until he had time to conduct further research. He planned to print a copy from his computer for his field studies and give it to me for safekeeping when he finished his survey. It wasn't found in the car when he … died, but it should have been. I've turned his house upside down, but haven't been able to find it."

"What about his cellphone?"

"It's missing too, along with the iPad he used in the field. And I've checked his home computer files. There's no evidence of the document or map there, either."

"So, Jake didn't want a bunch of copies of the document or map floating around where others might get their hands on them?"

"I think that was his reasoning."

"Do you have access to Jake's place?"

She nodded. "Laurel hasn't put it on the market yet, and I have a key. She walked in on me one day while I was there, and wasn't happy about it. I made up an excuse about looking for photos and personal items Jake and I owned when we were kids. She told me not to mess with his things. She wanted the key back, so I gave it to her. But I happen to have another."

"Do you have it with you?"

"No, it's in a safe place. I don't want to take a chance of losing it."

"The safe deposit box?"

She smiled. "No. Let's just say it's in good hands."

I let the guessing game drop. Something told me the missing copy of the old Spanish document had more than a little to do with Jake's untimely demise, if in fact he hadn't offed himself, as Jessie assured me was the case. The missing cellphone and iPad added another layer of doubt about the supposed suicide. Why would Jake have ditched the phone and iPad before he killed himself? And if it wasn't a suicide, maybe whoever did Jake in had conveniently lifted the items after killing him.

"Mac?"

Jessie's voice snapped me out of my who, what, and why mode. "Yeah?"

She leaned forward, both arms resting on the table. "This might be important. A few months after the boys were born, Laurel urged Jake to take out a life insurance policy. Five hundred thousand dollars."

I whistled. "What about a suicide clause?"

She sighed. "The company's policy had a two-year waiting period requirement. Laurel collected every penny. I know Jake took out the policy to take care of Laurel and the boys in case something should happen to him, but the first thing Laurel did was buy a brand new Corvette Grand Sport. That's hardly a soccer mom vehicle."

Probably to assuage her grief, I almost said, but didn't. I could sense more than a hint of sisterly jealousy in Jessie's voice.

"I've also heard she's looking at a foreclosure home on Lake Jackson," she continued before I could comment. "I doubt there'll be anything left of the insurance money for the boys' education."

Sweet Laurel seemed like the epitome of a doting mother—doting on herself, that is. "You think Laurel had anything to do with your brother's death?"

Jessie's brow furrowed and her lips pressed tightly together. "At first, no, but now I'm not so sure."

"Do you have a photo of Laurel with you?"

Jessie thought for a moment. "Of course I have photos on my phone … but yes, I do have one I can give you that shows Jake and Laurel together. It was taken not long after they were married. Laurel hasn't changed much, except she wears her hair shorter nowadays." She retrieved a wallet from her purse, took out a snapshot, and handed it to me.

The smiling newlyweds stood beside a white sedan, each with an arm wrapped around the other's waist. Laurel's free hand touched Jake's chest, conveniently showing off her wedding and engagement rings. Jake Lofton bore a close resemblance to Jessie in bone structure and coloration—a studious young man with a full shock of red hair, not exactly handsome but certainly not bad looking either. Laurel was either wearing heels or was a good inch or so taller than Jake. She had a pretty, heart-shaped face and a model's figure—slinky, with nicely flared hips. Telltale dark roots hinted the blonde locks cascading past her shoulders came from a bottle. "You said I can keep this for now?"

"Sure." Jessie closed the wallet and slipped it back in her purse.

I thanked her and put the photo in my wallet. "What's Jake and Laurel's home address?"

"Why do you need that?"

I hesitated a moment as our eyes met. "It's part of the job, Jessie. You never know."

She pinched the bridge of her nose again, and then opened her purse and took out a small notepad and a pen. She took a couple of minutes jotting down info and then tore off the sheet and handed it to me. "That's Jake's home address on top. The others are the school where Laurel and her boyfriend Steve Vann work, his apartment, and both their cellphone numbers."

Jessie had certainly done her homework. I questioned her a few more minutes, but she'd already spilled about as much as she knew about her brother's supposed suicide and the Five Mile Island project he'd been researching. I thanked her for coming and said I'd keep her updated on anything I found relating to the case. She promised to do the same.

Jessie reached for her purse and pulled out a checkbook. I held up a hand like a traffic cop. "You'll be paying Frank. He'll bill you, and make sure I get my cut. I'll do my best to talk him into giving you a good discount."

She smiled and slipped the checkbook back into her purse. "Thanks."

I started to stand but Jessie reached across the table and grabbed my wrist. "Wait, Mac, there's something else you should know."

I eased back onto the bench and waited. Jessie released her grip and fiddled with the teacup. Her hands shook slightly, and she seemed to struggle finding the right words. Finally she looked up and I noticed her eyes moistening. "When my brother was a child he was under the care of a psychologist for several years." She hesitated a moment. "The hunting accident I mentioned? It was Jake who shot his best friend."

Chapter 2

————————•————————

Jessie's last-minute revelation threw a big monkey wrench into her contention that Jake hadn't offed himself, just as the Jackson County medical examiner concluded and the media reported. The fact that a young Jake was responsible for his best friend's accidental death twenty years ago might have led to lingering psychological problems. Maybe he felt guilty for stealing possibly priceless artifacts on private property without permission. Toss in a cheating wife and not being able to be a full-time dad to his twin boys, and you had plenty of factors that might have pushed him over the edge. Jessie's argument was leaking water like a rusted-out sieve.

On the drive back to St. George, I gave Frank a call and brought him up to date, conveniently leaving out any mention of the artifacts Jake pilfered. "That tidbit does put a damper on Miss Lofton's theory," Frank said after I'd told him about the eleventh-hour bombshell Jessie dropped in my lap.

"Understatement of the year. Do you have any deputy friends working in Jackson or Leon County?"

Frank hesitated a moment. "A couple, maybe, if they're still around. It's been a while since we've made contact."

"Can you find out, and pick their brains on what they know about Lofton's suicide?"

Frank let out a big sigh. "This is supposed to be your case."

"So dock my pay. Look Frank, those guys wouldn't know me from Adam's second cousin. I doubt they'd give me the time of day even if I got on my knees and spit-shined their shoes. You cops are a fraternity. They'll talk to you."

"And what do you intend to do in the meantime?"

"I'm going fishing."

"Should I ask?"

"No, but I'll tell you anyway. Jessie showed me a copy of a copy of a map of Five Mile Island she got from her brother. It could be related to a project Lofton was working on when he supposedly killed himself. Jessie thinks it's important, so I thought I'd check it out and see what I can turn up."

"Sounds to me like you're chasing wild geese and wasting company time."

"Hey, Frank?"

"Yeah?"

"Don't forget to find out what happened to Lofton's car, and if the forensics are airtight. If there's any possibility of a loophole, I want to know about it."

Another grumbled sigh. "Anything else I can do for you while I'm doing your job, Mac?"

"That about covers it … for now."

———

To MY EVERLASTING EMBARRASSMENT and the detriment of my male ego, I'd missed the Final Jeopardy answer by a year. I could've sworn the New York Giant's Bobby Thomson belted the "Shot Heard 'Round the World" to beat the Dodgers for the pennant in 1952. Adding salt to the wound, Kate correctly picked 1951. I'd never live it down.

Gulf Grocery wasn't running any steak specials, but an ad in the morning newspaper I'd read before my meeting with

Jessie Lofton informed me the Piggly Wiggly in Parkersville was. I stopped there on my way back to St. George and bought two thick rib eyes and a bottle of Kendall-Jackson Cabernet Sauvignon, one of Kate's favorite reds.

I killed the afternoon in my travel trailer, a twenty-two foot Grey Wolf, watching a Braves rubber match game with the Cubs. I'd rented site 44 at Gulf Pines Campground when I'd arrived in St. George, and it had been home sweet home ever since. After the game I booted up my laptop and researched Hernando de Soto's winter layover in Tallahassee. Anhaica was the name of the Apalachee Nation's capital village. The center of de Soto's encampment was located on the grounds of the Governor John Martin House, almost within sight of the present Florida State Capitol building. I even learned the correct spelling of the explorer's name.

At six o'clock sharp I showed up on Kate's front porch with the wine, steaks, and my self-concocted secret rub—only the dearly departed are entitled to know its ingredients. She greeted me with a lingering happy birthday kiss. I could hardly wait for dessert.

I did the grilling honors while Kate made her special bacon and cheddar double-stuffed baked potatoes and a salad. We enjoyed the feast at the picnic table on the deck, listening to the murmur of the surf and watching the sun disappear behind the backyard neighbor's house.

Dinner left me as stuffed as the leftover potato Kate planned to send home with me. The steaks hadn't survived. Neither of us were big on sweets, so after Kate sang the obligatory "Happy Birthday Song," we shared a cupcake she'd bought with a single candle and "43" iced on the top. Kate was looking particularly sexy tonight. At thirty-six, she had hardly any wrinkles, despite living her entire life on the gulf coast. I hoped the wish I'd made before blowing out the candle came true.

I poured Kate a refill of wine and stepped into the kitchen to switch to Scotch on the rocks. On my way out the door, I heard whimpering from the general direction of Kate's bedroom. I listened closely for a minute, wondering if a child was crying outside the house, but it had stopped. I chalked it up to my imagination and sat beside Kate on the glider.

"Where's my present?" I said, my voice competing with a symphony of crickets and tree frogs.

Kate glanced at me for a second, and then stared out at the yard and the growing darkness dotted by the occasional flash of a firefly. "What on earth makes you think you deserve a present?"

I sipped my Scotch and stared at her. She was fighting back a smile. "Well, the way you laid it on me at the door when I showed up, I was hoping there'd be more where that came from."

"What? Oh, you!" She gave my forearm a playful slap. "You're incorrigible, MacArthur McClellan." She leaned over and pecked me on the cheek. "I do have a little something for you, but you have to promise not to peek."

I grinned. "Something warm and snuggly, I hope."

Another slap, harder this time. "Dang, you have a one-track mind sometimes, you know that?"

"I—"

"But it just so happens you're right. It *is* something warm and snuggly. Now, promise you won't peek and I'll go get your present."

I promised and Kate disappeared into the house. I was having visions of her prancing out in a skimpy, furry Victoria's Secret outfit when she broke my reverie. "Hands over the eyes and keep 'em shut tight," she commanded from the door as it swung open.

I held my free palm over my left eye and covered the other with the back of my hand holding the tumbler. I tracked her footsteps until she stood in front of me.

"Okay, you can look now."

I opened my eyes and there stood the cutest damn Doberman

puppy trying to wriggle out of a squatting Kate's grasp. She turned the pup loose and he ran two or three tight circles and then tried to jump into my lap. The black and tan ball of energy fell back and tumbled for his effort, but he regained his footing in a flash and tried again. This time I caught him, christening him with a slosh of Dewar's as he stood on my lap and slathered my face with his tongue.

"Happy birthday, Mac!" Kate was grinning like a Cheshire cat.

I set the almost-empty tumbler down and stood with my gift under one arm and the other wrapped around Kate. As I kissed her, I felt the puppy licking my neck and chin, obviously trying to help me with my task. "Thanks, I love him," I said, having noted the big blue ribbon tied around the pup's neck.

"Well, I'm glad, and relieved. I wasn't quite sure how you'd react."

"Are you kidding? A Devil Dog? I couldn't have asked for a better gift." Then I grinned. "Well, there is *one* thing."

Kate arched an eyebrow but spared the slap. "Okay, he's not AKC registered, but he is full-blooded. He has all his puppy shots and as you can see, he's been cropped and docked."

"He's been what?"

"His ears and tail, Mac. They don't come like that, you know."

"What about—?"

"Don't worry, his manhood is intact. Best of all, he's a rescue dog."

"A rescue? He's just a pup."

"Don't ask, because it's a sad story and I'd rather not talk about it. All he needs now is a good home."

I gave Kate another one-armed hug, and the Dobie and I both smothered her with kisses. "He's got one now." It would be nice having full-time company. The Grey Wolf felt lonesome at times. "What's his name?"

Kate crossed her arms and pressed an index finger below her pursed lips. "I've thought of one, but it's up to you."

The puppy was trying to wriggle out of my arms, so I gave in and set him down. He launched off the deck like a bottle rocket, chasing and snapping at fireflies as he sped around Kate's fenced-in backyard. "Okay, shoot."

"Well, you were born on August eighth, so I thought, 'What would be unique to the month of August, or the number eight or eighth?'"

"And?"

"My first thought was Augustus Caesar, but I didn't think you'd like either name, so I concentrated on the number. Then I thought, 'What oversexed cad from history would you admire for his unbridled behavior?' Kate hesitated a moment, and then swept an arm toward the bounding Dobie. "Behold, Henry the Eighth!"

I scrunched up my nose at Kate's good-natured insult about the cad I admired and tried not to laugh at the name. Henry? Kate pouted and pretended to look crestfallen. "Can I at least nickname him Hank?"

Her smile returned and she gave me a warm hug. "Behold, Hank the Eighth!"

"Hank. Period."

Another wave of the arm. "Behold, Hank!"

———

A COUPLE OF HOURS and drinks later, Kate and I were sitting hip to hip on the glider, listening to soothing waves rolling ashore and gazing at the sky for shooting stars. Hank wore himself out in his futile attempt to catch fireflies and was snoozing at our feet, snoring lightly. Now and then one body part or another twitched in reaction to his puppy dream.

Kate snuggled tighter against me and pressed her cheek against mine. I smelled her hair and was just getting warmed up as she pushed me away. "Your cheek feels like sandpaper. You need to shave."

Kate had never been one to mince words. I felt my cheeks

above the beard. Not too bad. *"Mañana."*

Kate frowned. *"Esta noche,* if you want your other birthday present."

I knew when I was licked. I was about to head for the half-bath where I kept a ditty bag containing a toothbrush and razor and other toiletries when my phone rang. Hank looked up and yawned, and then rested his head back on his big paws. I grabbed the phone. "This is Mac."

"Mac, it's Frank. I'm afraid I have bad news."

I sat up straight, my fatigue gone in a rush. Frank had my full attention. "What is it?"

"I heard from a deputy friend of mine in Walton County a few minutes ago. Jessie Lofton's car hit a bridge abutment west of Freeport this afternoon. The car rolled down the bank and wound up in the drink."

"Damn." I felt Kate's hands tighten around my arm and saw the concern in her face. "How is she?"

"She's dead, Mac."

Chapter 3

———•———

THE NEWS OF JESSIE Lofton's death blew away any air of romance. The first thing I did when Hank and I got home from Kate's was to walk behind my camper and take a leak. It was a private enough area for the task at hand—nothing but pine trees and bushes, and well-shielded from the glow of the campground's street lamps. The pup was a smart one and seemed to catch on right away. He sniffed around and then squatted and peed next to where I'd gone. I praised him and he followed me inside. I skipped a nightcap and we crawled into my double bed.

The bad news about Jessie kept me awake. I got up and read awhile, but the book didn't hold my interest. I hit the rack again and tried to sleep. No dice. A couple of times I got up to make an outside head call with Hank. The Dobie proved to be a fast learner and did all his business outside throughout the night. We needed to have a little discussion about his snoring, though.

The next morning around ten I guided my rental boat slowly out of City Canal and across the sandbar, and then gunned the motor. I'd rented this same twenty-one-foot center console from Gillman's Marina for over a year now. I kept threatening to buy a boat of my own, but somehow managed to talk myself out of it for one reason or the other. Maybe next week, or month.

Hank was quite a sight, suited up in his brand-new fluorescent-orange doggie life jacket. He stood on his hind legs with his front paws propped on the bow deck. I'd placed a rubber floor mat from my Silverado on the main deck so Hank would have better footing. His ears lay back in the wind and his tongue lolled out the right side of his mouth. Even with Kate's employee discount, the jacket cost me over fifty bucks, but I figured Hank was worth it. Besides, Kate would be more than a little pissed if my birthday gift was to drown and become crab bait on our maiden voyage together.

It was a beautiful morning. High wisps of clouds like shredded cotton shared the blue sky with wheeling gulls riding the thermals. Low-flying terns searched the bay waters for their breakfast. The salt air smelled great and a brisk southerly breeze kept the heat down, but I had to slack back the throttle to avoid giving Hank a shower as I steered for the Stumps near the border of Five Mile Island State Park.

When I was about fifty yards from the most outlying of the dead pine trunks I cut the throttle to a leave-no-wake speed and steered to the west side of the Stumps to adjust for the strengthening wind now blowing across our port. A few feet from the sandy shore I cut the motor and heaved the fifty horsepower Mercury's shaft to a tilting position. With a light jolt the bow skidded ashore a couple of feet, but the contact was enough to throw Hank off balance. He tumbled sideways and slid toward the stern, then scrambled up and regained his footing.

I stepped onto the gunnels, jumped to dry beach, and clapped my hands at Hank. Bounding up and over, he landed belly deep in the shallows. Instead of coming to me, he scampered off after a flock of sandpipers feeding along the shoreline. I tugged the boat a couple of more feet ashore, grabbed the anchor, and tossed it a few yards inland. I stretched and jogged after Hank, only to find he was hustling back my way with tongue flapping, chasing the sandpipers, who'd doubled back.

The area called the Stumps by the locals was once a forest of virgin longleaf pines on a spit of land jutting into the bay from Five Mile Island. Decades ago an unnamed hurricane churned its way up the bay and cut the pine forest off from the rest of the main island. Over time the small forested island gradually eroded, leaving the big pines to a watery fate. The resin in many of the trunks hardened and turned the trees into fat lighter, a much-sought-after wood that's impervious to rot and is mostly used to light fireplaces or campfires.

About midpoint through the Stumps, I stood on the beach and gazed inland at the dunes. They started upward in a gentle slope and then veered sharply into a high vegetated bluff. Somewhere up there the late Jacob Lofton recently discovered evidence of a possible encampment by a contingent of Hernando de Soto's 16th-century band of explorers. I wondered if Jake had noticed the prominent No Trespassing signs posted up and down the beach beyond the legally recognized high-water mark. I hadn't fished this area in over three months. The signs hadn't been there then.

I whistled and clapped for Hank to come. He broke off his frolicking and obeyed, though he did get distracted a couple of times before he finally reached me. I tied a ten-foot length of yellow polyester line to the clasp between the shoulders of Hank's vest, and we headed east along the beach. We traveled a good two miles before turning back. With few exceptions, about every fifty yards one of the new No Trespassing signs was spiked into the sand. It didn't take a rocket scientist to figure out someone had been buying up a huge portion of Five Mile Island, and fairly recently. I did notice one sizeable strip of beach, maybe a hundred and fifty yards or so, with no signs in sight. A dilapidated dock jutted several yards into the bay, and an old wooden boat had been dragged ashore. Whoever was gobbling up the bay front property hadn't gotten their hands on that prime piece yet.

Back in the boat, we cruised eastward twenty yards offshore. I sketched a rough map on the back of a fuel receipt ticket given to me by Donnie Hoover, the new chief mechanic at Gillman's, when I gassed up before setting out this morning. I'm no artist, but I jotted down landmarks along the shore and made a note of roughly where the signs ended and began again. My best guess was there were only four or five parcels of bayside land that hadn't been sold or resold to whoever was buying up the island. A trip to the county courthouse was in order.

The last of the signs was about a quarter-mile west of the Trade Winds Lodge, near where I'd found the body last year. A short distance east of the Trade Winds was the causeway leading back to the mainland. We'd covered the area between the state park and the causeway, so I steered a north-northwest course across the bay toward the marina.

———·———

FRANK DID A LOT of phone and footwork on Tuesday while Hank and I had our little adventure on Five Mile Island. Frank called around noon Wednesday to bring me up to date on what he'd learned.

Topping the good news was that Jessie's daughter would be taken care of by her godparents, Ron and Angie Decker of Destin. They'd accepted the role at Sydni's christening when she was a few months old. The Deckers had three children of their own, a daughter who was two years older than Sydni and happened to be one of her closest friends, and two younger sons.

The good news out of the way, it was time to hear the bad. "According to the FHP report, Jessie's right front tire suffered a catastrophic failure at the worst possible moment," Frank said. "She was probably speeding, and when the tire blew and came apart, her car veered right onto the narrow shoulder. She tried to steer back toward the road but the bridge abutment was blocking her path. The car hit right of center and tumbled down the embankment, landing upside down in the bayou. A passing motorist noticed the rear tires sticking out of the water, but by then it was too late."

"Catastrophic failure?"

"Basically it means the tire exploded and caused the driver to lose control of the vehicle."

"What kind of car was she driving?"

"Brand new Mustang convertible. It still had temporary plates."

"Red?"

"Yeah."

"I saw it parked outside the coffeehouse where Jessie and I met. What would cause a tire with only a few miles on it to blow like that?"

"Your guess is as good as mine. Factory defect, under-inflation, act of God. I don't know, Mac, but it happens."

"But for it to happen exactly when and where it did, Jessie couldn't have asked for worse luck."

"I won't argue the point."

"Was the top up or down?" I doubt it would've done much to increase Jessie's odds of surviving the crash given the circumstances, but I wondered about the manila envelope containing the artifacts her brother discovered on Five Mile Island.

"Down. The report states she survived the initial crash but was trapped underneath the vehicle and apparently drowned. The official autopsy results won't be available for a few days."

"Damn." I felt sick to my stomach, realizing the horrible fate that had befallen the vibrant young woman I'd talked with Monday morning. Not to mention the grief her daughter must be feeling. "Any personal effects recovered? Jessie had a manila envelope with her. It contained a few items important to the case."

"The FHP said unidentified paraphernalia were found scattered along the embankment. The car rolled, remember."

"Can you find out if they recovered the envelope?"

"I'll do my best."

"Thanks. Hey, Frank?"

"Yeah?"

"I don't want to drop the case. There's too much on the table to let it go. Jessie was positive her brother was murdered, and then she dies on her way home after our meeting. A little too coincidental, don't you think?"

Frank exhaled. "Somehow I figured you'd say that. It'll have to be on your nickel, Mac. We no longer have a paying client."

"I know, but my gut tells me I need to dig into this until I at least turn up some answers, one way or the other. I think Jessie deserves that much. And I damn well know her daughter does."

———

I WAS TIRED OF my own cooking, so Thursday morning I drove to Carl's Sandwich Shop for breakfast. Carl's was located directly across Highway 98 from Gillman's Marina, and Kate and I often met there for lunch. I'd never met Carl and I wasn't certain he even existed, but Denise, who worked the counter most days, was as friendly as they come and not at all hard on the eyes. Plus she made the best damn BLTs this side of wherever.

While I was sitting at the counter drinking coffee and waiting for my BLT, I thought about where I stood in the Lofton case. Jake Lofton was found dead in his car from a gunshot wound to the right temple on June eighth. That was around the same time the case I'd been working on came to a head at the Palmetto Royale Casino and Resort. Exactly two months to the day later, Jessie Lofton is killed in a single-car accident a few hours after our meeting in Panama City. There was too much coincidence here. If Jessie was correct in her assumption Jake was murdered, then somebody must've known she was sniffing the trail. Jake's murder and Jessie's "accident" had to be connected. All that was left for me to do was find out how and why. Simple task. *Yeah, right.*

Frank had called again the night before. His contact in Jackson County came through with the information I'd wanted, although the results weren't what I'd hoped for. Forensics backed up the finding that Mr. Jacob Devon Lofton committed suicide. His fingerprints were all over the weapon, a cheapo nine-millimeter pistol manufactured by Barrco Arms of California. There were powder burns on his temple area and traces of gunpowder on Jake's fingers consistent with him doing the honors. The blood spray and brain splatter patterns were also within the parameters of a normal aiming angle for someone bent on doing away with himself. It all seemed cut and dried, except for one interesting fact.

"The autopsy found drugs in Lofton's system," Frank said.

"Damn. What kind?"

"Lunesta and Xanax."

"Lunesta? The sleeping pill with all the butterflies in the commercials?"

"Yeah, powerful stuff. Xanax is a chill pill; it's used to treat anxiety disorders and panic attacks."

"Sort of like Valium?"

"Same family, yeah. There was enough of both in Lofton's system to knock out Sonny Liston."

"Who?"

"Never mind. He was before your time."

"Jessie didn't mention anything about Jake being on medications."

"That might be because the prescriptions belonged to his wife."

"Damn. Why would Jake take that crap when he was facing

a day's work and a two-hundred-mile roundtrip?"

"Listen, Mac. The accepted theory is Lofton drugged himself up so he'd have the balls to pull the trigger. Let's face it, he was depressed—never mind what his sister believed. The guy's wife was shacking up with another man, he missed not having his kids around, and he was seeing a shrink. And don't forget ... he shot his best friend to death when he was a kid. Jacob Lofton was a troubled young man."

Everything Frank said made sense, but for whatever reason my instincts told me not to buy into the theory the cops had worked out. "What about Jake's car?"

After Jake's 2004 Dodge Caravan underwent the fine-tooth combing required to satisfy the authorities, it was released to his grieving widow. Mrs. Laurel O'Donnell Lofton wasted no time having the minivan's interior cleaned and refurbished, and then sold to a wholesaler who auctioned it to a used-car dealer from Thomasville, Georgia. Out of sight, out of mind.

My wishing well had run dry. It was time to get off my butt and act. After I finished my sandwich and a third cup of coffee, I drove back to my trailer to do a little research. Henry nearly knocked me off the steps when I opened the door. I'd decided to rechristen the Dobie with Kate's original suggested moniker after having called Frank Hank and Hank Frank about a dozen times in the past two days. So, Henry the Eighth it was, for better or worse.

After running a few circles around the front yard, he followed me around back. He was getting used to the routine. He sniffed around and then did his business in the usual place, almost lifting a leg this time. I praised him and scratched behind his ears. He followed me back inside the Grey Wolf, negotiating the steps like a pro without so much as a stumble.

I refilled his bowls with puppy chow and water, then booted up my laptop and typed in the URL for White Pages. I typed Ronald Decker and Destin, Florida, under the Find People section, and then punched Find. Voilà! A Ronald and

Angela Decker lived on Indian Mound Trail, and their phone number was listed. I jotted down the info and then pulled up googlemaps.com for Destin, Florida. A few mouse clicks later, I was looking at a photo of their two-story brick and stucco home in what appeared to be a well-maintained, upper-middleclass neighborhood. Another positive was the Deckers lived only a mile or so from Kate's parents, so I was semi-familiar with the area, should a visit be in order.

I dialed the number and a woman answered after the second ring. "Is this the Decker residence?"

"Yes." The word was drawn out and sounded a bit irritated. My guess was she thought I was trying to sell her something. "This is Mrs. Decker. May I ask who's calling?"

I figured it was best to get right to the point. "My name is Mac McClellan, from St. George, east of Panama City. I was an acquaintance of Jessie Lofton."

There was silence for a moment as my words sank in. "You knew Jessie?" The voice almost broke on the last word.

"Yes ma'am, briefly. Please hear me out, Mrs. Decker. I work for Hightower Investigations, a private investigation agency. Our home office is located in downtown Destin. Miss Lofton recently hired me to look into her brother's death."

There was a cough and sniff. "Jessie hired a private investigator? But Jake's death was ruled a suicide."

"I know, but Jessie had reason to believe he might've been murdered."

More silence, then, "I don't know what to say, Mr. ...?"

"McClellan. Please, call me Mac."

"This isn't a good time, Mac," she managed to choke out. "Jessie's daughter is very upset, and the funeral is tomorrow and we're ... we're all devastated right now. I lost both my mom and dad in the past three years, and now this."

"I understand, and I apologize for the poor timing, but I believe Jessie might've been right about Jake not committing suicide. He was headed for St. George to do research on a project at the time of his death. Could you and your husband possibly meet with me soon … maybe sometime next week?"

Angie sniffled. "My husband will be busy at work, but I suppose I could meet with you, if you feel it's important."

"I do, and thanks. Why don't I give you a call Monday and we can arrange something. In the meantime, feel free to call Frank Hightower. He'll vouch for me. His number's in the book. Hightower Investigations, on Harbor Boulevard."

She sniffed again and I heard the muffled noise as she turned away from the phone and blew her nose. "Thank you, I will. And thank you for caring about Jessie."

Damn, now I was about to choke up. "I'll call Monday. My condolences to your family, and to Sydni."

Chapter 4

———•———

HENRY COULDN'T STAY LOCKED inside my camper all day while I was in Destin for my meeting with Angie Decker, so Tuesday morning with Kate's blessings I dropped the pup off in her fenced and locked backyard, along with the insulated igloo doghouse I'd bought Saturday at the Wal-Mart in Parkersville. I placed the doghouse under the sprawling live oak in Kate's yard where Henry would have shade all day.

I stayed on Highway 98 all the way to Destin, resisting the urge to detour north and take a look at the scene of Jessie Lofton's accident. It wasn't so much the extra time or miles it would cost me; it was damn depressing thinking about a life snuffed out so senselessly. My first official client hadn't lasted a day.

When we'd talked yesterday, Angie asked if we could meet at her house. The new school year began Monday, so the children would be gone. Her husband was working out of town for a couple of days. My guess was she had dependable neighbors and a topnotch security system, and would feel safer at home rather than meeting elsewhere or speaking with a voice over the phone. She'd also talked with Frank, so maybe her contact with him had something to do with the arrangements.

I had no trouble finding the Deckers' lavish Indian Mound Trail home. From the looks of things, they'd done well for themselves for a couple in their mid-thirties. A fancy white wall with decorative corner posts surrounded the property. I drove through the open gate down a concrete drive bordered with palm trees. Scattered native pines towered above the manicured lawn. Trimmed azalea and gardenia bushes dotted the landscape. The driveway ended in a circle in front of the two-story house. The brick and stucco façade was painted the same bright white as the wall. The roof was shingled with half-round terracotta tiles. There was a four-car garage at one end of the house, and a glass-enclosed sunroom at the other. A metallic black late-model Jaguar was parked in front of the garage, making quite a contrast against all the white.

I negotiated the circle and parked the Silverado aimed back toward Indian Mound Trail. The steps leading to the double front doors were the same white bordered by terracotta brick. The low porch was inlaid with fancy white marble. I was almost afraid to walk on it, and decided it might be time to shop around for an upgrade camper.

Checking my watch a second time I saw I was right on the button for our eleven o'clock rendezvous. I pushed the doorbell, half-expecting a fancy classical chime, but heard the familiar *ding dong* that most people fortunate enough to have doorbells settle for. I glanced through the beveled leaded panes in the door. A few seconds later a blurred figure approached. From inside a handle turned and one of the doors swung open.

Across the threshold an attractive woman welcomed me with a smile. She was average height with a healthy, tanned complexion. Her dark-brown hair was pulled back in a ponytail. For her height she was probably carrying an extra eight or ten pounds, but they were nicely distributed, and she carried them well. She offered her hand. "Mac?"

I nodded and shook the silky-smooth hand. "Nice to meet

you, Angie," I said, making sure to keep my eyes above her chin.

Angie invited me in and I followed her through the spacious foyer into a great room, admiring the view. The form-fitting jeans looked great, and the loose-fitting sage pullover accentuated her topside assets, balancing out a nice full figure. Ronald Decker was a lucky man.

The room wasn't bad either. With its high walls and vaulted ceiling, it didn't fall short of my expectations. I was pleased to see the walls were painted a pastel gold instead of white. Or were the walls gilded?

"I think we'll be more comfortable in the kitchenette," Angie said, glancing over her shoulder. We passed under an archway at the far end of the room, and through a short hallway. It led to a kitchen damn near twice the size of my Grey Wolf. I definitely needed to upgrade my home on wheels.

Angie stopped in front of a granite-topped island with a full double sink and more appliances and features than most American Dreamers ever envision. She offered refreshments, and I settled on coffee, black. She waved a manicured hand toward another archway. An exterior wall was lined with three rectangular tables and padded benches. Angie told me to make myself comfortable while she brought the coffee.

I strolled into what I guessed was the kitchenette and sat on one of the benches at the center table. Beyond the glass wall running the length of the room was a large curved swimming pool wrapping around a flowing waterfall. A diving board stood at one end, and near the middle was a loop-de-loop waterslide. I couldn't see the area past where the pool disappeared around the far side of the waterfall, but I would've bet money there was a Jacuzzi and a kiddy pool in the vicinity.

"Here we are." Angie reappeared with a large serving tray loaded with a coffee decanter, cups, and accessories—platters filled with small sandwiches and assorted raw vegetables and diced melons. She was keeping up a brave front for someone who'd recently lost a close friend and been promoted from godparent to legal guardian in the blink of an eye. "It's almost lunchtime. I thought you might be hungry."

Angie unloaded the tray and filled the two flower-print cups with fresh-brewed coffee. "Help yourself," she said and eased onto the padded bench opposite me. I took a sip of the rich brew and clanged the cup onto the saucer. I wasn't used to such amenities. "How's Sydni doing?" I decided that was as good a start as any to get things flowing.

Angie lifted her cup and gently blew to cool the coffee. "As well as can be expected, I suppose." Her brown eyes peered over the top of the cup. She took another sip and set the cup onto the saucer. "We managed to get Sydni enrolled at Fort Walton High last week. It was no easy task considering everything else that was going on. Riley has been such a big help."

She went on to explain that Riley, the Deckers' sixteen-year-old daughter, was like a big sister to Sydni, and helped ease Sydni's quick transition from orphan to family member. "Riley got her driver's license last month. She's taking Sydni to the mall to shop after school today. It was Riley's idea that we try to keep Sydni as busy as possible for a while."

I pictured the shiny black Jag parked outside, and wondered what set of wheels young Miss Riley Decker was driving as her first car. My money was on a showroom model, not a bargain from a pre-owned lot. The chit-chat went on for a few more minutes and then I decided it was time to get down to business. "How long had you known Jessie?"

Angie placed the piece of cantaloupe she'd been nibbling on a small plate and sighed. "Since we were students at Niceville High. Jake and Jessie's dad was career Air Force. He transferred to Eglin the summer before my and Jake's junior year. The Loftons bought a house about a block away from where my family lived. Jessie was only a freshman, but we became good friends, especially after Jake and I began dating later."

I raised my eyebrows. "You and Jake dated?"

She nodded. "We started going together shortly after Ron and I broke up."

This was beginning to sound like a soap opera. "You broke up with Ron to go out with Jake Lofton?"

Angie offered a weak smile and shook her head. "It's a little more complicated than that. Ron was a year ahead of me, a freshman at Okaloosa Junior College. We'd been going steady for over two years, but then I found out he'd dated a girl from one of his classes at the JuCo behind my back, so I broke it off. That's when Jake and I started going together."

The soap opera plot was thickening, but I wasn't exactly sitting on the edge of my seat. I figured somehow it had to lead to the reason Jessie Lofton chose the Deckers as her daughter's godparents. "What happened between you and Jake?" I hoped the climax was coming sooner than later.

Angie picked up the decanter and I held out my cup as she topped it off. "Nothing, really. Jake was a sweetheart, but Ron was … I don't know … more exciting, maybe? I know that's a poor excuse to break up with someone, but it's the truth. I'd never gotten over Ron. My relationship with Jake was more of a rebound thing, I suppose. Anyway, when Ron came begging his way back to me, I broke up with Jake. I know he was crushed for a while, but he was a good sport about it, and we stayed close friends."

I wondered how "close" a friend Jake considered Angie to be after she dumped him. Her attitude seemed a little snooty for my tastes. I would've been royally pissed at her. *Semper Fidelis* my ass. Angie Decker dropped down a couple of notches on my favorite people list. No more beating around the bush. "How did you and your husband wind up being named as Sydni's godparents?"

Another deep sigh. "After I graduated high school, I followed Ron to Okaloosa JuCo for a year. That summer I got pregnant with Riley. Ron shelved his plans to attend FSU, we got married, and he went to work full-time for his dad's construction business. After Riley was born, Jessie became our go-to babysitter. I was an only child and my parents moved to New Jersey for my dad's job. Jessie and I were practically like sisters by then, and she was crazy about Riley. She would've babysat for nothing."

Angie paused and finished the piece of melon. "One day Jessie came to see me while Ron was at work. She was crying. She told me she'd missed her last two periods and was overdue again. I finally talked her into seeing my OB/GYN. She was three-months pregnant.

"Jessie was only sixteen at the time, and in her junior year at Niceville High. Her parents weren't thrilled about the situation, as you can well imagine, especially after Jessie refused to tell anyone who the father was. They wanted her to give the baby up for adoption, but she refused. Her father was as strict as they come. He practically disowned her then, after calling her every name in the book. Jessie was devastated and moved in with Ron and me until Sydni was born. Jessie's dad finally came to his senses once he saw his granddaughter. Jessie moved back home and finished school, and then worked her way through nursing school to make a life for her and Sydni."

Angie studied the contents of her cup for a moment before looking up. "She never would reveal who the father was, as much as we all tried to encourage her to. She said she wanted nothing to do with a sorry bastard who would turn his back on his own flesh and blood. We finally gave up and dropped the subject."

I finished the last of my lukewarm coffee. "And so, I can assume Jessie named you and Ron as Sydni's godparents because of your close friendship and the kindness you showed her while she was pregnant?"

Angie laughed. "I never answered your question directly, did I? But yes, 'and now you know the rest of the story,' as Paul Harvey used to say."

One question down, several more to go. "Did Jake ever use drugs?"

She laughed. "Jake? That's a hoot. Jake didn't even drink coffee that I'm aware of. One night while he and I were dating, a bunch of our crowd from high school threw a party on the beach. You know—bonfire, music, beer and booze, a couple of joints passed around, that sort of thing. I had to talk Jake into it, but he finally agreed to go. Everyone was sitting around the fire, drinking and having a good time, except Jake. He wouldn't touch any of the stuff. You know what he brought?"

I played along. "What's that?"

"A thermos full of hot chocolate." She laughed again. "When Jake wasn't looking, I whispered to my girlfriend sitting next to me that it was spiked with vodka. It was sort of embarrassing to be there with the one person who wouldn't join in on the fun. And from talking to Jessie, I know that hot chocolate remained Jake's beverage of choice after all these years."

Angie sat there smiling at the memory as I knocked her down a couple of more notches on my favorite people list. No wonder she'd gone back to Ron. Hot chocolate wasn't nearly as exciting as getting wasted on pot and booze. "You and Jessie were best friends, right?"

"Yes. I like to think so, anyway."

I finished the last bite of a pimento cheese on crustless whole wheat and swore off my diet as I grabbed another. "Do you have a key to her place in Niceville?"

Angie turned her head and her eyes narrowed. "Jessie owned her own home. She carried credit life, so it belongs to Sydni now. I suppose we'll eventually sell it and put the money away for Sydni. And yes, I have a key. Why do you ask?"

"Because I might need to take a look around her house. With your permission, of course. What can you tell me about Jake's wife?"

Angie frowned. "Laurel? Honestly?"

I nodded.

There was a long sigh. "She's a conniving slut."

No mincing words there. "What makes you say that?"

Angie chewed on her lower lip. "Laurel had a reputation as far back as middle school. She slept with half the guys at Niceville High. There were even rumors about her fooling around with one of the boys' PE teachers." She emptied the last of the coffee into her cup. "For the life of me I'll never understand why Jessie encouraged Jake to date Laurel while they were at nursing school together. And I'll never understand what Jake saw in her. He deserved better."

Yeah, someone loyal like you, I thought, but kept my trap shut. "Then you know about the current affair with the coach?"

Angie crunched a bite of celery dipped in ranch dressing. She finished chewing and swallowed. "Yes. Jessie said Laurel left Jake and moved in with the guy a few months ago. But I guess it's no longer officially an affair, now that Jake's gone."

"I guess not. Did Jessie mention that Laurel caught her in Jake's apartment and tossed her out?"

Angie's brow furrowed. "No. Did Jessie say what she was looking for?"

It was nitty-gritty time. I stared into Angie's big brown eyes, hoping there was a soul behind them. "I can't go into specifics, but Jessie was convinced the items might lead to the person or persons responsible for her brother's death."

Angie dabbed her lips with a cloth napkin. "Then she truly believed Jake's death wasn't a suicide?"

Since they were best friends, I was a little surprised that Jessie hadn't discussed her suspicions with Angie. "Yeah, and I believed her. She never discussed it with you?"

"Not that I recall. Tell me something, Mac."

"Shoot."

She frowned. "Why are you doing this? Jessie can't pay you, and I doubt you're the type to bill Sydni for services rendered on behalf of her late mother."

"It's not about money. Jessie showed me enough evidence

to convince me she was on the right track. I'm doing this for Jessie, and for Sydni."

Angie was silent for a moment. She glanced out the glass wall toward the pool, and then locked her big browns on me. "What can I do to help?"

I didn't blink. "A lot, I hope. Jessie mentioned she rented a safe-deposit box, and that a trustworthy friend was listed as co-signer. Is that you?"

Angie opened her mouth to answer, and then hesitated and glanced down at her plate. "Yes." She looked up and sighed, her eyes searching mine. "I wasn't supposed to tell anyone, but under the circumstances …. I'm listed as co-renter. I signed the necessary paperwork, but I promised Jessie I'd never open it unless she asked me to."

"Then you do have a key?"

Angie nodded.

"I need you to open the box."

Her eyes widened. "Why?"

"Because Jessie said there were items in there that she was keeping for Jake. They might have something to do with why he was killed."

She sighed again. "Then you're convinced Jake was murdered."

What part of "yes" did this lady not understand? "Yeah."

Angie brushed a hand across her bangs. "What sort of items are they?"

"Relics from a new archaeological site Jake discovered. Iron arrow points, old coins, stuff like that. Jessie didn't go into too much detail."

Angie propped her chin in one hand and drummed the manicured nails of the other on the tabletop. "Give me ten minutes to freshen up. You can follow me to the bank."

As soon as I saw Angie's face when she returned from the vault where the safe deposit boxes were kept, I knew something was wrong. She walked across the lobby and took the seat next to mine. "There was nothing in there, Mac."

Damn. "Nothing? The box was empty?"

Angie fiddled with the strap of the purse sitting in her lap. "Not empty. There was Jessie's legal paperwork, birth certificates and mortgage papers and the like, but no sign of any artifacts or old maps or documents."

Jessie had flat-out assured me there were other artifacts in the box. Why would she lie? "When was the last time Jessie signed in to access the box?"

Angie glanced up at the ceiling as if the info was written there. "According to the register, it was the morning of her accident, right after the bank opened."

Math was never my favorite subject, but I ran the numbers. Jessie and I met at ten thirty in downtown Panama City. The First Community Bank of Destin opened at nine. That meant she would've been doing at least the legal speed limit to get there on time, *if* there was no traffic to contend with. And she was already waiting at Panama Joe's when I'd arrived at ten thirty sharp.

But this was vacation season for a lot of out-of-state visitors. With traffic the way it was this time of year, you'd have to be awfully damn lucky to get to the bank when it opened, access the box, and then make the drive to PC all in less than an hour and a half. Something was out of whack.

"Are you sure only you and Jessie had access to the box?"

"I'm positive, and today is the first and only time I've opened it. I told you that's the way Jessie wanted it."

I wasn't fond of asking my next question, but it had to be done. "Is there any possibility that your husband, or maybe even your daughter, might've gotten hold of the key?"

Angie flashed the expected hostile frown, and the words that came next burned my ears. "That question doesn't deserve an answer, but I'll give you one anyway. No one else knew about the box other than Jessie and me. And even if Ron or Riley found the key and tried to use it, they would've been denied access. Bank policy requires matching signatures, and there's no one else listed on the box account besides Jessie and me."

The frown stayed on Angie's face, so I figured I'd try to calm the waters. "I apologize. But I don't think Jessie could've made the drive from here to the place we met in Panama City in less than an hour and a half. Not with the summer traffic. How long does it take to drive from Jessie's place to here?"

The frown faded. Angie pressed her lips together and stared blankly over my shoulder for a moment. "It's around twenty miles; I'd say thirty, maybe thirty-five minutes or so, depending on traffic."

I nodded as I clasped my hands together and rested my arms on my thighs. I stared across the lobby at the teller windows. After a minute of deflating disappointment I sat up straight and looked at Angie. "I appreciate your help and cooperation. One last thing?"

She chewed her bottom lip before answering. "What?"

"Jessie kept a spare key to Jake's house. She told me it wasn't in the safe deposit box, and that she didn't keep it on her person. I need to get into her house and look for it."

Angie's eyes narrowed. "You're planning to break into Jake's house?"

"No, I'm planning to let myself in with Jessie's key, if I can find it."

She shook her head slowly. "That's still breaking and entering, Mac. You could wind up in jail."

"I've been in worse places. Look, Jake hid a file somewhere with information that might've cost him his life, and maybe Jessie's, too. My guess is it's somewhere in his house like Jessie believed. I need to find out, one way or another. Sydni deserves that much."

Angie stared at me a couple of seconds and then let out a big sigh. "I must be out of my mind," she said as she began fishing through her purse.

Chapter 5

———•———

ANGIE NOT ONLY TRUSTED me with the key, she also composed a signed note stating she was now the legal custodian of the late Jessie Lofton's house and property, and granted me permission to be on the premises. On another slip of paper she jotted down a rough map and directions to Jessie's Honeysuckle Drive home. I promised to overnight the key back to Angie via FedEx.

Jessie's house was a modest ranch style structure with beige vinyl siding and a single-car attached garage. The backyard was enclosed with a chain-link fence, much like Kate's. It was a nice middleclass neighborhood, nothing fancy, but most of the houses were fairly new and well-kept. There were a couple of kids riding skateboards on the sidewalks, and a mixed group of teens cruising the streets on their bicycles. Two older boys were shooting hoops a few houses down.

Parking in front of the garage, I climbed the steps to the front porch, slid the key into the deadbolt, and swung the front door open. The power was turned off, so I pulled the living room drapes back and sunlight streamed through the double windows behind the sofa. Remembering Jessie's words that the key was "in good hands," I glanced around, looking for anything that might be from the Allstate Insurance Company. I spent the next fifteen minutes wandering from room to room, searching through magazine racks, small stacks of mail, anything that might have to do with Allstate, but came up empty.

As I searched I noticed several framed photos of Jessie and Sydni on the walls and dresser tops, and a few of a man I recognized as Jake. There was a strong family resemblance between brother and sister, but the girl had dark hair and lacked the fine-boned features of her mother and uncle. Elvis's daughter, when she was around the same age, came to mind.

I headed back through the living room and was working up the courage to rummage through Jessie's bedroom dresser drawers when something caught my eye. A bronzed pair of hands with fingers pressed together in prayer stood on the coffee table in front of the sofa. Good thing it wasn't a snake or I would've been bitten a couple of times already. I picked up the statue. It was about eight-inches high and weighed close to five pounds. Sunlight shined through the hollow space between the thumbs and pinkies when I turned it to the window for a better look. I gently shook the sculpture and heard a light tinkling sound. As I tipped the hollow end down, a key fell out and clanked on the coffee table.

Good hands, indeed.

I'd found what I'd come for, and luckily without any nosey neighbors asking questions. I locked the door and drove back to the bank in Destin, retracing my route. It was a little out of the way, but since I was here I figured I might as well conduct a little experiment.

I pulled into the bank's parking lot, circled around and stopped to check the time before exiting. Two-twenty. I punched the timer on my watch, turned onto Highway 98 and headed east for Panama City. Traffic permitting, I drove like a bat-out-of-hell, weaving in and out of lanes around vehicles and generally making myself a target of road rage for other drivers heading the same direction. I was bucking for a speeding and/or reckless driving ticket, but that was a chance I had to take if my experiment had any chance of succeeding.

I kept my eyes peeled for cops and off my watch as I played road racer. The miles flew by, and I finally made the turn onto Harrison Avenue leading to the heart of downtown Panama City. Several blocks later I slowed and angle-parked in front of Panama Joe's. I checked my watch: an hour and thirty-eight minutes. Jessie supposedly left Destin a little after nine the morning of our meeting, had already been served and was waiting when I arrived. I'd made the trip during mid-afternoon, so traffic was bound to be somewhat worse, but I'd hit speeds above eighty for several miles at a time and been slowed by heavy traffic only a couple of times.

If Jessie was waiting by the door when the bank opened at nine, and she'd pulled-off a super-quick visit to her safe deposit box, it was possible, but not likely, that she'd made it to PC in an hour-fifteen with no traffic. But that Mustang would've been running like a scalded dog, or in this case, horse. My horse sense said no way.

———

WEDNESDAY MORNING I DROVE to the FedEx office in Parkersville and overnighted Jessie's house key to Angie Decker with a note telling her my search was successful and that I'd keep her updated.

After leaving FedEx I stopped at Redmond's Sporting Goods. I'd done a little online research on metal detectors last night and decided that a Bounty Hunter would suit my needs. It was lightweight, reasonably priced, and could detect metal objects at a depth of five feet. The coil was also fully submersible in case I decided to wade the shallows around the

Stumps. Fortunately, Redmond's happened to be an authorized
dealer for the Bounty Hunter line.

On the way back to St. George, I called Kate at Gillman's.
She was free for lunch at one. I planned to head for Five Mile
Island early the next day, so I spent the rest of the morning
reading the detector's instruction booklet and practicing with
the different settings while searching around the campground
with Henry. My booty consisted of two finishing nails, a rusted
bolt, a dozen or so old pop tops and bottle caps, and twenty-
eight cents in coins: a dime, three nickels, and three pennies,
to be exact—none pre-dating the twenty-first century. I hoped
I'd have better luck on the island. Henry found a battered golf
ball and a hunk of a Snickers bar with a piece of wrapper still
attached. He managed to woof it down before I could stop
him. *Yum.*

"You'll never guess who called me last night," Kate said as
she dipped a french fry into a small cup of ketchup sitting next
to her shrimp basket. I figured this must be the one day out of
the week that Kate allowed herself to splurge and eat whatever
she wanted.

I swallowed a bite of the chicken salad on a bed of mixed
greens that Kate insisted I would enjoy. "Matt Damon?"
Denise might make the best BLTs this side of wherever, but I
can't vouch for her chicken salad.

The french fry stalled a couple of inches from Kate's mouth.
She arched a brow and smiled. "Now there's a nice thought.
But no, it wasn't Matt, it was Megan."

I perked up. My daughter had rattled me a couple of months
back with a phone call announcing she was in love with a fellow
veterinarian student and on the verge of getting engaged. "Let
me guess … she came to her senses and dumped that Trey guy
she thought she couldn't live without."

The fry found its mark and Kate kept me in suspense while

she finished chewing, following up with a sip of iced tea. "Not even close. Actually, she mentioned a wedding."

I almost dropped my fork as I felt the heat rise to my face. "Megan's marrying that son-of-a—"

"Dang Mac, quit jumping to conclusions." Kate was grinning like a bear in a bee tree. "It's your ex. Jill and her Captain Riddick have set a date."

I set the fork down and rubbed my eyes. I felt relieved, yet somehow jealous at the same time. Jill had waylaid me when I returned from my last deployment dodging death overseas by announcing she'd fallen in love and wanted a divorce. She and John Riddick had dated steadily almost two years now, and I suspected they'd been spending a lot of time together in what was to have been my and Jill's dream retirement home. I'd already deduced from talking to the kids that things were getting serious between them. Riddick was a naval officer, a helicopter pilot stationed at Cherry Point Naval Air Depot, located near Camp Lejeune where I'd retired. He'd recently been promoted from commander to captain—equivalent to a full bird colonel in the Marines. I guess the extra bucks and prestige were enough to take the two lovebirds to the next stage.

"And when is this happy event supposed to take place?"

Kate's eyes grew wide. "What on earth? You ... are ... jealous!"

"Don't be ridiculous. I couldn't care less. In fact, I'm glad to hear it. They deserve each other."

Kate leaned forward and stared at me with narrowed eyes. "It's all over your face. I think your nose is growing as I speak. Anyway, Megan said we're both on the guest list. Sorry, but you weren't chosen to be the best man."

My appetite was shot. "Now that breaks my heart. I'm not going."

"Yes we are. For Megan and Mike's sake."

"I'd rather do another tour in Iraq."

Kate bit a fry in half and pointed the remainder at me. "Just make sure you're back by October sixteenth." She grabbed a napkin from the holder and blotted a smear of ketchup off her lower lip. "How was your meeting in Destin?"

I pushed my half-finished plate aside and rested both elbows on the table. "Interesting. Back in high school Angie Decker dumped her boyfriend and future husband, Ron, and started dating Jessie Lofton's brother, Jake. Then she dumped Jake and went back to Ron because she found him, quote, 'more exciting.' Then Angie got pregnant and Ron had to drop out of college and go to work for his father's construction business. Meanwhile, Jessie got knocked up and kicked out of the family home because she wouldn't reveal who the father was. She moved in with the Deckers until she had her baby. After the baby was born all was forgiven and she moved back into the family home, attended nursing school, and introduced her brother to the town floozy, who he eventually married. Then they all lived happily ever after—excluding Jake—until Monday a week ago when Jessie was killed shortly after convincing me that her brother didn't commit suicide after all, but was murdered."

"Wow, a regular As the Stomach Churns."

"Yeah. Oh, and I found a key."

———

A CHILL RAN DOWN my spine when I drove up and saw Henry lying in the shade at the foot of the Grey Wolf's steps. I damn well knew I'd locked him inside when I left to meet Kate for lunch. He woke up and yawned and then started running in circles when I pulled to a stop on the gravel drive. I heard his nails scratching at the driver's door as I reached under the seat and grabbed my Smith & Wesson .357 Magnum and slipped it out of the zippered case. I had my concealed weapons permit, but hadn't bothered to get a holster yet. I eased the Silverado's door shut, scratched between Henry's ears to calm him and whispered, "Who's in there, boy?" No answer. Big help my partner was.

August being the hottest month of the year in Florida, the Grey Wolf's rooftop A/C was blasting away, and I'd made sure all the window shades were drawn to help keep the heat out. I eased up to the door, *Messieurs* S & W at the ready, and grabbed the handle. It turned and I swung the door open, expecting somebody to come flying out or start popping rounds my way. A black and tan blur dashed up the steps. Henry was barking up a storm as I crouched and crept inside the camper, ready as I'd ever be for a showdown.

The place appeared empty except for Henry and me. I did a quick clearance to make sure. Nobody was home but us, but he/she/they had damn well left behind their calling card before vamoosing. The place was a mess. There wasn't a cabinet or drawer or closet that wasn't standing open, and contents were strewn everywhere. Every cushion and mattress was upended, every book and magazine and newspaper flipped through.

A closer inspection convinced me that robbery wasn't the motive. Nothing was missing that I could tell, at least nothing major. Whoever was here was looking for something. That's when it hit me. I patted the left front pocket of my shorts and then remembered I'd left my keys, including the one I'd added to the ring last night, in the Silverado.

I grabbed my phone and started to punch in Sergeant JD Owens's private cellphone number. JD is the young St. George police officer who'd saved my bacon last summer. My finger hesitated a half-inch from the button, and then I put the phone away. Why get the local authorities involved at this point? Nothing was missing, and I was convinced the break-in wasn't a random act by anyone local. I hurried out to the truck, retrieved the keys and stepped back inside the Grey Wolf, Henry guarding my heels the whole time.

What the hell was going on? My mind was going in circles. Jessie Lofton, dead from a strategically blown tire a few hours after hiring me to look into her brother's suspicious death. Angie Decker, entrusting me with the key to her late best friend's house after I'd confided that I needed to find the key to Jake's house that Jessie had hidden. And now, less than twenty-four hours later, somebody ransacks my trailer looking for something, that something no doubt being the key to Jake Lofton's Tallahassee residence.

None of this made much sense, unless you came to the conclusion that someone had known of Jessie's suspicions well before she'd ever laid eyes on me at Panama Joe's. He, she, or they must've known about our meeting in advance, and probably followed Jessie to our Panama City rendezvous. Said person or persons might've been inside the coffee house during our meeting, or waiting outside in a parked vehicle until Jessie and I parted ways. Was that scenario instrumental in Jessie's accident a few hours later?

And how the hell would anybody know that I'd managed to get hold of the key to Jake's apartment? Did somebody have Jessie's house under surveillance twenty-four/seven? Was Angie Decker somehow involved in the sordid deal? Angie seemed genuinely surprised when I mentioned that Jessie believed Jake's death wasn't a suicide. Maybe she was a damn good actress. I didn't want to believe that, although the more I thought about it, the more likely it seemed. But looking the other way while somebody made sure her best friend permanently stopped snooping into her brother's death? I couldn't quite swallow that scenario.

One thing was certain, at least in my mind: whoever was responsible for, or connected to, Jake Lofton's death and Jessie Lofton's "accident" knew I had the key to Jake's house. I needed to move fast, and that meant searching Jake's place ASAP. First thing in the morning I aimed to be in Tallahassee.

FOR THE SECOND TIME I drove past the Widow Lofton's

Camellia Circle house, located about two miles west of downtown Tallahassee in what once had passed for a middle-class neighborhood. Most of the houses along the wooded street were of '60s or '70s vintage, with low-peaked roofs and carports instead of enclosed garages. There were a few newer homes mixed in here and there, enough to give the longtime residents or first-time homeowners something to aspire to.

I parked Jerry Meadows's Dodge Ram pickup the next block down from the Lofton place in front of a house sporting a For Sale sign in the yard. Jerry and Donna Meadows were the owners of Gulf Pines Campground, and we'd become fast friends since I'd rented site 44 from them over a year ago. I'd let Jerry in on my plans last night, and after I'd dropped Henry off at Kate's this morning, I'd headed north in Jerry's truck, leaving my Silverado parked in the driveway of my campsite.

It was a quarter to nine when I exited the Ram and walked the block to Laurel Lofton's red-brick house. The air was already hot and muggy and sweat trickled down the back of my neck. I'd worn Dockers and a button-down shirt as part of my cover; if anyone questioned my presence at the residence, I was a real estate agent who'd heard the place might be coming on the market soon, and I was there to check it out for a prospective client.

I stopped in front of the house and took in the scene. The shaded lawn had seen better days; sparse centipede grass and weeds crept over the edges of the concrete driveway located on the house's right. A slanted roof came off the main structure and covered a two-vehicle carport. There was a smaller concrete pad with a flat roof, maybe a boat shed. If Jake Lofton owned a boat, Laurel had probably sold it. With Jake's insurance money she could afford a bigger and better one.

I took the four brick steps that led to a small inset porch two at a time, glanced around to see if anyone was looking, and pushed the key into the lock. I had to jiggle it back and forth several times, but it finally opened. Easing into the house, I closed the door behind me and locked it. Congratulations, I was now officially a lawbreaker. I hoped Frank would make my bail if my B&E skills weren't up to snuff.

It was dark inside, but there was no way I was going to open the curtains for better light. I stood there a couple of minutes, letting my eyes adjust. A quick glance around showed me the front part of the house was mostly living room with a dark hallway leading to the other end on the house. My eyes finally semi-adjusted to the poor light; it was time to begin my search, though I wasn't sure what I was looking for. Jessie had mentioned she'd turned the place upside down searching for files or documents that might relate to the Five Mile Island project. My best guess was that Jake had transferred his findings to a flash drive or the like, and hidden it somewhere in the house. The proverbial needle in a haystack seemed like an easy task compared to what I was facing.

I did have one hunch that came to me while I'd been unable to sleep last night, and I acted on it first. According to the toxicology report, drugs were found in Jake's system, drugs prescribed for his wife, Laurel. When I'd asked Angie Decker if she'd known of Jake using drugs, she laughed. Apparently Jacob Lofton was as squeaky clean and proper as Mister Rogers. I also recalled how Angie said Jake's drink of choice was hot chocolate. During my discussions with Angie and Jessie there'd been no talk of Jake's religion of choice, but I wondered if he might've been a closet Mormon.

Putting two and two together, I headed for the kitchen that was located through an archway leading from the living room to the back of the house. A side door led outside to the carport. The refrigerator was silent and the clock on the stove panel had stopped, so I figured the electricity was off. I reached to open the refrigerator. Who knew, maybe Jake's hiding place was a butter dish or vegetable bin. The stench almost gagged me, and after a quick inspection I shut the door. Whatever Laurel's intentions were for the house, keeping it spotless wasn't high on her list of priorities.

I checked the lower cabinets first and found an array of pots and pans, a slow cooker, an electric deep fryer and waffle iron. Two of the lowers contained shelves with a scattering of canned goods and an assortment of dried beans, rice, and boxed pasta. The upper cabinets were next. Plates, bowls, glasses and cups; more canned goods and canisters of flour, cornmeal and sugar. There was also what looked like an ample supply of mouse poop scattered among the staples.

I reached for the small cabinet above the stove where it was vented through the roof. Bingo. A mostly full bottle of Folger's Crystals—Laurel's, I assumed—powdered creamer, Sweet & Low, and a box with several packets of instant hot chocolate. A few were opened, carefully folded closed, and secured with rubber bands. Old Sherlock himself would've been proud when I deduced that the reason for the partial packs was that Jake sometimes wanted more than a cup of cocoa, as in when he wanted a thermos-full to take with him to work at the university or in the field.

That could explain why the drugs were found in Jake's body. My guess was that before leaving home that fateful morning for St. George, he'd made himself a thermos of hot chocolate. Only this time someone had pre-spiked an open packet of mix with ground-up sleeping and chill pills.

While enjoying a cup of hot chocolate as he hit the road, Jake had suddenly grown tired, so much so that after a while he could barely keep his eyes open. It got so bad that he'd been forced to pull off the road to rest and clear his head. Having never indulged in anything stronger than cocoa, he might've even fallen asleep, leaving himself easy prey for whoever was tailing him. With Jake passed out cold, it would've been a fairly simple matter to place the pistol in his hand and use Jake's own finger to squeeze the trigger. Move over, Inspector Clouseau.

After rummaging through the garbage can looking for empties, I grabbed a couple of the opened packets and slipped them in the front right pocket of my Dockers. Frank had a contact who could test them for drugs. Rather proud of my deductive reasoning, I exited the kitchen and followed a back hallway that led past the kids' bedroom with bunk beds and a ton of toys. Farther on was a hall bathroom with a tub and shower combo, and another small room that served as an office. At the end of the hall was the master bedroom with half-bath. Between the kids' bedroom and the bath was a small foyer that led outside to a covered deck. I didn't bother checking to see if the key matched that door's lock, but I assumed it did.

I hurried back to what I assumed was Jake's office. Laurel was obviously spooked when she'd found Jessie snooping around the house. There was no trace of a computer, but I did notice a cord under the desk that might've led to a printer or other hardware. I searched through the desk drawers but came up empty. In a closet I found an old printer cartridge inside a box and a couple of opened packs of letter-sized printer paper and colored card stock. I gave the closet a quick once-over. Nothing.

Behind the desk stood chrome and black metal shelving. A couple of shelves sagged under the weight of stacked books, mostly archaeology and history textbooks. The third shelf from the top held a collection of the Hardy Boys mysteries. I remembered Jessie mentioning Jake was a big fan of Frank and Joe Hardy. Here was the proof. I scanned the book spines from left to right and found they were in order, from book one, *The Tower Treasure,* to book forty-four, *The Haunted Fort.* Double-checking, I noticed one of the books was leaning against another instead of standing upright like the others. I took a closer look and saw that book eleven in the series was missing. Then I recalled Jessie saying that Jake would sometimes read the books to the twins at bedtime.

Another hunch sent me back to the boys' bedroom. Sure enough, there on top of a chest of drawers next to the bunks was a blue-spined hardcover book matching the rest of the set in Jake's office. I picked it up and glanced at the cover. It was number eleven, *While the Clock Ticked.* In the foreground two teens who I assumed were our heroes Frank and Joe Hardy sat bound and gagged, facing each other. In the background, a sinister-looking man emerged from a hidden door behind a grandfather clock. I flipped through the pages, half expecting a copy of the lost Rodrigo Rangel document or another treasured piece of evidence to come falling out. Nothing but a bookmark facing page thirty-seven. I thumbed through the pages once more in case I'd overlooked a clue. Nothing. *Crap,* I was sure I was on to something.

After making sure that everything was as I'd found it in the bedroom and office, I hustled to the master bedroom to see if anything would turn up there. No such luck. I stepped back into the hallway and through another arch that led to the front hallway and back to the living room. Something in the shadows of my right peripheral vision caught my attention. I glanced that way and damn near went jelly-legged. At the end of the hall stood a tall grandfather clock. I'd missed seeing it from the living room because of the darkness. The adrenaline rushed as I remembered the cover art and title of the mystery I'd found in the boys' bedroom minutes ago—*While the Clock Ticked.* Only this clock wasn't ticking. The pendulum had given up the ghost at eleven twenty. The clock might not be ticking, but my mind was. Could this grandfather clock have anything to do with the case, or was it simply a coincidence that Jake had been reading that particular volume to the boys at the time of his death? Could the clock on the book's cover have given Jake the idea to hide the info Jessie was searching for somewhere inside this clock? My enquiring mind sure as hell wanted to know.

I gave old granddad a closer gander. It was an antique, maybe passed down from the Lofton family or bought on a weekend outing when Jake and Laurel had been newlyweds with pipe dreams of sharing a happy life together before reality stepped in the way. I wondered how many years had passed since its last tick. Of course there was always the chance the clock worked perfectly and the works had simply run down after Jake met his untimely demise. I resisted the urge to open the clock face and wind it. Good thing too, because I heard the front door lock rattling as someone worked a key back and forth in the mechanism.

A cold double-shot of adrenaline surged through me as I stood there like a possum frozen in the headlights of an oncoming car. I was in the middle of a deep breath, trying to calm myself enough to think, when the handle turned and the front door creaked open. Sunlight swarmed into the dark house. I was about to dash the few feet to the back hall and take my chances hiding in a bedroom closet, but caught sight of a small alcove recessed in the hallway wall a couple of feet from where I stood. Squatting down, I wedged my six-one frame inside the shallow opening with my back toward the living room and my knees scrunched up under my chin.

My left leg was barely hidden inside the narrow recess. Glancing up, I noticed a fuse box a couple of feet above my head near the middle of the alcove. There were screw holes and chiseled hinge insets on the top and bottom of the opposite frame where a small door panel had once covered my slim hiding place. The thought of the fuse box bothered me. What if the power to the house was turned off at the box? If so, and if whoever the visitor was decided to flip the power back on, I was screwed.

Shadows danced on the wall behind the clock as my uninvited guest moved farther into the living room. "You'll have to forgive the mess," a woman said. "I haven't had much chance to keep up the place since my husband's death." A deep male voice mumbled something in return that I couldn't make out.

"So, we have the front door locks," she said, her voice trailing off slightly as they moved into the kitchen, "and this door here. I'd like a deadbolt here, also." The man mumbled more unintelligible words. I listened as their footsteps clattered on the tile across the kitchen and down the back hallway. The woman said something I couldn't make out, probably regarding the back door. My guess was they were in the foyer leading to the deck. I resisted the urge to sprint for the front door. No way could I leave without being heard, so I took a few deep breaths and decided to stay put.

I heard more mumbling and then laughter as the footsteps continued down the back hall toward my end of the house. "No problem at all, Mrs. Lofton. We'll have the new locks installed by two this afternoon. I'll have one of my guys drop the keys and the old hardware off at the school for you."

I tried to make myself smaller as the footsteps passed from one hallway into the other. I hadn't felt so exposed since my company had been caught by a mortar barrage in an open area during the fight for Fallujah. They decided to stop a mere couple of feet from where I cowered. I'd skipped breakfast that morning, and hoped my stomach wouldn't growl above the sound of their voices as they went on and on for what seemed like an hour.

"Thank you, Jim, I appreciate it. I'll certainly recommend you to my friends and co-workers." Their shadows, looking like the Incredible Hulk standing alongside Popeye's heartthrob, Olive Oyl, flitted on the wall opposite my cubbyhole. They exchanged more niceties and Jim gave Laurel his best sales pitch to convince her to replace all the inside door hardware.

Thankfully, Laurel declined the offer. The sound of their footsteps followed them into the living room and out the door. I waited another five minutes in case Jim's crew was already onsite before I unlimbered my stiff carcass from the hole in the wall. Easing down the hall into the living room, I pulled the curtain aside and peeked out. The coast looked clear.

Hightailing it back down the hall to the clock, I opened the face. The winding key was there, but nothing else. I shut the clock face and ran my hands down both sides, hoping to find a panel that opened. As far as I could tell, the sides were all solid wood. The lower front opened, giving access to the pendulum. I braced one palm against the clock and pulled it open. I pulled the penlight from my trousers pocket and clicked it on, my heart beating fast in anticipation. Cobwebs and a couple of dead bugs were the only clues I found, telling me the clock could stand a good cleaning and probably hadn't been used in quite a while.

The old grandfather stood too close to the wall for me to examine the back thoroughly. I thought about pulling it away from the wall, and then realized there was enough room for my hand to fit between the back and the wall. The lighting was piss-poor, but as I ran my hand along the upper part where the works were located, I felt the outline of a panel that provided access. I traced my fingers along it until I came across two metal stays at the bottom. I shined the light back there and squinted for details. I managed to grab one of the stays with my fingertips and give it a twist. It moved down a half-turn to where it cleared the panel. I forced my hand farther behind the clock and was able to grasp the second stay and turn it. I tapped along the top of the panel a couple of times. It moved, but fell back into place. I tapped a little harder and the top of the panel tilted out and rested against the wall. *Bingo!*

I retrieved my right hand, shook the numbness out of my fingers, and then eased my hand toward the edge of the now-freed panel cover. I slipped my thumb and forefinger around the panel, lifted it up and away from the back of the clock, and brought it out from the small space between it and the wall. Resting the dusty cover against the bottom of the clock, I craned my head as close to the opening as I could. I shined the thin beam of the penlight around what I could see inside the clock works. Nothing.

As I moved my hand from inside the works, the penlight bumped against the jamb of the opening and slipped from my grasp. The small flashlight clattered to the floor and rolled, flashing this way and that until it settled somewhere underneath the clock with the beam shining against the wall opposite where I stood.

Damn. Decision time. I decided against trying to move the clock to retrieve the light. It would die out in a few hours, and from what I could see you'd have to be looking for the beam to notice it. I figured Jim's crew would be too occupied changing the locks and handles of the outside doors to discover it. Unless somebody decided to use the front bathroom between the clock and the living room and happened to be staring at the correct angle toward the clock, or ....

Enough speculating. Either this old clock held something useful to the Lofton case or it didn't, and I didn't have all day long to find out. Jim's crew could show up any minute. I slipped my right hand and arm as far behind the clock as I could, and then forward into the works. I felt the touch of the toothed metal gears, and the flat springs and other unidentifiable parts. Nada. I braced my left hand against the front of the clock and forced the old timekeeper into a slight tilt forward. The damn thing was heavy, and it took all the strength I could muster in my awkward position to keep it from tipping over. I shoved my hand farther into the works and pushed my fingers into every nook and cranny I could find. I was about to give up when my pinkie touched something that moved, and it wasn't metal. Whatever it was lay on the far side between the works and the clock wall. I strained a little harder and managed to gain another couple of inches.

Pay dirt! The target was paper, and I was barely able to grasp it between my pinkie and ring finger and pull. It was slow going. If it slipped or tore I might not get another shot. Sweat was dripping down my face and back as I maintained my fragile grip and coaxed the object toward the back of the works. It finally came free. Carefully I retracted my now nearly numb hand from the back of the clock. The object dropped from my fingers before I could get my hand all the way free, but luckily it came to rest between the back of the clock and the wall, within easy reach.

It was a letter-size white envelope with a small flat object sealed inside, smaller than any flash drive I'd ever seen. On the bright side, it definitely hadn't been in the dusty old clock long. I slid the envelope inside my pocket with the cocoa packets and turned my attention to putting the panel back in place and getting the hell out. Easier said than done. It seemed to take forever before the panel would stay in place, and even then I was only able to turn the nearest of the stays securely in place. For a couple of minutes I tried like hell to get the other stay turned, but it was a no go. I'd been inside the house way too long for comfort already, so I left the panel as it was, swallowed my heart and beat feet for the door.

I could now add petty theft to my figurative rap sheet.

Chapter 6

—— · ——

Turns out the envelope I'd discovered contained a flash drive after all, the smallest I'd ever seen. The brand name was Verbatim, and at four gigs it measured a mere one and three-eighths-inch long by a half-inch wide, and was wafer-thin. It's a mystery to me how so much info can be stored on such a small device, but then again, I'm baffled at how the hell radio works, never mind television.

When I popped the drive into my laptop, a single file named "X" appeared. It opened without a problem; however, there was no trace of the Rodrigo Rangel document that Jake had supposedly taken digital shots of inside the state library's Spanish Land Grants room. Instead, it displayed several rows of random letters and numbers and symbols. I mentally kicked myself in the ass for not searching the grandfather clock more thoroughly while I had the chance. With the locks being changed, there was no way in hell I was going to risk another B&E.

The Lofton case was quickly going south. First, no Rangel document on the flash drive, then Frank's latest cheery news that the manila envelope containing the artifacts hadn't been recovered from the scene of Jessie's accident. Toss in the missing artifacts from Jessie's safe deposit box and things weren't looking so rosy.

———•———

I called Kate on the drive back from Tallahassee and dropped by her house as soon as she'd gotten off work that evening. "It looks like some kind of code," she said, peering over my shoulder at the laptop's screen and handing me a beer.

I took a swig. "Yeah. Were you ever in the Girl Scouts?"

"I was a Brownie, but we never dabbled with codes that I can remember."

I stared at the screen and scrolled down. There were four pages of double-spaced rows of letters and numerals of varying length, some containing Roman numerals mixed among them in no particular order. There were also a lot of what appeared to be Greek letters or symbols scattered here and there, most separated with plus or minus signs. "You ever see anything like this?"

Kate took a seat beside me on the sofa, gave the screen another look and shook her head. "Mark was in the Boy Scouts. I remember seeing a book or magazine he had when his troop was working on simple codes. It was mostly swapping a letter for a number, like 'a' equals 'one' or vice versa."

Mark was Kate's younger brother; he worked in graphics and had restored and enhanced several old photos that proved helpful in solving Maddie Harper's murder last year. "If we emailed him a copy of the file, do you think he'd be willing to give it a shot?"

Kate laughed. "Are you kidding? Mark thinks he's Tom Sawyer, Detective. He'd jump at the chance to be in on something like this. What about Uncle Frank?"

"I'd rather not bug him. He already thinks I'm a boil on his butt for wanting to keep on the case. Let's see if we can figure it out ourselves. If not, I'll ask if he can contact his retired FBI buddy and see what they can come up with.

"Oh, I almost forgot. Frank heard back from a friend of his in the sheriff's department about Jessie's autopsy. Guess what?"

Kate swallowed a sip of beer. "I give up."

"Turns out she was ten weeks pregnant."

Kate's eyes widened. "What on earth? Any idea who the sperm donor might be?"

I took another slug of Michelob and set the bottle on a coaster on Kate's glass-topped coffee table. "We can rule out the Man in the Moon and Eugene the Eunuch, but after that it's anybody's guess. Jessie never mentioned that she was involved with anyone, and neither did Angie Decker. I guess I need to talk to Angie again. That ought to be fun."

"You don't believe she's in on this, do you?"

"I don't know what to believe right now. Angie trusted me with the key to Jessie's house so I could search for the hidden key to Jake's place. The next day somebody ransacks my camper looking for something. What else could that something have been but the key to Jake's? And the next morning I'm inside Jake's house when Laurel shows up with a locksmith. That's one hell of a coincidence. You got any better ideas?"

Kate sighed. "No, but it seems odd that Angie would be so cooperative and then turn right around and sic the dogs on you. That makes her involvement seem way too obvious."

"Yeah." I drained the last of my beer, placed the laptop on the coffee table, and headed for the kitchen to get another Mich. I opened it and leaned on the bar separating the kitchen from the living room. "Unless …."

Kate turned and looked at me, waiting while my brain juggled puzzle pieces. "Unless what?" she said after a long pause.

I tapped four-four time with the bottle cap on the Formica top. "Unless someone close to Angie Decker happens to be involved up to their neck in whatever's going on with the Jake Lofton case."

My first order of business Friday morning was to head for the Palmetto County Courthouse in Parkersville and the property appraiser's office to see who was leading the run on Five Mile Island property. The buy-out was nearly complete, if all the No Trespassing signs Henry and I had seen were any indication. I was waited on by a perky young brunette named Ginny who looked like she belonged in high school. As I started my spiel about the specific properties I was looking for, her face lit up like a marquee.

"That would be Mr. Kreuzberger," she said, flashing a smile full of glistening enamel. Ginny turned and walked to a waist-high set of bookshelves that ran parallel to the front counter for damn near the length of the room. I stood admiring the scenery as she bent over and pulled a huge property records ledger from the shelf and lugged it back using both arms to support the weight against her chest. She set it on the counter, flipped through a fistful of pages, and turned the volume one-eighty to face me. "Here we go," she said, pointing a slender finger with a glittery-green nail about halfway down the page. "They begin here, and run to … here." She gave the opposite page a tap a third of the way down. "If you need any more help, I'll be right over there." She waved a hand at an empty desk.

I watched Ginny stroll back to her desk, and then turned my attention to the task at hand. Kreuzberger and Sons, Inc., a real estate development company from Dothan, Alabama, had, in the last six months, purchased a total of twenty-two properties on Five Mile Island for a nifty sum of seventeen million-plus dollars, according to my quick calculation by long addition. I jotted down all the property numbers that were recently gobbled up by Kreuzberger, and then called for Ginny's help.

"Could you make a copy of this plat?"

She flashed her bright smile again. "Sure. It's a dollar a copy. How many would you like?"

"One should do it," I said. At that price I'd visit the nearest Office Depot if I needed more.

Five minutes later I was out the door with my legal-size copy of Five Mile Island properties in-hand. I crossed the street to the Silverado where I'd left Henry parked in the shade of a sprawling live oak. I blocked the open door with my body while Henry greeted me with his lapping tongue. I pulled a plastic baggie from a box on the console, snapped the leash on Henry's twenty-buck harness, and held on tight as he leaped off the seat and sprawled headlong onto the pavement. Kate had said Henry was full-blooded Doberman, but I was beginning to wonder if a little squirrel hadn't snuck into the bloodline somewhere along the line. At this young age, the pup definitely had more cojones than brains.

When we got home I Googled Kreuzberger and Sons. Karl Kreuzberger Sr. founded the company. He emigrated with his parents and siblings from Germany to the U.S. at age fifteen, shortly after Hitler's forces blitzkrieged their way through Poland in late 1939. He fought in Europe with the U.S. Army during WWII and started Kreuzberger Realty from scratch after graduating from Alabama Polytechnic Institute, now known as Auburn University, in 1950. Married in 1960, he and his wife had three sons, each joining the business in the early '80s as the business evolved and morphed into Kreuzberger and Sons, Incorporated. When the old man died in 2004, Karl Jr. took command as president and CEO, with brothers Kurtis and Klifford assuming roles as vice-presidents. According to the company website:

> Kreuzberger and Sons, Inc. is a full-service, privately held commercial and residential real estate investment and development company. Over the past six decades we've established a distinguished résumé and reputation. A full-service developer, we have the ability to move any project from site selection,

acquisition, financing, construction, leasing, property management, and maintenance. The core principles that define the Kreuzberger organization are the stability, creativity, and professional expertise of our management team; a long-term, aggressive business plan; an unwavering commitment to excellence and tenant service; a close relationship with strategic partners, tenants, lenders, municipalities, and real estate professionals; a consistent ability to add value; and an unwavering pursuit of visionary development.

It was quite a mouthful, especially the part about their "unwavering pursuit of visionary development." How "unwavering" were the Kreuzberger brothers willing to be in their quest to buy up and develop Five Mile Island property? Whatever it took, I was determined to find out.

———

LATER THAT AFTERNOON I dropped Henry off in Kate's backyard and drove to Crowley's Ace Hardware to UPS the packets of hot chocolate I'd lifted from Jake's house to Frank. Frank had a friend of a friend at the FDLE crime lab in Tallahassee who agreed to examine the stuff on the sly for drugs. If the cocoa mix turned up positive, I'd have concrete evidence that somebody wanted to permanently halt Jake Lofton's research into the Five Mile Island project.

Leaving Crowley's, I turned the Silverado east on Highway 98 and headed for the causeway leading to Five Mile Island. I passed Barfield Fisheries and hung a right on Island Causeway. It was strange to see the once bustling Barfield's looking like a ghost town. State and federal authorities had shut the business down following the bust I'd instigated last summer while gathering evidence for the case I was determined to solve. Most of the people involved were out on bail and awaiting trial.

That didn't do much for my score on the Behavioral Relaxation Scale.

A little farther on I noticed a green and white county sheriff's cruiser approaching from the opposite direction. I eased off the gas until the Silverado slowed to the posted 45 mph. Sheriff Bocephus Pickron had me near the top of his shit list for past head-butting, and I had no doubt that he'd put the word out to his deputies to nail me for anything minutely pushing the letter of the law. I lifted my hand in a friendly gesture as we passed, but the glare on the cruiser's windshield blinded me from recognizing the deputy. In my dealings with the department I'd made the acquaintance of several friendly officers, but there were a few ass-kissing bad eggs wearing the uniform, too.

About a half-mile from the island I glanced in the rearview mirror and saw a county car trailing along behind. *Damn.* Probably one of Pickron's unfriendlies. I'd have to watch my Ps and Qs if I wanted to avoid trouble and accomplish what I'd set out to do. I needed to talk with the four businesses and homeowners on the bayside of the island who'd not yet sold out to Kreuzberger and Sons. I kept an eye on the car as I navigated the wide turn west onto the island. It had closed the gap by about half. The blue light flashed, but no siren.

Crap. I cleared the curve and pulled into the parking lot of the 7-Eleven, the only chain business on the island. It was located near the Trade Winds Lodge, the two separated by four upscale bayside homes built in the past couple of years. The cruiser followed. I parked and got out of the pickup, pretending to ignore my tail, and stepped onto the raised concrete walkway that ran the length of the storefront.

"Hey, McClellan!"

The voice stopped me in my tracks before I reached the door. There was no mistaking it. I turned in time to see a female deputy remove her sunglasses and flash a bright smile. Even the cop getup couldn't hide the knockout figure of young Deputy Dakota Blaire Owens. Dakota had worked undercover for the department on a case I happened to stumble onto a few months back, and despite being pummeled black and blue by a couple of hired thugs, she'd been instrumental in getting my butt out of a deep-shit, last-minute situation. She had also developed a crush on me, which I hoped was over.

Beneath the ball cap county deputies wore as part of the uniform, I noticed that her hair was the same reddish-blonde she'd dyed it months ago. The nine-millimeter Glock 19 Dakota used to carry concealed was now strapped to her hip, and all the buttons of her uniform blouse were buttoned according to regulation. Quite a change from the disheveled, vampish Dakota I'd first met as she was being escorted from the premises of the Green Parrot by her cousin JD after a brawl she'd instigated on the beach.

"Dakota, well I'll be damned. You're looking good."

She grinned, placed a hand on a hip and thrust the other to the side in a model's pose. "You like?"

What wasn't to like? Dakota was one hell of a sexy-looking woman, even if she was half my age. "Yeah. Good to see you again. How're you doing?"

"All healed up and back on the job. What's up with you, McClellan? I heard you got your PI license."

"News travels fast. Just taking a leisurely afternoon drive. Has Pickron got you tailing me?"

The smile faded and her upper lip curled into her signature Elvis snarl. "Give me a friggin' break. You can be a real asshole sometimes, you know that?"

It wasn't anything I hadn't heard from Dakota's potty mouth before, but it was true. "I apologize," I said, and meant it. "How about a cup of coffee? I'd like to talk to you if you got a few minutes."

A hint of a grin crept back onto her tanned face. "Anything for you, McClellan, but make mine a Red Bull. I'm pulling a double tonight."

Taking our drinks outside the 7-Eleven, we sat at one of the sheltered picnic tables. We talked for a good twenty minutes. Dakota was born and raised in St. George and turned out to be a well of information. Kreuzberger and Sons had been buying up island property for several months with the intention of building a planned beach resort community similar to Seaside in Walton County, located between Panama City and Destin. I hadn't heard about it yet because at this point nothing was official and the plans were being kept under wraps. The sheriff's department had been notified by Kreuzberger and Sons, requesting they crack down on people trespassing on their newly acquired properties. Jake Lofton popped into my mind.

I moved my coffee out of the way and spread the plat of the island on the table. I pointed out the bayside properties not yet under Kreuzberger's umbrella.

"You can scratch off the Little Birmingham here," Dakota said, tapping a fingernail on the mom and pop motel and gift shop. "It's been in business since the mid fifties. The word is Mr. Vernon and his old lady sold the place last week." The Little Birmingham had once been a popular destination not only for vacationers, but also for celebrating high school graduates and illicit lovers. Irate parents and the county law finally cracked down several years back and put an end to most of the partying and hanky-panky.

Two other parcels were owned by out-of-towners, but Dakota had no info on them. Then she ran a fingertip across a large tract of land located about midway in the proposed idyllic bayside community. "Old Man Moats owns this place, the crazy old coot. He's lived there like forever. His daddy bought up a bunch of property back during the Depression or World War Two or something like that. I heard Moats turned down over three million for his property."

I cut loose a whistle. "Three million? Why wouldn't he take that offer?"

Dakota snorted. "That old hermit's already got more money

than he could ever spend from selling all the gulf-front property his old man left him."

I heard static as a call came in over Dakota's shoulder-mounted radio. A resident of one of the island's upscale gulf-front homes reported that a neighbor's dog was crapping in her yard for the umpteenth time. Dakota rolled her eyes and informed the dispatcher she was on her way. From the tirade she cut loose as she stomped the few feet to her cruiser, I could tell she was more than a little peeved. It was a world away from her previous duty. Life as a uniformed deputy on routine patrol might not be as exciting as working undercover, but it was one hell of a lot safer. I was glad Dakota was out of that racket for now.

I caught up with the fuming deputy as she slammed the cruiser's door. "I think I'll go pay Mr. Moats a visit and see if he's got anything interesting to say."

Dakota lifted her sunglasses and raised both eyebrows. "You better watch your ass, McClellan. That old fart would just as soon shoot you as look at you." And with those parting words of comfort, Dakota gunned the engine and laid rubber as the county car squealed out of the parking lot heading west.

———

ACCORDING TO THE PLAT, Amos Moats's property covered a little over four-hundred feet of road frontage, and nearly that much bordering the bay. It didn't take an engineer to see his parcel was key to the success of the Kreuzbergers' proposed development. I slowed to check the number on the rusting mailbox to confirm the address, and then turned onto the rutted sandy drive. The drive weaved through low dunes carpeted with coarse grasses and sandspurs. On either side, stunted oaks bent toward the bay like posed ballerinas. The worn track stopped in front of a ramshackle concrete block house standing about seventy-five yards off the road. Most of what once was aqua or sea-green paint had long since faded and peeled away.

I parked the Silverado to the side of the drive, such as it was, and had made it about halfway to the house when a thunderclap cut the air. Instinctively I dropped prone and hugged Mother Earth—or sand, to be more accurate. The adrenaline rushed and it took a couple of seconds to remember the sky was blue and this wasn't a war zone. Then my eye caught movement at the left front corner of the house.

A thin, wiry elf of a man stepped around the corner and stood facing me with a scowl on his leathery face. The old double-barrel shotgun clutched in his hands was damn near as long as he was tall. He had to be all of five feet two, and thin enough that a gusting wind might pick him up and carry him away unless he kept a couple of good-size rocks in each pocket of the patched overalls he wore. Dakota wasn't bullshitting when she said Amos Moats would just as soon shoot you as look at you.

He spit a brown stream toward me and then shifted the wad of tobacco to his other cheek. As he cocked his head to one side, his scowl grew and the lines in his prune-like face deepened. I noticed his finger inside the trigger guard, not a comforting sign. "What in Satan's lair you doin' here?" said the gravelly voice. "Damnation, ain't you got eyes, boy?"

I lay there dumbfounded.

"The sign out front yonder," he said, when I didn't answer. He spit again, shifted the scattergun to one hand and pointed a gnarly finger toward the road. "It says 'No trespassin' and no solicitors,' plain as the day is long, yes sir, plain as the day is long. So what bidniz you got comin' on my property again? I done told you fellers a dozen times if I told you once that I ain't sellin', come hell or high water or snow in August."

I pushed myself up to my knees, making sure I kept both hands raised above my head, and stood. I was relieved to see his itchy finger was no longer fiddling with the triggers.

"I didn't see your sign, Mr. Moats, and I'm not trying to buy anything. I stopped by for a quick chat."

Amos craned his neck in the opposite direction. "So, you know my name, and I can see you know my address. Stole my sign again, did they? Well, you wastin' your time anyways, 'cause I ain't buyin' nothin' neither."

By this time I was getting a little ticked. "Look, I'm not trying to buy your place, and I'm not trying to sell you anything. Now, can I put my hands down so we can talk face to face like men?"

He waved the barrel of the shotgun in a circle. "Reckon so. Go on and put 'em down then, but you try somethin' funny and I'll give you both barrels."

I lowered my hands to my sides and breathed a little easier. I resisted the urge to tell Pruneface he'd have to reload if he intended to give me both barrels, since he'd already emptied one over my head. I stood my ground and let him cut the distance between us. He stopped well out of arm's reach but within lethal range of what I now saw was an old Savage Stevens Model 311 twelve-gauge. I'd hunted with the same model when I was a kid.

Amos waved the barrel in a circle again and craned his neck back the other way. "Well?"

"What do you know about the Kreuzberger people who're buying up all the land around here?"

"I know they's a bunch 'a damn hooligans that won't take no for a answer and go around hasslin' everybody on the island. Been here a dozen times if they been here once."

"Do you know about the big project they plan to build along the bay?"

An osprey with a fish clutched in its talons flew parallel to the bay shoreline heading west. Amos tracked it for a moment and then turned his eyes back to me. "Yep."

"Did you know your place sits almost right in the middle of it?"

Amos chuckled and turned his head to spit. "Reckon they'll

hafta build their little paradise around me then, won't they, boy?" He wiped his stubbled chin with the back of a hand.

I grinned. "Reckon they will. Is it true they offered you three million for your place?"

His eyes narrowed to slits and his face wrinkled up around his mouth. "That ain't none 'a your damn bidniz. Say, did that boy 'a mine send you here to try to talk me into sellin'?"

I shook my head. "I didn't know you had a son."

"Highfalutin lawyer over in Panama City. Leastways he thinks he is. Him and that sorry-ass wife 'a mine been tryin' to get me to dump this place ever since them varmints first come snoopin' around."

Wife? Dakota had called Amos an old hermit. I was missing something here. "Oh, so you're married?"

Amos turned his head and spit again and cut loose a sarcastic laugh. "Name only, boy. Cherry and that son 'a mine been shacked up damn near a year now, yes sir. And in the same damn house I give him the money to buy. S'posed to 've been a loan, but I reckon you know how that goes."

Cherry? I almost busted out laughing. Dakota had evidently left out a few minor details about the life and times of Amos Moats. "Your wife and son are living together?"

Amos scooped the tobacco from his cheek with an index finger and flipped the slimy wad onto the sand. He ran his tongue around his mouth and spit a couple of times to get rid of the rest, leaving a couple of specks on his grizzled chin. He nodded. "Fourth wife. Buried the first two; the third run off when I wouldn't let her get her sticky paws on my money. You believe that, boy? I give that woman three-hun'erd dollars a month to do with as she damn well pleased, but it weren't enough, no sir. Greedy sort, she was. Divorced her and married up with Cherry 'bout a year later."

I mulled over Amos's marriage record while he fished in a pocket of his overalls, pulled out a pack of Beech-Nut, and stuffed a fresh wad into his mouth.

"If you don't mind my asking, if your wife left you for your son, why haven't you divorced her?"

He chuckled and slipped the tobacco back into the pocket. "Bidniz 'rangement. Cherry's a fine-lookin' woman, and I'm getting' a little long in the tooth. Man my age ain't got time to go chasin' after fresh cooter. I keep 'er on the payroll and she visits a couple 'a weekends a month to perform her wifely duties."

"And your son's okay with that?"

Amos chuckled and tongued the fresh wad to his cheek. "One thing that boy 'a mine likes more'n coochie is money. Hell, I knew them two was conjugatin' before me and Cherry ever tied the knot. Only reason I kicked her out was she kept pesterin' me to sell out to them developers. I ain't no fool, boy. I know them two's after my money. They figure they'll get it too, soon's I'm in my grave feedin' the worms. Hell, I ain't got no other use for it, done got all I need right here. But I got a little surprise for them two after I'm gone to my heavenly re-ward."

I was wondering what to say next when Amos's eyes lit up and I heard a low bark behind me. I turned and saw a huge, one-eyed brindle dog of questionable heritage lift a leg and piss all over the left rear tire of my Silverado. When he was finished, he sniffed the tire a few seconds to make sure he'd marked this new intruder on his territory properly.

"Rascal, where the hell you been, boy?" Amos laid the shotgun across a saw palmetto bush and knelt down as the popeyed old cur trotted over to him. He ruffled the dog's ears and scrunched up the loose skin of his neck. "You been off shittin' in Miz Ogden's yard again, boy. Huh, that it? Good boy!"

Amos gave Rascal another pat on his broad head, and then stood up and retrieved the scattergun. "Say, you never did tell me what you doin' here."

"I'm looking into the possible murder of a man who might've had a run-in with the Kreuzbergers." That was stretching the truth a little, but what the hell. The old geezer might be more cooperative if he thought we were on the same side.

"Murder? I ain't heard 'bout no murder. You a cop?"

"No sir, I work for Hightower Investigations out of Destin. The incident happened about two months ago along the highway a little south of Marianna. The authorities ruled it a suicide, but I've got my doubts."

"Humph. Wouldn't put it past them scoundrels, no sir. What'd you say your name was, boy?" His tone had changed from threatening to almost friendly. Maybe Rascal was a good influence on the old geezer.

"Mac McClellan. I've got a business card in my pocket I'd like to leave with you." I eased my hand into my shorts pocket and pulled out one of the cards Frank had given me when I'd earned my PI license. I held it out as Amos walked over and took it. "I'm local. Give me a call if they keep harassing you, or if you see or hear anything suspicious going on."

He glanced at the card. "McClellan …. Say, ain't you the feller found that Harper girl's body a while back?"

My claim to fame. "That's me. You'll let me know if you hear anything?"

Amos turned his head and spit a long stream that the loose sand quickly swallowed, leaving a damp brown stain. "I'll do 'er. Feller never knows when he might could use a friend."

Chapter 7

———•———

Ａfter talking with Dakota and visiting Amos Moats, I decided my next order of business should be putting my new metal detector to work. The Kreuzbergers had notified the sheriff's department about trespassers, and I had little doubt that they would soon hire their own private security guards to patrol their newly gotten gains, if they hadn't done so already. Snooping ashore around the Stumps would be risky, but I needed to find out for myself if that's indeed where Jake Lofton had found the artifacts Jessie had shown me during our meeting.

After negotiating Amos's sand rut of a driveway back to the highway, I turned west and headed toward the state park. The Stumps were located near the park's eastern border. I wasn't certain if another parcel of land lay between them and the park or not, because they didn't appear on the plat I'd gotten from the property appraiser's office. As I approached the small brick building near the park's entrance, several No Trespassing signs leading up to it gave me the answer. Except for Amos's land and the two lots owned by out-of-towners, the bayside of Five Mile Island was now all Kreuzberger property from the state park to the Trade Winds Lodge. And I would've given odds to any takers that the two other parcels were as good as in the bag. I pulled over to the right shoulder of the road, checked my mirrors, and made a U-turn.

It was after four when I got back to Gulf Pines. I pulled to a stop in front of the doublewide that Jerry and Donna Meadows had converted into the campground store and office. There were a handful of customers milling about the aisles with shopping baskets. Donna was sitting in her usual place behind the counter, knitting needles clacking, as she watched a TV talk show. I headed for the coolers in back and grabbed a dozen eggs, a pound of ground sausage, and a six-pack of canned Bud.

"Hey, good looking," I said, placing the items on the counter and reaching in my back pocket for my wallet.

Donna looked up and smiled. "Hey there, Mac, where you been keeping yourself lately?" She set the knitting aside and got up to man the register. The sunlight streaming through the window behind highlighted the bluish tones in her gray hair.

"Oh, here and about. That old man of yours around?"

"He's over by the north end, weed-whacking," she said, keying in numbers.

"Well, shoot. I was hoping me and you could go out and shake a leg tonight."

She laughed. "If you'd 'a asked me that twenty years ago I might've took you up on it."

I counted out the total and set the bills and change on the counter. "Can't blame a man for trying," I said, grabbing the paper sack and giving her a wink on my way out.

To pull off what I wanted to do, I needed a partner to back me up in case things didn't go as smoothly as I hoped. Tomorrow being Saturday, I knew Kate had to work. Jerry Meadows was next on my list. He was getting on in years, but was active as a man twenty years his junior. I knew for damn sure he was trustworthy. I followed the whine of the gas Weed Eater and parked the Silverado off the crushed shell road near where Jerry was attacking grass and weeds encroaching the drive of a vacant campsite. He glanced up and waved when he noticed me climbing out of the pickup, and shut off the trimmer as I crossed the road. Propping the Weed Eater against a hip, Jerry pulled a handkerchief from a back pocket and wiped his brow as we exchanged greetings.

I wasted no time giving him a brief spiel of the case I was working on, and my plans for early tomorrow morning. After I'd finished, he said, "Your boat or mine?" without blinking an eye.

"Mine. If anything goes wrong you tagged along to wet a line. I don't want you getting your butt in a sling because of me."

———

THUNDER RUMBLED FROM A distant squall to the southwest as I eased off the throttle. Dark clouds muddled the southern horizon and lightning zigzagged across the low sky. The Stumps loomed like ghostly sentinels intent on guarding whatever secret the land beyond held. I hoped the old resin-filled pines were the only guards hanging around the area.

Jerry glanced over his shoulder and pointed to the east side of the Stumps. "Better head yonder with this wind coming on."

I nodded and turned the wheel. We skirted the backside of the old pine forest and then eased along the eastern side toward shore. I put the Mercury into neutral and let it idle as the boat drifted closer to the narrow sandy beach. With a slight jolt, the bow ran aground. I moved toward the bow while Jerry headed for the steering station.

"I'm gonna back her up about halfway out and tie off to a stump," he said. "How long you reckon to be?"

"No longer than it takes," I said, grabbing the Bounty Hunter in my right hand and using the left to grip the starboard gunnel as I stepped over the side into knee-deep water. I sloshed ashore as Jerry backed the boat into deeper water. After turning to give him a quick wave, I scrambled up the steep bank using handholds of coarse grass to pull against and trying my damndest to avoid a fistful of sandspurs.

By the time I crested the dunes, Jerry had already tied the boat off and was casting a stingray grub into the Stumps for flounder. I took a quick glance around. Nobody seemed to be stirring, so keeping a wary eye out for diamondback rattlers, I worked my way inland for about twenty yards.

During our meeting at Panama Joe's, Jessie had mentioned that her brother found the artifacts near the bay overlooking what appeared to be a dead forest sticking out of the water. That had to be the Stumps, and most likely the location of the Spaniards' winter fort, if it had existed. But there was no telling how far out into the bay the small forested peninsula had extended during de Soto's time. My guess was the main part of the fort was now under several feet of water. From my front pocket, I pulled the map Jessie had given me of what during the 16th century was a seven-mile-long peninsula. I took it out of the protective Ziploc bag. After studying it a minute or so, I slipped it back in the bag and back in my shorts pocket.

My plan was to start inland and work my way in a crisscross pattern toward the bay. Not being familiar with the metal detector, and knowing I was looking for iron objects as well as coins, I turned the discrimination knob low and the sensitivity setting to about midrange and pressed the "All Metal" display. With those settings I'd probably come across a lot of trash, but it was my best shot at finding something worthwhile.

Sweeping the coil back and forth, I almost immediately picked up several beeps of different tones. I pinpointed the object as best I could, then dropped to one knee, pulled the garden trowel I'd borrowed from Kate from my back pocket, and dug into the sand. A few seconds later I flipped up the rim of an old drink can that predated all-aluminum cans.

The next ten or fifteen minutes produced nothing but pull

tabs, rusted cans, and other junk. Finally the detector let out a beep different from the ones I'd been hearing. Digging down about four or five inches, I heard the trowel strike something solid and metallic. My adrenaline rushed as I lifted a coin with a trowel-full of sand. Brushing the coin clean, I saw it was an Indian Head penny in rough condition, dated either 1903 or 1908. It was no 16th-century Spanish coin, but what the hell, I figured it had to be worth at least a few cents. The trip wouldn't be a total loss.

The wind was picking up, and the thunder was getting louder by the minute. Deciding my chances would probably be better closer to the bay, I hurried in that direction. Jerry and I had to motor back to St. George, and I damn sure didn't want to do it while fighting a gale. About ten feet from the edge where the dunes began to slope downward to the bay the detector cut loose again. I dropped to both knees and began digging. I dug about a foot deep and came up empty, so I passed the coil over the pile of sand I'd excavated to make sure I hadn't missed anything. Nothing.

I kept digging for another six or eight inches and then an object hit the pile and slid down a couple of inches. At first I thought it was an old bracelet someone had lost years ago. Closer inspection proved it to be several small rusted oblong or circular loops linked tightly together, forming a patch-like object a couple of inches long and maybe an inch and a half wide. I had no idea what it was, but I slipped it into my pocket. You never know.

A few feet away the Bounty Hunter beeped again. Down and digging, I soon turned up a similar object, although this one was a little smaller in length. I dropped it in my pocket with the other one as a voice called out, "Hey, you!"

Oops. I turned and saw a tall lanky man with bushy hair approaching from about fifty yards away. He wore a tan shirt and trousers and a brown ball cap. It wasn't a county sheriff's uniform, but I had no intentions of hanging around long enough to find out who the guy worked for.

I scrambled to my feet and trotted toward the ledge as a shot rang out. The SOB was *shooting* at me, at least in my general direction. I hit the deck, cradling the detector in both arms. Low crawling to the dune wall, I went over head first. I spit out a mouthful of sand and tried to let loose a warning whistle to Jerry, but I doubt you could've heard it five feet away.

Turning feet-first, I slid on down the slope and hit the beach running. Jerry had the boat waiting a few feet off the shoreline. I high-stepped through the shallows. Tossing the detector into the boat, I grabbed the bow and pushed for all I was worth. Jerry gunned the motor in reverse. I hung on until I managed to pull myself aboard and flop onto the deck.

"Turn this thing around and get the hell out of here!" I shouted, but Jerry was way ahead of the game. We were thirty or forty yards past the end of the Stumps when another shot rang out, barely discernable above the roar of the Merc 50. By then I was more pissed than scared, and if the Bounty Hunter was an M16 I would've had that chicken-shit wannabe cop hugging Mother Earth for all he was worth.

Chapter 8

———•———

BACK AT THE CAMPGROUND, I stripped down and spent a good hour tweezing and plucking broken-off sandspur burrs out of my ass and other strategic body areas. Luckily, during my less-than-graceful descent down the dune face, the Indian Head penny and two odd pieces of rusted metal I'd found had stayed put in the pocket where I'd stowed them. Kate's trowel hadn't fared as well, lost somewhere during my inglorious retreat back to the boat.

Under the bathroom sink I found an old toothbrush and went to work scrubbing the encrusted sand and rust from the metallic objects. Twenty minutes later I'd managed to remove most of the crud from the centers of the loops, although I inadvertently broke a link or two that crumbled free of the others. It looked like a couple of crude rusted bracelets connected together, but keeping in mind where I'd found them, I figured they might be something of interest or of use to the Jake Lofton case. I booted up my laptop and googled "de Soto's Tallahassee encampment."

I almost dropped my beer when I came across a photo of objects that closely resembled what lay on the table beside my computer. It was chain mail, a type of light armor that the Spanish explorers wore to protect themselves from hostile Indian arrows and spears. According to the accompanying text, the armor proved to be ineffective and was, for the most part, soon discarded.

I picked up the rusted objects and jiggled them, realizing I was holding a part of history in the palm of my hand. Here was probable proof that Jake was correct in his theory. A party of Hernando de Soto's band had indeed trekked south to the coast and built a fort during the winter of 1539–40 on what became Five Mile Island. The question now was, where the hell was I going with this case next?

When I called the marina, I recognized Sara Gillman's perky voice. We exchanged a few pleasant words and then she informed me that Kate was outside showing a boat to a prospective buyer. She'd have her call me as soon as she was free. The Gillman's cute teenage daughter and I had hit a rough patch back when I was trying to solve Maddie Harper's murder. I was glad things were smooth between us again.

"Sorry, Mac, but I'm leaving for my parents' house right after work," Kate said when she returned my call and I'd asked if she'd like to meet me at the Green Parrot for happy hour and dinner. "By the way, how did your trip to the island turn out?"

"Good, and not so good."

"Meaning?"

"I found evidence to back up Jake Lofton's theory, and I owe you a garden trowel." I decided to leave out the part about getting shot at, at least for now.

"Can't you ever give a straight answer?"

"I found some small pieces of what I think might be Spanish armor."

"Really? Well that's great news, isn't it? Somehow you don't sound too thrilled."

"Two people are already dead because of this mess, Kate. My

gut tells me somebody's playing for keeps in this crap game. How thrilled am I supposed to sound?"

"Well, excuse me for being interested in your life."

"I'm sorry. I don't want you getting involved this time." A few months back somebody had gone after Kate because of her ties to a case I was working on. I didn't want to risk that happening again.

"I'm not a helpless little girl, Mac. I'll call you when I get back Sunday night. Maybe." *Click.*

———

THAT EVENING I WAS sitting on my picnic table nursing a Dewar's over ice and pretending to watch the sun go down over the gulf when "The Marines' Hymn" rang out from my cargo shorts' pocket. I thumbed loose the Velcro tab and answered.

"Mac, this is Angie Decker. I need to see you again."

I snickered and slapped at a mosquito that was bugging the hell out of me. "What does *Mr.* Decker have to say about that?"

"Damn it, this is no joke."

When it came to conversing with women, I was batting a big fat zero for the day. "Sorry. I'm all ears." In the background I heard a racket and voices arguing, probably the Deckers' young sons getting into a scrap.

"I can't talk now," Angie said, her voice dropping almost to a whisper. "Can you meet me here, Monday morning, ten sharp?"

"Okay, but what—"

Click.

———

MAN OF MY WORD, I pulled into Angie Decker's driveway promptly at ten Monday morning. Before I'd even turned off the engine, she opened the front door and stepped out, closing the door behind her. I hadn't taken two steps her way before she lifted an index finger to her lips, signaling me to be quiet.

The gesture stopped me in my tracks, but she motioned me forward and led the way back inside the house.

Once inside, she turned back to me and repeated the "be quiet" signal. *Okay, I get the message, Angie, but what the hell are you up to?* I wondered. I didn't think she was about to throw me a surprise party, at least not a fun one. I practically tiptoed as I followed her through the great room and into the spacious kitchen. She walked past the large granite-topped island and then stopped beside the edge nearest the kitchenette where we'd sat and talked during my previous visit. I followed suit.

Flashing the quiet sign again, she pointed at the bullnose edging of the granite countertop extending about three inches past the oak island base. She pointed to the underside of the granite overhang. I assumed a catcher's squat, craned my neck to the side and glanced up. *Aha!* There was a small black rectangular object stuck to the underside of the countertop. It was about two and a half inches long, maybe three-quarters of an inch wide, and less than a half-inch thick. I started to reach for it, but thought better of it. I grabbed my cellphone from my pocket and snapped a few shots from various angles. I stood, and for a change of pace, crooked a finger for Angie to follow me.

Fortunately the wall and trees surrounding the Deckers' property provided a lot of privacy against any potential nosey neighbors. But if somebody had bugged the house, there was the possibility the yard was under surveillance, too. It was a risk we'd have to take. We both kept our traps shut until we reached my truck and climbed inside the cab of the Silverado, where I was reasonably certain we could talk freely.

I started the engine and switched on the air-conditioner so we wouldn't suffocate in the August heat. "My guess is it's a digital mini-recorder, probably voice-activated. When did you find it?"

Angie drummed her manicured nails on the console between us. "Late Saturday afternoon, about an hour before I called you. I saw a spider crawling up the island. I can't stand those things, so I grabbed a can of spray from the cabinet. By then it had disappeared, so I looked under the countertop and there it was."

I offered a slight grin to lighten the mood. "Did you get the spider?"

She glanced my way and then stared through the windshield. "I was so stunned I forgot all about the damn spider. Ron must've put it there, but I have no idea why."

"Are you having an affair?"

If looks could kill, I would've been a goner. "*That* is none of *your* damn business!"

"Jessie hired me to find out what happened to Jake," I fired back. "You were her best friend and she trusted you with the safe deposit box, so that sort of makes it my business. Your husband planted a listening device in your home for a reason. Is he checking up on you, or what?"

Angie sighed and sat back in her seat, facing forward again. "No, I'm not having an affair, if that's what you mean," she said, her voice calmer now. "I've never cheated on my husband. There's no reason I can think of why he'd even suspect I was. None."

"Thanks. I'm sorry I had to ask, but it's important."

"Why?"

I turned the A/C down a little. "Because if your husband has no reason to suspect you're having a fling, that means he probably planted the recorder to find out other information. Where is he now?"

"Out of town on a job. What information?"

I rested my elbow against the door panel and cupped my chin in my hand. "Remember what we talked about when I was here before? How Jessie was convinced that Jake was murdered? The new archaeological site he'd discovered? The artifacts Jessie was keeping for him in the safe deposit box?"

Angie frowned and nodded.

"Remember where we were sitting?"

The frown deepened. "Yes."

"Within range of that recorder." I grabbed the steering wheel with both hands and turned my head to face Angie. "Just how well do you trust your husband?"

Angie's mouth fell open. "Wait. You can't think Ron had anything to do with this. No, he ... he couldn't."

"What else am I supposed to think? You found the recorder. My guess is your husband, or somebody, had Jessie's house bugged, too. The day after I found the key to Jake's house at Jessie's, somebody ransacked my trailer. Nothing was stolen, but whoever did it almost turned the place inside out looking for something. I'd bet my bottom dollar it was the key to Jake's place. And the next day Laurel had all the locks changed."

Angie shifted in the seat and gave me a wounded look as tears clouded her eyes. "I think Ron and Jessie were having an affair."

Chapter 9

————•————

"IT'S A TOP-OF-THE-LINE MICRO-RECORDER, voice activated," Frank said. "Probably has a range of thirty feet or more."

"Then I'm screwed. Ron Decker heard every word we said that day."

Frank ran a hand through his thick gray hair and adjusted his glasses as he gave the photos on his monitor another look. "You might want to think about getting a new phone. These photos suck."

"Thanks. Angie Decker thinks her husband and Jessie Lofton were screwing around."

That got Frank's full attention. "What makes her think that?"

I got up and headed for Frank's coffee maker for a refill. "She overheard her daughter and Sydni talking. Seems Uncle Ron was visiting Jessie at her house a couple of times when he was supposed to be working out of town. You want coffee?"

"No thanks." Frank rocked back in his chair. "Then Decker might've been Jessie's unborn baby's father."

"Yep. And I wouldn't be surprised if he's Sydni's father, too."

Frank sat up straight and rested both arms on the desktop. "That's a reach."

"He sure as hell had opportunity. Don't forget, the Deckers took Jessie in when she got knocked up by the mysterious unnamed sperm donor and her father kicked her out of the house. And she was their go-to babysitter when their daughter Riley was little. Angie mentioned she had to work part-time for a couple of years when Ron first started with his old man at the family construction business. My guess is there were plenty of chances for him and Jessie to hook up. Then there's the fact that Jessie never got married, or even had a serious relationship, according to Angie. Sounds like unrequited love to me, with a little sex on the side."

"I think I will have that coffee," Frank said. He got up and poured the dregs of the decanter into his mug. "You better watch yourself. I doubt Decker is working by himself, *if* he's involved in this mess."

I grinned. "I'm touched that you care."

"Don't flatter yourself, Mac. You haven't worked off your classes and license fees yet."

———

Leaving Destin, I crossed Choctawhatchee Bay on the Mid-Bay Bridge and turned west on Highway 20. One of Frank's contacts learned Jessie Lofton's totaled Mustang had wound up at Simon's Auto and Salvage, a little east of Niceville. I found the sign and turned right onto a short gravel road leading to the salvage yard's open front gate. I parked beside a shiny new Snap-on tool truck in front of an old concrete block building with chalky white paint and a rusting metal roof.

Inside, a window-unit air conditioner hummed noisily behind the counter. The Snap-on man was talking shop with a Ben Franklin lookalike at the near end of the oil-stained counter. I walked past a couple of guys sitting on stools to where a tall, thin younger man with a shock of red hair stood staring at a computer monitor. He glanced up when I stopped in front of him. *Brian* was sewn in cursive on the patch above the left pocket of his dark-blue work shirt.

His Adam's apple bobbed when he spoke. "Can I help you?"

"Yeah. I'm looking for a late-model Mustang convertible I heard you guys got in a week or so ago. Red."

"What'cha need off it?"

"Looking for some rims."

"Might still have 'em." He turned toward the tool man and Ben Franklin and spoke above the noise of the A/C. "Hey, Bill, the rims still on that red Mustang ragtop out back?"

Bill looked annoyed at being interrupted. "Far's I know."

Brian lifted a hand and pointed his thumb over his shoulder like a hitchhiker. " 'Bout ten, twelve rows back, near the fence. If they what you want, let me know and we'll get 'em for you."

I thanked him, put on my sunglasses and headed outside into the hot and humid August air. I worked my way down a sandy trail with crabgrass and sandspurs growing on either side past row after row of wrecked and rusting hulks that had been somebody's pride and joy back in the day.

I forgot to count the rows, but it didn't take long to find Jessie Lofton's deathtrap. It was sitting with three other late-model autos in a new row a few feet from the high, weather-beaten chain-link fence topped with barbed-wire standoffs. The metallic candy-red body looked like somebody had worked it over with a sledgehammer, and the paint was splattered with dry, dark mud. I grabbed my phone and snapped a few pictures, including a close-up of the VIN plate, and tried not to think about the young woman trapped upside down in the water. All four wheels were on the vehicle, but the two left-side tires were flat. There wasn't a trace of rubber on the right-front.

I looked around and found a piece of half-rotted plywood near the fence. Placing it over a patch of sandspurs near the naked wheel, I took off my sunglasses and knelt down. Using the hard plastic ice scraper I kept in my Silverado, I scrubbed away the mud and other debris from the front of the tarnished chrome wheel that the tire had covered. There was no damage that I could see, so I moved the piece of plywood to the back edge of the wheel and went to work on what I could see and reach.

I'd about given up when I noticed a shallow gouge and scarring about two inches long, running from side to side across the concave part of the wheel. It was only a couple of inches from the ground, so I carefully pulled the weeds and grass away for a better look. Whatever had caused the tire to blow, this was probably evidence of it. I cleaned around the area, being careful not to scrape over the gouge itself. I took a closer look, then slipped the scraper in my back pocket and had started to stand when a voice called out.

"Them what you after?" Brian said, blowing a puff of cigarette smoke out with the words.

"I don't know. They look a little rough. Looks like this thing rolled a couple of times."

"Yeah, but they'll clean up real nice."

"How much?"

"Seventy-five each. I'll let 'em go for two hunnard if you buy the set."

I scratched at my beard. "Sounds a little steep, coming off a junker."

"Naw, them's top of the line rims. Oughta be askin' least a hunnard apiece."

I hesitated a couple of seconds. "That right-front's dinged-up some."

Brian gave the wheel a quick glance. "She'll clean up and hold a bead fine."

"Will you take a hundred for the set?"

He laughed. "Mister, I do that and I'm out a job. Two's as low's I can go."

I scratched the back of my head. "You take VISA?"

Brian took a final drag and flipped the butt toward the fence. "Sure do."

Thirty minutes later I drove out the gate of Simon's Auto and Salvage with the rims off Jessie Lofton's Mustang in the bed of my pickup.

———⊹———

ACCORDING TO THE ACCIDENT report Frank was able to get hold of, Jessie was killed when her car struck the eastern abutment of the bridge that crosses Suggs Bayou, about eight miles west of Freeport, and then rolled down the bank and ended up upside down in the shallow water. Approaching the bridge from the west, I gave the map a final glance and pulled onto the shoulder of Highway 20. I checked for traffic, crossed the road, and walked up to the bridge.

The approach from the east followed the shore of the bayou as it made a sharp curve southward and then back to the west right before the bridge crossing. I stood and watched a couple of vehicles negotiate the curve and cross the bridge. I retraced my steps west along the shoulder for about twenty yards and turned to watch a couple of more vehicles cross Suggs Bayou. The angle as they rounded the curve confirmed my hunch. From this vantage point, anyone who was a decent shot with a rifle could place a round into the front right tire of an approaching car. Add a good scope to the scenario and it was a no-brainer. The only problem was, how the hell could the shooter stand, kneel, or lie prone in broad daylight and not be seen? There was no nearby brush or any other concealment anywhere in the general area. This was pretty much the spot where a person would have to be to pull off such a shot.

I squatted and watched as another car approached and passed by, returning the friendly wave the driver offered. This height was dead on to take out a tire for a vehicle the size and profile of Jessie's Mustang. I fished my cellphone out of my pocket and casually snapped a couple of pictures as cars rounded the curve and approached the bridge. Then I headed back to the Silverado and home.

Chapter 10

⸻

I BROUGHT KATE UP to date on the case while we were enjoying happy hour that evening at the Green Parrot. She wasn't pleased, especially when I mentioned my theory about why Jessie's tire blew. "I think you should leave this one alone," she said, sipping her beer. "Uncle Frank does, too."

I smiled to lighten the mood. "So, you two've been conspiring behind my back, huh? That cheapskate doesn't want me on the case because we're not being paid."

She didn't appreciate my little attempt at humor. "It's not funny. You said it yourself: two people are dead already. I don't want you joining them."

I sang a few bars of "Don't Worry Baby" in my best imitation of the Beach Boys, which wasn't so hot. "That's not on my agenda."

Kate dipped a piece of fried calamari in tartar sauce and narrowed her eyes, never a good sign. "I suppose that's why you didn't tell me about getting shot at on the island the other day."

Oops. "How'd you find out about that?"

"I don't appreciate being lied to, dang it!"

I slugged down a couple of gulps of draft Bud. "I didn't lie. I simply left out a few boring details. Besides, the guy wasn't shooting *at* me. He fired over my head to scare me off."

"Not according to Jerry Meadows."

"Jerry exaggerates. The rounds never came close." I made a mental note to thank Jerry for spilling the beans. "I've been shot at a few times before, you know."

"Yeah, and *hit* a few times, too," Kate fired back, scowling.

This was a firefight I knew I couldn't win, so I reached across the table and took Kate's hands in mine. "Hey, let's enjoy the evening and not worry about this other stuff, okay? I value our time together. How about company tonight?"

"Meaning you and Henry?"

"Yeah."

The scowl faded and she almost broke a smile. "Does this mean you're dropping the case?"

I let out a deep breath. "I can't. I have an obligation to Jessie's daughter."

She pulled her hands free. "And *I* have a splitting headache!"

———

IN THE MORNING I drove out to the island to see Amos Moats. His phone number was unlisted, and there were a couple of questions I wanted to ask him. When I parked near his house Rascal was nowhere to be seen. That was fine with me. I hoped he was off fertilizing his neighbor's yard.

Easing up to the front door of the house like I expected to be ambushed any second, I pushed the doorbell. It stuck, but I didn't hear a chime. So I knocked a couple of times and got no answer. I walked around the back of the house and detached garage, calling out Amos's name every few yards. I didn't relish having that double-barrel barking my way again. Finding a well-worn path, I followed it down the back of Amos's property to the bay. There was a rickety pier of weathered pilings and warped planks jutting about thirty feet into St. George Bay.

Nearby, an old wooden boat listed on the shore above the high-tide mark. Its Florida registration number was hand painted on the bow in faded black letters and numbers. It was the same location Henry and I had come across on our earlier beach reconnaissance. There was no sign of Amos. I made my way back to the truck and waited another ten minutes, hoping he'd show. No such luck. Maybe he'd driven into town for something.

After giving up on seeing Amos, I cruised west down Island Drive and turned around at the state park entrance. The two properties previously owned by out-of-towners now sported new No Trespassing signs, making Amos Moats the lone holdout property owner of available bayside land on Five Mile Island.

When I got back to the campground Henry was chomping at the bit to go for a walk, so I hooked up his leash, grabbed my metal detector, and we headed for the beach. We spent a couple of hours searching for coins or other treasure, chasing sandpipers, and enjoying the salt air and scenery. I dug up a few coins and a broken silver-plated bracelet. Henry made out like a bandit, getting fawned over and petted by several admiring female sun worshipers. I should be so lucky.

———

THAT EVENING I RESEARCHED artifacts and archaeological websites and found a couple of clubs in the area, one in Tallahassee, the other in Fort Walton Beach, another popular tourist destination a few miles past Destin. I decided to listen to Horace Greeley and go west. I called Ed Duncan, who was listed as Research Director for the Emerald Shores Archaeology Society. Ed seemed excited by my news and agreed to meet for lunch at noon the next day at the Crab Shack in Fort Walton Beach. I was hoping he'd be able to confirm whether or not the rusted iron links I'd found near the Stumps were the real deal.

Next morning I set out on Highway 98, bound for Fort

Walton Beach. I'd talked to Frank last night after arranging the meeting with Ed Duncan and told him I was stopping by the office to drop off the right-front wheel from the Mustang. He said I'd probably wasted more of my time and the two hundred bucks, but did promise to have his retired FBI buddy examine it.

"She could've run over a bolt or a piece of scrap metal to cause that damage," he said when I lugged the wheel inside his office and showed him the gouge and scar.

"Yep. And somebody might've used a rifle on the tire. Don't forget, the tire blew out quick enough to cause Jessie to lose control. Did you take a good look at the photos I emailed?"

"Yeah, but like you said, a person would be taking a huge risk shooting at a vehicle in broad daylight on a well-traveled road."

"I've thought about that. Remember those two snipers up around D.C. a few years back? They took out something like ten people in a couple of weeks."

"Muhammad and Malvo."

"Good memory, Frank. Anyway, they cut a port in the trunk lid of their car to make a sniper's nest. Somebody could've done the same thing in this case."

"Okay, it's possible, but where's the motive?"

I reached in the pocket of my Dockers, pulled out the envelope containing what I'd dug up on the island and dumped the contents in my open palm.

Frank looked unimpressed. "What is it?"

"I think they're pieces of old Spanish chain-mail armor. I'm meeting with an archaeology expert in Fort Walton Beach who might be able to confirm it."

"Where did you get it?"

"On Five Mile Island, right where Jake Lofton found the artifacts Jessie was keeping for him in her safe deposit box. If de Soto's men *did* have a winter camp on the island, discovery of such a rare archaeological site might throw a monkey wrench in the Kreuzbergers' plans for their development. My guess is saving a multi-million dollar project such as the Dunes could get the right people *very* motivated."

———

ED DUNCAN AND I met on the back deck of the Crab Shack overlooking Santa Rosa Sound. Stoic brown pelicans rested on most of the dock pilings, sparing a few for double-crested cormorants and royal terns. Raucous mixed gulls begging for handouts swarmed above a boat steering for the yacht basin next door. A waitress showed and took our orders. Ed and I passed the next few minutes swapping small talk.

Duncan was a fit-looking man in his mid sixties with thinning salt and pepper hair and a handlebar moustache. He'd served in Vietnam with the First Air Cavalry Division, and was a retired master plumber whose sons had taken over the family-owned business. Archaeology had been his true passion for nearly forty years. When I slipped the rusted pieces of iron from the envelope and laid them on the table, Ed cut loose a low whistle, took a pair of eyeglasses from the pocket of his loud red and blue Hawaiian shirt, and put them on. Reaching for the artifacts, he stopped and glanced up at me. "You mind?"

"That's what we're here for."

Carefully he picked one up and laid it flat in his palm, adjusting the glasses as he turned the patch of loops gently this way and that. When he'd finished, he placed it on the envelope and repeated the procedure with the other piece. "It's Spanish chain mail, all right. Most likely sixteenth century."

He paused as the waitress arrived with our orders: fried oyster po'boys with a side of onion rings each—Ed's recommendation—along with iced tea, mine unsweetened. We thanked the young lady and she strolled away to wait on another table.

I took a bite of my sandwich as Ed nudged the larger of the

rusted pieces with an index finger. He scratched his temple and rested both forearms on the table. "Do you know you're probably the first person to touch this armor in nearly five-hundred years?"

The thought had already occurred to me. "Yeah, sort of puts things in perspective."

"I hope you realize the significance of what you have here. This is a rare find. Where did you discover it, if you don't mind my asking?"

I finished squeezing the lemon into my tea and stirred it. "Sorry, but I can't tell you right now. It would be a conflict of interest in a case I'm working on."

His shoulders slumped. "I see." He reached out and nudged one of the pieces again, keeping his eyes glued to it. "I worked on the de Soto dig in Tallahassee back in 1987. These pieces look similar to the ones we recovered there."

I finished swallowing a bite of onion ring. "Did you ever hear of the possibility that a detachment of de Soto's men might've spent the winter along the coast?"

Ed's eyes grew wide. "No. Did you find these somewhere near the coast?"

I hesitated. "I have to plead the Fifth again."

"Damn it, Mac, this find could be historically significant. You can't keep this to yourself. It's not fair to the public, never mind the ethical implications."

His words made my ears burn. "Look, I'm not a private collector trying to hoard artifacts. And I agree with you a hundred percent that the public has every right to know, *if* it turns out to be legit. But right now I have to think of my client. I've got good reason to believe someone was murdered because of the location where these were found. I can't take the chance that whoever is responsible will get away scot-free by blowing the lid off my case before I can finger them."

Ed took a moment to let my little tirade sink in. "I see your point." He sipped his tea and stared out at the sound. "Promise me one thing, will you, Mac?"

"If I can."

We locked eyes. "Promise me that once the case is over and your obligations to your client have been fulfilled, you'll apprise me of what you know. My group would love to volunteer our services for any survey or excavation that might be warranted."

"Okay, if you'll promise to keep what I've told you to yourself. If this leaks out, things could get real nasty."

Ed extended his hand. "You have my word."

It was a firm grip, and my gut told me I could trust the man. "And you've got mine."

———•———

Friday evening Kate and I were about to enjoy a Cajun seafood boil I'd prepared outside on my propane fish cooker when Frank called. It was disappointing news. The opened packs of hot chocolate I'd lifted from Jake Lofton's kitchen had all tested negative for drugs or any other foreign substances. That didn't prove that Jake hadn't been drugged. Laurel or someone else could have easily crushed up the pills and dumped them into Jake's thermos when he wasn't around. Frank wasn't sold on me pursuing the case. He didn't come right out and say so, but I could tell he thought it was mostly a waste of my time and effort, not to mention the agency wasn't making a dime for my trouble.

Finally he cut to the chase. "There's a wandering spouse case in Panama City I want you to take," he said. "The client is one Mrs. Bonnie Youngblood, and she's actually willing to pay for your time."

I knew there was no sense in arguing priorities, so I kept my mouth shut. Frank briefed me on the particulars. I jotted down the name and number and said I'd get on it first thing in the morning.

"Dang, Mac, you've hardly touched your food," Kate said,

looking at my plate, which was still piled high with spicy boiled shrimp, smoked sausage, corn on the cob, and potatoes.

I dropped the shrimp I'd been peeling onto the plate and took a swig of Michelob. "Your Uncle Frank ruined my appetite."

"The new case?"

"Yeah. I'm already going in circles with the Lofton case, and now he throws me this curveball. Who gives a crap about a cheating husband?"

"Hmm, maybe the wife who's being cheated on, or their kids, or—"

"Okay, I get the picture. I'll go play voyeur for the next week or so."

Kate put her arms around me and kissed my cheek. "It's part of the job. It doesn't mean you have to give up on the Lofton investigation. So, you spend a couple of hours a day checking this guy out. Meanwhile, you keep digging and find out what you can on the other."

I tossed a half-eaten hushpuppy to Henry, who'd taken up vigil beside the picnic table since I'd dumped the feast onto a thick layer of newspaper. He caught it on the fly and swallowed it with barely a chew. "Yeah, you're right," I said, turning my attention back to Kate. "Hey, who knows, maybe the guy I'm supposed to tail will turn out to be related to the Kreuzberger brothers."

Kate clucked her tongue. "Poor Mac. He doesn't get his way for once and thinks the whole world's against him."

I was searching for a smartass response when her cellphone broke the silence. She answered and strolled around my front yard, such as it is, while she talked. Henry shadowed her. I managed to catch bits and pieces of her end of the conversation, but none of it made much sense. I heard Kate laugh and say, "See you tomorrow," and then she slipped the phone back into the case that hung on the thin belt looped around her jeans.

"Ready for some good news?" she said, smiling and revealing

the tiny space between her front teeth I found so sexy. She didn't wait for an answer. "Mark's driving over after work tomorrow to spend the night. He thinks he's got most of the code from Jake Lofton's flash drive figured out."

———·———

I TRIED THE NUMBER Frank had given me for Bonnie Youngblood several times throughout the day on Saturday, but got no answer. A recording directed me to voicemail, but I decided against leaving a message in case hubby somehow had access to her phone. Frank had given her my number, so I decided to wait until Monday to try contacting her again.

That evening after supper Mark Bell spread the printouts and notes he'd compiled on top of the bar dividing Kate's kitchen from the living room. Mark was a few years younger than his sister, but the family traits were strong and the two could've been mistaken for twins. "This was a real bitch to figure out," he said, "but I think I've got it, most of it, anyway."

Kate elbowed him in the ribs. "Don't use that word around me."

"Ow! Damn. Sorry, Moolah."

Kate shot Mark the evil eye. "And I can do without your filthy mouth, too."

"Moolah" was short for "The Fabulous Moolah," a famous lady wrestler from the heyday of professional wrestling. The nickname was bestowed upon Kate by her brothers because she'd been a rough and tumble tomboy growing up, always giving as good as she got.

I stepped between the two. "I hate to break up this family bonding, but could we get on with business here?"

Kate puffed out a breath, stomped the few steps to the refrigerator, and grabbed three beers.

Mark leaned closer to the bar and pointed to a series of letters, numbers, and symbols Jake Lofton had copied to the flash drive I'd found in the grandfather clock. "This thing is complicated, so you'll have to trust me. We'll be wasting hours if I have to explain everything in detail."

"Kate said you could handle it. You've got the floor."

Mark took a sip of his beer. "Okay. I've made an entire translation we can use later, but let's work with the code first. This Jake guy was slick, and probably a genius. I'll make this as simple as I can." He ran an index finger across the first horizontal line. "Most of the narrative is simply what we learned in Boy Scouts, substituting a number for a letter. One equals 'a,' two equals 'b' and so on. He did use a trick or two. See these big Alpha and Omega characters? Numbers following the Alphas are in order, from one to twenty-six or whatever they happen to represent. But whenever he used the big Omega, the letters and their values were reversed from that point."

I finished a slug of beer that burned down my throat. "Hold on, you're losing me."

Mark glanced at me like I was missing a couple of marbles. "You weren't a Boy Scout, were you? It's simply counting backwards. One equals 'z,' two equals 'y.' Got it?"

I nodded and tipped back my beer. "And the numbers and letters count that way until the next big Alpha or Omega."

"Right." Mark turned back to his work. "Now, a lot of these are Greek letters that Jake had to translate from the original Spanish. Each Greek letter has a numeric value. Notice how he used plus or minus signs between groupings of the letters. It took a while, but I finally figured out that the Greek letters stand for distances."

"As in leagues?"

"If this came from de Soto's expedition, that's a safe assumption. Approximately two point six miles in a league."

Kate leaned in and tapped a fingernail on the printout. "What about all these Roman numerals?"

"That was a real bi—" Mark barely managed to catch himself. "That was a real tough one, but then it dawned on me. Look how each Roman numeral either precedes or follows a series of Greek letters. Now, if these letters represent such-and-such a distance, then it stands to reason the Romans stand for … what?"

"Directions?" Kate said.

Mark lifted his bottle of Bud and tapped it against Kate's. "Three points for the Fabulous Moolah." He pointed to the numeral IXX. "For example, the letter S is the nineteenth number in the alphabet. It follows these Greek letters," he said, tracing a finger over a portion of the printout. "If I'm right, and I'm sure I am, this part says the group traveled twelve leagues south, and then another six leagues southwest—IXX-XXIII— before turning south again."

I drained my beer. "So Jake translated the Rodrigo Rangel document he discovered in the state library into code and copied it to the flash drive I found."

"Two points for a lay-up, Mac. I haven't figured out what these last few lines represent." He pointed to the lines that were separated from the others by several blank spaces. "They don't seem to fit the code. But I'm working on it."

Grabbing the bottle of Dewar's I kept in Kate's cabinet, I put ice in a rock glass and poured myself a Scotch. "Now for the big test." I pulled a folded, detailed map of the Florida panhandle from my cargo pocket and handed it to Mark. "If these coded directions lead from Tallahassee to anywhere near Five Mile Island, then *you're* the genius."

Using the English translation he'd made from Jake's coded message, Mark went to work matching Rodrigo Rangel's 16th-century report of the de Soto detachment's route to the coast with the roadmap I'd given him. There were a bunch of small directional changes, and what seemed to be a few discrepancies. But the route basically followed Highway 20 from Tallahassee west to Blountstown, and then southwest and south to Wewahitchka on State Road 71, and then on to the coast near St. George and Five Mile Island.

"The route makes perfect sense," Mark said when he'd finished. "It stands to reason the Spaniards would use trails already long established by the indigenous people, that being the Apalachee Indians and other minor tribes in the area."

A quick search using MapQuest showed the distance being approximately a hundred miles. Jessie Lofton had mentioned her brother stating the entire route from de Soto's main encampment at Tallahassee to the coast as being thirty-eight leagues. That checked out with Mark's calculations. If you did the math, the detachment had traveled a hair under one hundred miles on their journey to the gulf. That was damn sure close enough for horseshoes and hand grenades in my book.

Mark Bell *was* a genius.

Chapter 11

———•———

BONNIE YOUNGBLOOD WAS WAITING on a bench near the southeast corner of McKenzie Park, a large square of land shaded by sprawling live oaks a block off Harrison Avenue, near its termination at the city marina. It was only a short walk to Panama Joe's. I'd almost balked when she suggested we meet there Monday morning at nine. Considering what happened to my previous client, I found the park a little too close for comfort.

To make matters worse, as I approached I noticed she was drinking a cup of coffee with Panama Joe's logo printed on it. If she was eating one of their croissants, I was going to turn around and get the hell out of there.

"Mac?" she said when I was within earshot. We had dispensed with formalities during yesterday's phone call.

I offered a hand. Her grip was firm. "Nice to meet you, Bonnie." She wore jeans and a desert camouflage T-shirt with *Army Strong!* printed in gold and black across the front. I pointed at the opposite end of the large wood and concrete bench. "Mind if I sit?"

Bonnie was late twenties, early thirties, with natural dark-blonde hair cut along the jaw line. Her toned body indicated regular exercise. You could call her attractive except for the dark circles under her eyes and an overall drawn and tired expression weighing on her face. I also noticed a faint bruise under her left eye that makeup had failed to conceal.

She didn't waste any time getting down to business. "My husband's cheating on me again."

"Again?"

She nodded and sipped her coffee. "I met Ray at Fort Jackson, in South Carolina. I was a mechanic with the 187th Ordnance Battalion. Ray was a drill sergeant. I'd recently returned from Iraq and been welcomed home with divorce papers from my first husband. I suppose as a civilian my ex got tired of being both Dad and Mom to our son while Mommy was away playing soldier."

"That's tough. I can relate. The same thing happened to me during my last deployment with the Marines. At least our kids were about ready to leave the nest at the time."

I was trying to connect with the client like the book says all good PIs should do, but Bonnie acted like she hadn't heard me. She set the cup on the bench and fumbled in her purse for a pack of Marlboros. Her hands shook a little as she thumbed the lighter and lit up. She took a puff, turned her head and exhaled. "About a week after reporting in, I spent an evening drowning my sorrows at the NCO club. This hunk walked in and sat next to me at the bar. He started talking me up and buying me drinks. I wound up spending the night with him at his apartment off base."

She must've read my face. "Yeah, I know, not the wisest move I ever made."

"I'm not being judgmental, but were you married at the time?"

She frowned and her eyes narrowed. "No. My ex and I both grew up here. He wanted out of the marriage, and frankly, so did I. He got the ball rolling before I got home. The whole thing took less than six weeks."

"What about your kid?"

Bonnie took a draw on her cigarette and let it out with a deep sigh. "I left Tyler with my parents until I could get settled in at Fort Jackson. Ray and I hit it off right away and decided to live together at his place. A couple of weeks later we got married by a justice of the peace. As soon as we could, we both got three-day passes and drove down to Panama City so Ray could meet the family and we could pick up Tyler."

Talk about a whirlwind romance. "Wasn't that rushing things a little? You get divorced, meet somebody new and get married in what, a month or so? You hardly knew the guy."

She took a final drag and dropped the half-smoked cigarette into the dregs of her coffee. "Do you believe in love at first sight, Mac?"

"No."

"I do, or did. Ray was Army, I was Army—both career. My son needed a father figure. He damn sure never had one with my ex."

It was past time to zero in on why I was here. "When did the cheating begin?"

"About three months after we were married. At least that's when I found out about it. He was screwing around with another drill sergeant's wife."

Nothing like esprit de corps. "How'd you find out?"

"A friend. She saw them coming out of a motel together one afternoon while she was in Columbia shopping. Ray had tried to hit on her, too, and she figured I ought to know about it."

"What happened when you confronted him?"

Bonnie lit another cigarette. "He denied it. But when I named names and told him my friend had seen the two of them at the motel, he went ballistic. He punched a couple of holes in the wall and kicked the coffee table over. When I tried to stop him from tearing the place apart he slapped me. Hard. Thank god Tyler wasn't home."

"In the face?"

"Yes."

"Did it leave a mark?"

She nodded and turned her head again to exhale. "I told the guys at the shop that I tripped and bumped my cheek against a chair. I don't think they bought it."

Bonnie glanced at me and then stared ahead. "It was the PTSD. Ray did multiple tours and saw a lot of combat. I begged, but he refused to go for help. He said it would be a sign of weakness and ruin his chances for promotion."

I understood the problems PTSD could cause; been there and done that. But there were ways to deal with it that didn't include slapping women around. Manning up and getting help was one. I'd heard enough to know this guy was a royal prick and a wife beater, but I sensed Bonnie needed to vent. "Anything else?"

She leaned forward, placed both hands beside her thighs, and began to rock back and forth. A thin trail of smoke snaked upward and dissipated in the light breeze. "He had sex with a female private while the platoon was on a field training exercise."

For a moment I was damn near speechless. "A recruit? Are you serious? That's enough to warrant brig time and a dishonorable discharge."

Bonnie sat back and folded her arms across her chest like she was suddenly cold, despite the warm and muggy August morning. "Another female private saw the girl giving my husband oral. Of course Ray and the girl both denied it. The only thing that saved him was that the two privates had a history of bad blood between them all during training. The battalion CO handled it, so it never went to trial. The privates were transferred to different training companies, and the matter was dropped."

"And you believe your husband did it?"

"Yes. He'd cheated before, and since."

"You mentioned that you and your husband were both career Army. What happened with that?"

Bonnie finished with the barely smoked cigarette. It hissed when she dropped it in the cup. "Ray beat the shit out of a couple of privates in his platoon. One of them reported him. He was court-martialed and convicted."

"What kind of discharge?"

"BCD. Twelve years of service down the piss-tube."

Bad Conduct. That meant Ray Youngblood was screwed as far as ever receiving veterans' benefits. Getting a decent job as a civilian probably wouldn't be easy either. "Why did you get out?"

She glanced up at the blue-white sky. "Because of Ray. I loved him despite everything, believe it or not. I thought I could help him. I'd completed eight years and was up for promotion if I reenlisted. But I gave it up for him, the sorry bastard."

A small flock of pigeons landed a few yards away and waddled toward us, expecting a free meal. I reached down, picked up an acorn, and tossed it their way. They scattered. "What is it you want from me?"

"I've been talking with the local recruiter. I've only been out for eight months, so if I reenlist I can retain my sergeant's rank. I know Ray's screwing around again, but I need solid proof."

"As in photos?"

Bonnie nodded. "I want to nail the bastard when I take him to divorce court. Without photos, it's his word against mine."

"What happened to wanting to help him?"

"I tried. There *is* no helping that son-of-a-bitch. He stays drunk half the time, and he's taken a belt to my son."

"He's also slapping you around," I said, pointing to the mark under her eye."

Bonnie ignored my last remark. "Will you take the case?"

I hesitated.

"Please. I'm trying to make a new life for Tyler and me."

Hanging around sleazy motels spying on horny lovers wasn't exactly what I had in mind when I'd signed on with Frank. But this young woman was hurting. She'd made some poor choices, but she had the intestinal fortitude to want to make things right for her son and herself. What the hell was I supposed to say? "Okay, but I'll need info."

———•———

BECAUSE HE COULDN'T KEEP his fly zipped, former Staff Sergeant Raymond Youngblood had gone from being a respected drill sergeant, United States Army, to bouncer at The Golden Pole, a strip club located on West Highway 98 in Panama City. It was the seedier part of town, with rundown motels that rented by the day, week or month, and hookers roaming the area shopping their wares.

It was easy duty. All I had to do was show up by eight when Ray's shift began and stay awake and alert until the joint closed at two in the morning. My biggest worry was finding a suitable parking spot each night where I could watch the front and the side door that exited into the parking lot. A local cop pulled up behind me the second night, wanting to know if I was a john on the hunt. After I showed him my PI license and explained what I was up to, he put out the word that I was okay.

For the first week Ray stayed on the straight and narrow. Shortly after closing time he'd exit the building through the side door and stand watch over the parking lot, making sure the departing customers behaved themselves until they vacated the premises. His duties also included seeing that the female employees made it safely to their rides home. If he'd treated Bonnie with half the respect and courtesy he showed these young women, I would've been out of a job.

Usually by three he'd climb into his dark-green Chevy Blazer and head home, with me on his tail. Traffic was light, so I'd stay a good distance behind and use another vehicle as a blocker. It was only a couple of miles to the house they rented in an older neighborhood near St. Andrew Bay. After Ray turned onto their street, I'd drive past the turnoff and double-back a few minutes later. When I saw the Blazer parked in the drive, my day was done. I was beginning to think that if Ray had been fooling around, the fling might be over. But Bonnie wanted me to keep bird-dogging him, sure that he'd trip up sooner or later.

Then things got interesting.

It was the Wednesday after Labor Day, and the action was slow at the Golden Pole. Around midnight the side door opened and Ray stepped out into the parking lot, his arm wrapped around the waist of a young dancer I'd noticed before. Hot pink hair and spiked-up bangs will stick in your mind that way. I knew she was a dancer because there was a photo of her hanging upside down on a pole in the strip club's show window. I'd scoped it out earlier with my zoom lens.

I was parked across the four-lane in front of an out-of-business pet store. I cranked the engine, but waited until they were a couple of blocks away before switching on the headlights and pulling onto 98 heading west. Less than a half mile from the club he slowed and hung a right into the parking lot of the Panama Motor Court, a single-story concrete block structure whose heyday probably dated back to the 1950s or '60s. Ray drove past the office and its fluorescent sign with a flashing red palm tree announcing *Vacancy,* bringing the Blazer to a stop in front of the right wing of the upside-down U-shaped structure. The Blazer was hidden in the shadows of a burned-out security light and was barely visible from the highway.

There wasn't time to stop and try to snap a photo of the two as they exited the Blazer and entered the second room from the wing's end. I'd have to wait them out and give it my best shot when they left. I hoped to hell it wasn't an all-nighter. Checking the mirrors, I made a U-turn and parked in the lot of a twenty-four hour McDonald's a block and a half away. I grabbed my camera—a new Canon digital SLR I'd laid out big bucks for—and locked the Silverado. Looking both ways first, I hustled across 98.

I cut across the parking lot of a minimart next door to the Panama Motor Court, taking care to keep the camera against my left hip in case any customers might wonder what the hell a man with a camera was planning to shoot at this hour of the night. There was a drainage ditch between the two establishments, and then an overgrown hedge skirting the Motor Court's property line. If I could work my way through the hedge, I'd probably have a good vantage point to snap away when Ray and Hot Pink exited their love nest.

In the darkness behind the minimart I underestimated the width of the ditch and landed short, my right foot finding water and mud that sent me sprawling to my knees. A sharp pain jolted through my left kneecap when I landed, but I managed to hang on to the camera. Struggling to my feet, I wondered if Frank carried workers' comp.

I limped out of the ditch and faced my next obstacle. The hedge looked like it hadn't been trimmed in years. I walked along the length of it, searching for an easy way through. No such luck, so I bit the bullet, picked a likely spot and plowed in. A couple of minutes and several scrapes and scratches later, I found myself on the other side, no more than fifty feet from the end of the motel's right wing. Keeping in the shadows, I crept along the hedge closer to the motel and found a spot where the growth bulged outward enough for concealment but provided a good view of the target room. I checked the ground for sharp objects and ant beds and settled down to wait.

I killed the next hour or so by putting a dent in the ranks of the mosquito horde that wasted no time finding my hideout. A couple of minutes before two, the door swung open and the girl stepped out, closing it behind her. She leaned back against the concrete wall, propped a foot against it and lit a cigarette. I trained the camera on her face and zoomed in. She took a drag and blew a long stream of smoke toward the overhang. In the glare of the bare bulb outside the door I was able to get a good look at her. Despite the wild hair and enhanced boobs bulging over the top of her low-cut blouse, she was a looker—almost eyes, full lips painted a matching hot pink, high cheekbones, and a slightly upturned nose. She didn't appear to be a day over eighteen, but I figured she had to be legal to pass muster for the Golden Pole to hire her.

The camera was set on silent mode and low-light conditions, and I snapped several shots of the girl before Ray Youngblood stepped out into the night to join her. He locked the door, and then reached down and pinched Hot Pink on the butt through the tight miniskirt she wore like a second skin. She reached down and grabbed his groin, and then they both laughed and hugged. While all the grab-assing was going on, I was firing off shot after shot of the two lovebirds. I made sure to get a few wide angles, too, so anyone looking at the photos would have no doubt that the location was a motel, namely the Panama Motor Court.

As soon as they climbed into the Blazer and headed back toward the Golden Pole, I beat feet across the parking lot to the office. When I stepped in, I was greeted by a cold blast of air coming from a noisy window unit and a thick cloud of cigarette smoke. The source was an overweight, balding man sitting behind the counter. Dressed in a pair of old gray slacks and a dingy white tank-top T-shirt, he was staring down at a girlie magazine spread across his lap.

He looked up when I leaned on the counter. "Need a room?"

"No, what I need is information."

The man set the magazine on a lamp table beside his ragged-out chair and stood. He scratched his belly and yawned, showing a cavernous mouth with several missing teeth as he stepped up to the counter. "Yeah? What kinda information?"

"Who's renting Room 38?"

The overhead light reflected off his head when he tilted it back a little and looked down his nose at me. "Who's asking?"

Grabbing my wallet, I slipped out a twenty and laid it on the countertop. "Andrew Jackson."

The man glanced down at the bill for a second, and then back at me. "Never been much of a Jackson fan."

I pulled another twenty out and dropped it next to the first one. "Andrew Jackson and his twin brother."

He reached for the bills but stopped short. "You a cop?"

"No," I said, wishing I had a twenty-dollar bill for every time I'd been asked that in the past year.

He scooped up the forty bucks and opened a register filled with dog-eared pages. After flipping through a few, he ran a chubby finger down a column of names. "Room 38. That would be Mr. John Smith."

"Not *the* John Smith?"

The man scratched an armpit and grinned. "I reckon so."

"Does Mr. Smith pay by the day or week or what?"

"Mister, I can't go giving out that kinda information. It's against regulations—'less you the law, that is."

I opened my wallet, flashed him my PI license, and pinched out another twenty. "Just so happens those Jackson boys are triplets. That do?"

He took the bill out of my fingers and looked down at the registry again. "Says here your Mr. Smith's been renting by the month."

Chapter 12

———◆———

"I NEED MORE," BONNIE Youngblood said, looking closely at one of the photos—a shot of her husband and Hot Pink with their arms wrapped around each other in a tight embrace. You couldn't have slipped a God particle between them.

"More?" I waved the handful of photos in front of her face. "We got him dead to rights."

Bonnie took a sip from her Panama Joe's coffee cup and shifted on the park bench. "There's more than one woman involved."

I tossed the pigeons a handful of popcorn from the bag I'd bought at the Winn Dixie. I figured I owed them a meal after scaring them away with an acorn during my last visit to McKenzie Park. "How do you know that?"

"A good sense of smell," she said, tapping a nostril. "Perfume and other odors, woman odors, I've smelled on Ray. He's fooling around with more than one woman. I'd bet a stripe on it."

"You can hang him with what we've got here."

"It's insurance, Mac," Bonnie said, lighting up a cigarette.

"You catch Ray with one more woman and I can walk into that courtroom with his balls in my hand."

———•———

I WAS ABOUT HALFWAY back to St. George when my phone rang. It was Kate.

"Mac, I've got exciting news!"

"You won the lotto!"

"I wish. Can't you be serious for even five dang minutes?"

"Sorry. What's the big news?"

"While Uncle Frank's had you playing voyeur, I've been doing a little investigating of my own. Guess what?"

I checked my mirrors and gunned past a lumbering waste oil truck that was traveling about half the posted speed limit. "I give up."

"The project the Kreuzbergers are developing is called The Dunes Bayside Resort, LLC."

"A limited liability company. How'd you find that out?" It was interesting news, but not exactly what I'd call exciting.

"It's a matter of public record. A trip to the courthouse was all it took."

"Smart move by the Kreuzbergers. They get several investors to each put up a good chunk of change for the project, form an LLC, and their assets are protected."

"Right. They filed last week. All that island property on the plat you have? It's now showing as one big parcel owned by The Dunes Bayside Resort."

I passed an older pickup truck loaded with fresh produce, probably headed for Gulf Grocery. "Except for one great big lot near the middle."

"Right again," Kate said. "Mr. Moats is the lone holdout. But guess who one of the partners is?"

"Donald Trump."

"Come on, Mac."

"You asked."

"Ron Decker."

I almost dropped the phone.

WHEN I CALLED ANGIE Decker later that afternoon she pled innocence and ignorance.

"I don't keep up with my husband's business affairs, and I've never heard of Kreuzberger and Sons. Ron has an accountant who handles all the paperwork for the business," she said. "He doesn't like to talk about work when he's home. And frankly, I don't care all that much. As long as he keeps my personal checking account fluid, that's all I give a damn about these days."

Talk about your happy camper.

Angie did say she'd do a little digging and see if she could come up with anything, but I wasn't going to hold my breath.

Meanwhile, back at the Golden Pole, I spent several more fruitless nights waiting for Casanova to make another move with a different woman. Thinking he might've noticed my Silverado in the area a little too often, I switched vehicles with Jerry Meadows and Kate a few times. I was a little pissed at Bonnie for wanting more evidence. I didn't think she needed more, and I was getting tired of growing calluses on my ass. So one night around ten thirty I decided to change things up and patronize the Golden Pole. What the hell, might as well enjoy a little entertainment while you're waiting, I figured.

Inside, the establishment was about what I'd imagined. Loud music, mirrored walls, and flashy neon lights of gold, pink, and red dominated. A circular stage stood in the center of the room, with three polished brass dancing poles. Individual stools circled the stage front, with dozens of small tables backing them up. There were two U-shaped bars, one on either side of the room. Wide-screen TVs hung on the wall behind both bars, along with monitors so customers could keep up with the center-stage action without having to turn around to gawk.

The joint was about half full, not bad for a Thursday night.

"Hey, there!" I looked away from the stage, where dancers spun around two of the poles in rhythm to the upbeat music blasting from surround sound speakers. A petite young brunette approached wearing a skimpy bikini with sequins sparkling in all the right places. She had a small tattoo of a blue butterfly on her left breast, and a Cupid with bow and arrow on her left shoulder. Beneath all the makeup she looked like she belonged in middle school. Taking my arm in her slender hand tipped with glittery nails, she guided me to an empty table and pulled out a chair facing the stage. "My name's Taylor, and I'll be your waitress for now. There's a two drink minimum, hon. Unlimited drinks for a hundred dollars."

The accent was Southern, maybe Georgia or Alabama—might even be native. She was a tiny thing. I barely had to look up to catch her big amber eyes. I flashed a smile. "I'll have a Scotch on the rocks."

Taylor returned the smile, her teeth bright white and even. "Be right back, and feel free to move up to the stage if you want to. I'll find you."

I watched her saunter between tables as she headed for the bar. My eyes wandered around the room for familiar faces. There was no sign of Ray Youngblood. Probably backstage somewhere, hitting on one of the dancers.

Onstage, one of the performers, a skinny redhead with cantaloupe boobs, skittered to the bottom of her pole and crawled on hands and knees toward a man with a beer belly. He was sporting a faded John Deere cap, and a five-dollar bill dangled from his fingers like a lure. She stopped short of his reach, rose to her knees, and shook her bare boobs in his face. The guy let out a war whoop as she spun around and wiggled her butt, the G-string concealing little. She backed up a couple of feet and the guy slipped the bill in the waistband of the G-string. He cut loose another whoop as she gave her backside an appreciative shake.

Taylor returned with my drink on a small tray as the lights dimmed and a spotlight zeroed in on the center pole. The two dancers abandoned their poles, gathered their tips, and disappeared backstage as the theme from *2001: A Space Odyssey* began to blare from the sound system.

"That'll be ten dollars, hon," Taylor said, leaning close to my ear, her breath blowing soft against my cheek. I grabbed a ten and a five from my wallet and dropped them on the tray. She mouthed a "Thank you."

"Ladies and gentlemen," a deep voice sounding like a ring announcer's bellowed above the music, "fresh from wildly successful engagements in Baltimore, Charlotte, and Atlanta's finest adult venues, please give a big round of applause for our featured performer, the beautiful, the luscious, the sexy ... Miss ... Kami ... Kae!"

Whoops and hollers and shrill whistles bounced off the walls as a gold-sequined curtain parted, and none other than Hot Pink herself pranced around the stage, throwing kisses to the audience with both hands. She'd completed two circuits when the music changed from the theme to a saucy Latino song I'd never heard.

Kami kicked off the high heels, swung the long robe she'd been wearing in a circle over her head a few times, and tossed it to the back of the stage. She was down to a tight powder-blue midriff blouse and white miniskirt. The skimpy outfit lit up under the house lights like it'd been dusted with silver glitter. The mostly male crowd roared its approval as Kami leapt into the spotlight, deftly grabbed the pole with both hands, and went to work.

For the next ten minutes Kami made sweet love to the pole, keeping perfect time with the music, spiraling and sliding and grinding. That pole wouldn't need polishing for a month. To the delight of the crowd she slowly shed one article of clothing and then another, teasing the most vocal guys gathered around the stage with money in hand, until finally only a wisp of a

G-string separated Kami from her birthday suit. She made repeated trips to the stage edge and back. So many bills bulged from the strings of her tiny bottoms that she was forced to make a pile of greenbacks on the stage floor.

Finally the music began to fade. Kami treated the audience to one more seductive thrust and grind, and then gathered her pile of cash and strutted off the stage to wild applause, hips bouncing like a Victoria's Secret model. Reaching the gold curtains, she turned and blew a final kiss and disappeared.

As the applause died down, the DJ assured the crowd that the lovely Miss Kae would be wowing them with another breathtaking performance in one short hour. Scantily clad cocktail waitresses appeared out of the shadows and began working the floor. I'd seen this routine before, during my first hitch in the Corps as a young single Marine. Get the audience's hormones stirring and then hit 'em up for a lap dance or two.

I watched as a few working girls huddled close and friendly with the guys they'd targeted. Here and there a customer stood up and he and his girl headed for a curtained room near the club's left side bar. I felt a hand on my shoulder. Hair brushed my neck and face as Taylor leaned in and asked if I'd like my second drink. I said yes, and she gave my shoulder a squeeze as she turned and made her way to the bar. I scoped out the place again through clouds of cigarette smoke turned pink and orange by neon lights. Still no sign of Ray.

Taylor was back in five minutes carrying a tray with my Scotch and another drink in a taller glass. She slid into the chair beside me without asking permission and scooted my way a little until our thighs were close to touching. She picked up the other glass and took a sip. "I took a chance that you might wanna buy me a drink," she said, gazing up at me.

I grabbed my wallet, fished out a twenty, and placed it on the tray. "Are we good?"

She set her drink down and smiled. "Sure."

I picked it up and took a quick sip and swirled it around my mouth. Not a trace of booze, straight Coke or Pepsi. I pushed the glass back to her. "How old are you, Taylor?"

She averted her eyes, staring down at the table. "Twenty-one."

"You're not a convincing liar. I laid out ten bucks for a watered-down Coke. You're not legal to drink, are you?"

She turned back to face me, her thigh brushing mine. "Sure I am," she said, placing a manicured hand on my forearm. "I gotta dance later, and I dance better straight. Listen, I think you're a hottie. I'll give you a special deal on a lap dance." She squeezed my arm. "I'll make it *real* up close and personal."

I smiled and shook my head as I looked at that little girl face buried under makeup. "What're you doing working in a crap hole like this? You should be in school."

Taylor's eyes narrowed and her lips pursed. "You want that dance or not?"

"How much?"

"Twenty."

I took a big swallow of Scotch and held the glass up, looking at the melting cubes swimming in the golden liquid. "Tell you what. I'll give you the twenty and we sit right here and talk some more."

Taylor glanced back at the big neon clock on the wall under the DJ's station. "I go on in a half hour. I gotta go get dressed and made up."

"Ten minutes."

She sipped her Coke and thought about it a few seconds. "Okay. What you wanna talk about?"

I dropped two tens on the tray. "Are you a runaway?"

Her eyelids fluttered rapidly. "No. Hey, are you a cop or something?" It was a question she was probably supposed to ask before hitting me up for a lap dance.

"No, I'm a retired Marine with a daughter and son older than you."

Taylor looked away and it seemed like her whole body

slumped a little. "My brother was in the Marines. He got killed in Afghanistan a couple years ago."

"I'm real sorry about your brother. I knew a lot of good Marines who didn't make it back."

A chair scraped the floor behind me, and heavy footsteps clacked on the wooden floor. "This gentleman giving you trouble, Taylor?"

I turned to see Ray Youngblood towering over me. He was a big man, maybe six-four or five, all muscle. He was no hunk to me, but I guess ruggedly handsome would fit the bill. There was a thin two-inch scar across his right cheek, probably a grazing bullet or shrapnel wound from the looks of it. He wore a black silk shirt, black trousers and Western boots, and his hair was cut high and tight.

Taylor held up her glass. "No trouble, Ray. He bought me a drink. We're just talking, is all."

He looked hard at the girl with narrowed eyes. "Yeah, well you behave yourself. You go on in twenty. Better get moving."

"He always that friendly?" I said after Ray was out of earshot and heading across the room.

"Ray's okay. He watches out for us. It's just …."

"Just what?"

"Nothing. Look, I gotta go." She gathered up the money. "Thanks for the drink."

I didn't stick around to watch Taylor dance.

———◦———

THAT NIGHT AFTER CLOSING, Ray and Kami Kae took off in his Blazer and headed toward the Panama Motor Court. There was no sense in following those two, so I headed home.

The next evening I decided to venture into the lion's den again. It was around ten thirty and the joint was maybe a third full. As luck would have it, Taylor was strutting her stuff at one of the poles, along with the redhead from the night before. A quick glance told me Taylor's petite body was natural. She was one of the few dancers I'd seen at the Golden Pole who could claim as much.

My eyes barely had time to adjust to the low light before I felt a hand on my forearm. "Good evening, sir. Table or stage?"

The girl was early- or mid-twenties with curly, tawny hair and skin darkened from hours of sunbathing. The accent was hard to place, maybe Midwestern. Right away I recognized her as the dancer who'd shared the stage with the redhead. She was fairly attractive, maybe five-eight counting the heels, and wore a sparkling jade-green bikini with a silvery lace shawl across her shoulders. Nice body. Enhanced, but a nice job. "A table will do fine."

She escorted me to a table near the one I'd had last night. I sat down and motioned for her to join me. She did. "Two drink minimum, right? I'm Andrew," I said, using my middle name.

"Yeah." She extended her hand. I gave it a light squeeze. "My name's Bambi. What can I get you, Andrew?"

"Bambi?" I said, faking surprise. "That was my mother's name."

She cocked her head, a hint of a smile curling her puffy lips. "Really?"

I crossed my heart and raised a hand with two fingers pointing skyward. "Scout's honor," I said, lying through my teeth.

Bambi put on a coy smile. "About that drink …."

"Dewar's on the rocks. And order something for yourself."

Bambi stood and weaved her way through the tables to the bar. The DJ said a few unintelligible words as the music morphed from one song into another without a break. I kept my eyes off the stage and scanned the room.

Several tables away I spotted Ray with his back to me. He was dressed all in black again. Maybe he was a Johnny Cash fan, or thought it made him look more intimidating. Sitting across from him was an attractive woman in a red dress with spaghetti straps and a plunging neckline. Her legs were crossed ladylike, right shoe dangling from the toes of her foot. She waggled it slowly up and down. She opened a matching handbag and tapped out a cigarette. Placing it between pursed lips, she leaned forward to accept a light from Ray. The dress barely maintained control of her bulging breasts.

I slipped my phone out of my pocket and pretended to text while snapping a few shots of the two. From where I sat the woman looked to be late thirties, maybe early forties. She sipped a tall drink from a straw, and then threw her head back laughing at something Ray said, her long chestnut mane tumbling across her shoulders.

"Dewar's on the rocks." Bambi leaned over and set the glass in front of me with a couple of napkins. "Mind if I join you? These damn heels are killing my feet."

"Please do." This time I remembered my manners. Bambi eased into the chair as I held it for her.

"Thanks," she said, reaching down and slipping off the tight heels. "Who said chivalry is dead?"

"What're you having?" I said, dropping a Jackson and Lincoln on the tray.

"Whiskey Sour. Care for a sip?"

"No thanks. How long've you been working here?"

Bambi idly stirred her drink. "Long enough. I'm outta here soon as I save what I need to get to Vegas. I got a good friend dancing out there. A girl can make a lot of money in Sin City if she knows what she's doing."

"And you do?"

Bambi leaned closer, put on a sultry look and batted her fake eyelashes at me. "Care to find out?"

I grinned and ignored the question. "That guy over there," I said, indicating the table where Ray and the lady in red sat, "you know him? He looks familiar."

Bambi pursed her lips around the straw and took a sip. "Ray? He's been working here awhile. I think he was in the Army before."

I took a drink of my Scotch. "Maybe that's it."

"Just between me and you, he's a real prick."

"Yeah? How so?"

"He's laid half the girls that work here. You didn't hear it from me, but he gets rough sometimes."

"You mean with the ladies?"

Bambi nodded while taking another sip. "Yeah, he's into that auto-erotic shit, you know, where the guy or girl chokes their partner while they're getting it on. Supposed to make the orgasm better."

"Then why sleep with the guy?"

"Truth?"

"Yeah."

"He's hung like a horse. Curiosity killed the cat. Take your pick."

I let it slide. "What about the lady friend?"

"That's the owner, or one of 'em. Name's Charlotte Mooney, used to dance up north somewheres, or so I heard. She's okay. Drops in a couple times a week, more since Ray hired on. I seen her and Ray leave together a time or two."

The music ended before I could come up with another question. The DJ spouted something or other as Taylor and Red gathered up their few tips and pranced offstage. Bambi grabbed her heels by the straps and plopped them on the tray, along with the money and her half-finished Whiskey Sour. A hard rock song blared from the speakers.

"That's my cue. I'm on in five. Thanks for the drink, Andrew."

"Good luck in Vegas," I said as she hurried away.

———•———

I BEAT FEET AS the house lights dimmed and Bambi strutted onstage. Crossing 98, I resumed the vigil from inside my Silverado. I was parked on a side street with a clear view of the parking lot. Less than thirty minutes later my hunch paid off. The lady in red strolled out of the nightclub into the lot with Ray on her heels like a hound tracking a hot scent. Ray's Blazer was parked in its usual spot next to the chain-link fence separating the Golden Pole from an adjacent vacant lot. Instead of walking to Ray's SUV, they disappeared around the back of the building. I started the engine. A minute later a silver Lexus sedan drove out of the lot traveling west.

The windows were tinted, and in the poor light I couldn't tell for sure if it was Ray and the lady in red. I eased up to the highway and waited. After a minute no other vehicle had exited the lot, so I turned and gunned it for the Panama Motor Court. Hanging a left, I drove into the McDonald's lot and parked. I grabbed my camera, checked traffic, and beat feet across the four-lane.

Not wanting to risk busting my ass jumping the ditch behind the minimart, I decided to use the hedgerow bordering the motel's property line as cover to sneak into position where I'd have a clear shot of Room 38. Hugging the hedge, I was soon at my old hideaway. Like I'd hoped, the Lexus was parked nearby. I double-checked the settings on the camera and hunkered down to wait on the lovebirds. Except for the flashing red palm tree and yellow bug lights outside the rooms, the place was dark.

"Ya wanna li'l drink?"

I damn near levitated at the sound of the voice in the hedge a few feet away. A thin, shadowy figure struggled to stand upright and staggered my way, a bottle clutched in his hand.

"I got Mad Dog 20/20 if ya wanna drink," the man said, weaving above me and taking a big swig. He swallowed and held the bottle out to me. "Good stuff. Here, have yerself a li'l drink."

By now my eyes had adjusted. The grizzled old man was probably on the backside of seventy, with long gray hair and a week's worth of stubble on his face and neck. He'd puked on the ragged checkered shirt he wore and stunk to high heaven. I don't know how the hell I'd missed him. I was getting careless. If this was Iraq, I'd be a dead man.

"No thanks, I'm fine."

"Wha', ya too good ta have a drink wit' me?" he said, way too loud for comfort.

Great, now I'd insulted the old geezer. I had to get rid of him quick, or else risk getting caught with my pants down. "No sir," I said, reaching up and taking the bottle from his hand. "Never too good to have a drink with an old friend." I put the bottle to my mouth and tilted my head back, wincing at the taste of the sour wine on my lips. I hoped it wasn't mixed with puke. I handed the bottle back and tried to unknot my stomach.

Swaying, the old man slugged down a couple of swallows and wiped his mouth with the back of his free hand. "Yer my buddy, yessir, my good ol' buddy." And with that, he plopped down beside me, sloshing wine on my leg and cackling like a hyena.

I had to act fast. I grabbed my wallet and pulled out a bill. Great, a twenty. "Here, old buddy, take this and go buy yourself another bottle over at the minimart," I said, pointing like a hitchhiker. "Get yourself something to eat, too."

He took the money and started crying, but managed to get to his feet. "Yer a good man, yessir," he said between sobs. "God bless ya, ol' buddy." He staggered toward the highway a few steps and then turned around to face me again, rocking like a sailor on a deck in high seas. "I won' ferget this, nossir, God bless ya."

I took a deep breath after he finally disappeared around the end of the hedge, hoping like hell he wouldn't show up again. Turns out I didn't have long to wait. I hadn't been there thirty minutes before the door to 38 opened. The stallion and lady in red must have settled for a quickie, or maybe she had to be elsewhere soon. I managed to fire off several damning shots before they climbed into the Lexus and headed east.

Mission accomplished.

Chapter 13

———•———

THE FOLLOWING SATURDAY I grilled amberjack steaks for dinner at Kate's house and spent the night. She'd taken Sunday off from work, and we hadn't gotten cozy in a while. I was up with the sun the next morning with a smile on my face, frying diced potatoes and ground sausage for my specialty omelet. Henry sat a few feet away, watching my every move with pleading eyes. Kate walked in, stifling a big yawn as the coffee finished dripping. She gave me a peck on the cheek.

"Morning, Mac." She was wearing one of my long-sleeved button up shirts, and maybe panties.

I set the spatula down and hugged her, enjoying the feel of our bodies pressed tightly together. "Morning yourself, sleepyhead."

She yawned again and scratched Henry's ears. "Coffee ready?"

"Yep. I'll pour you a cup as soon as you get the paper."

She disappeared into the bedroom, mumbling something that I'm sure wasn't complimentary. A couple of minutes later she walked through the kitchen wearing shorts and my shirt and went outside.

The front door closed and Kate came back in. "Here's your dang paper." She tossed the *Parkersville Independent* on the table.

"And here's your dang coffee." I handed her a cup full of my strong black brew. Kate drew in a quick breath as I opened the refrigerator and grabbed the egg carton.

"What on earth?"

I turned my head her way. "What's up?"

"They found Amos Moats's body floating in the bay."

———⊢———

EVER SINCE THE DAY I failed to locate Amos, I'd had a nagging feeling that something bad might have happened to the old man. Our introduction had been a little hairy, but we'd parted on a friendly note. Now, with Amos out of the picture, his property was fair game. The lawyer son and his stepmother lover were itching to sell. I doubted they would pass up a three mil-plus offer. Amos's demise definitely upped the ante. Now that Bonnie had what she needed to hang her cheating husband by the family jewels, I was chomping at the bit to get on with my investigation of the Five Mile Island fiasco.

On the local news broadcast I watched Dakota standing by as the Palmetto County Dive and Rescue team recovered Amos Moats's body and brought it ashore. A young married couple window-shopping for property in the proposed new development had spotted him about fifty yards out in the bay. Dakota had received the call from dispatch and was the first officer to arrive at the scene.

That evening I phoned Dakota and arranged to meet her Monday on the island so she could bring me up to speed on any details the press might not be privy to.

At high noon we sat in the narrow shade the roof covering the concrete table offered. It was hot and humid. A brisk onshore breeze saved us from heatstroke. Dakota took a sip of her 7-Eleven coffee and winced. "This crap tastes like burnt friggin' motor oil," she said, and then took another sip.

"You said he'd been in the water about two weeks."

She swallowed and made another face. "At least two weeks … that's what I heard. Maybe longer."

"Nobody reported him missing?"

"Nope. His son said it wasn't unusual for the old coot to take off for a couple of weeks without telling anybody he was leaving."

Another sip, another face. "Why do you keep drinking that stuff if it tastes so bad?"

Dakota grinned. "Because you paid for it, McClellan. I can't pass up free goodies, knowing how tight you are."

"Water in the lungs?"

"Yeah. Moats drowned."

"Any sign of trauma?"

Dakota tore open the Snickers I'd also bought for her impromptu lunch. Coffee, a large bag of corn chips, and a jumbo candy bar. How the hell did she keep that figure? "There was a contusion on the side of his head, and a big scrape on his jaw and chin," she said, chewing a mouthful of corn chips and candy. "They found splinters with creosote embedded in the scrape, probably from one of the pilings on his dock. The lab guys took samples to check for a match."

I sipped my coffee. It tasted okay, a little on the weak side. "So, the official theory is that Amos tripped or passed out, hit his head on a piling, and fell into the drink."

Dakota washed down the candy and chips with coffee. "You're sharp as a new razor, McClellan."

"Nobody suspects foul play?"

"Not that they're saying."

"Christ on a crutch, did Pickron even consider that Amos might've had help taking his swim? He owned the prime property the Kreuzbergers were salivating over, remember?"

Dakota stopped chewing and removed her sunglasses. Her big brown eyes bore into mine. "Between me and you, I think the sheriff missed the boat on this one. Either that or he's putting out false info hoping solid evidence will show up, or that the perp will relax or get careless and trip up."

"What do you think happened?"

Dakota put the shades back on and took another bite of her Snickers. "I think Old Man Moats was murdered."

———

WEDNESDAY AFTERNOON AT TWO I pulled into the parking lot of the Church of God, located a block inside the eastern city limits of St. George. The old church was built around 1950, largely from money donated by Amos Moats's father, Luther. I circled the lot twice, but it was packed. Driving a short distance east on 98, I made a U-turn and parked on the shoulder of the road.

Talk about surprises. A couple of days before his funeral, the *Parkersville Independent* ran an interesting article on Amos Moats on the page opposite the obits. Turns out old Amos had followed in his father's philanthropic footsteps and contributed regularly to the church throughout the years, although he rarely attended because of "medical issues." Translated, that probably meant he was considered nutty as your grandma's fruitcake. The old semi-hermit had also generously donated most of the land for the state park, and was a big supporter of the Salvation Army in Parkersville. You never know.

Inside the small church sanctuary it was standing room only for the closed casket service. I assumed the grieving relatives were sequestered in a private sitting area to the preacher's right. As he spoke, he glanced in that direction every now and then. St. George's mayor, Jim Crowley, owner of the local Ace Hardware, sat in a pew near the front, along with several city and county council members. Three rows back, I recognized the carrot-topped head of Chief Brian Tolliver. He was decked out in his spiffy dress uniform. Sitting beside him in a navy sheath was Beth Sowell, the young police dispatcher. Those two had become an item shortly after Tolliver was hired to replace the former disgraced police chief.

I stood in the back near the door as the preacher droned on about how Amos might not have had a multitude of friends in this world, but he did have the one friend who mattered most—the Lord Jesus Christ. I smiled, wondering if Amos would've greeted JC with a load of buckshot had he happened to pay Amos a personal visit.

When the preaching and praying and singing were over, I hurried outside to my truck. I got in line as the procession motored west on 98 for a mile, and then turned north on 13th Street. Who says thirteen is an unlucky number?

I parked and stood with a group a few yards away from the maroon funeral home awning covering the gravesite. Clouds had begun building to the west and south, and the wind was picking up. Distant thunder rumbled over the Gulf of Mexico. The preacher stood near the flower-covered casket and waited patiently for latecomers to arrive. He then read a few verses of scripture and offered a parting prayer for Amos Moats.

When he'd finished, he stepped away from the casket to offer condolences to the handful of people sitting on metal folding chairs at one side of the open grave. He leaned over and shook hands with a man around fifty with thinning but neatly styled hair. He wore what looked to be an expensive suit, and black patent leather shoes. Amos's son, Richard the lawyer, I guessed.

The preacher moved to the grieving widow sitting next to the suit. She was decked out in a black dress and veil. If poor Amos's carcass hadn't been lying there in that casket I might've busted out laughing at the hypocrisy. The dress had a low bodice and showcased a surprising bit of cleavage for such a solemn occasion. When I remembered that Cherry Moats was shacking up with her stepson, the outfit didn't seem all that out of place. She did have a lacy black shawl draped over her shoulders for a touch of modesty.

My phone vibrated. I reached in my pocket and checked

the number. It was Frank. The crowd was dispersing, and the people who'd been sitting under the awning began filing out. For propriety's sake I decided to wait a minute before returning Frank's call. The suit and widow were emerging from the shadows of the awning, angling away from me so I couldn't get a clear look at their faces. The wind gusted, blowing grit almost horizontally from the crushed shell road. The widow turned her back to the stiff breeze and faced my way. The veil lifted. My jaw dropped.

It was the lady in red.

———•———

Charlotte Michelle Mooney hailed from Indianapolis and had left a trail of her past as long as her shapely legs. She was all over the Internet, or at least her alter ego, Cherry Moon, was. Old clips of her dancing days abounded on Myspace, YouTube and other sites. Back then her locks were dyed cherry red, and the signature ending to her routine was to bend over, grab both ankles and moon the audience while alternately flexing her cheeks to the beat of a drum. It was damn impressive how fast she could do it. Cherry also dabbled in adult modeling. Googling her stage name brought up dozens of racy pics and videos from her prime days, posing with both men and women.

A visit to the courthouse in Parkersville turned up more interesting info. She'd been married to Amos Moats a little over four years; her age was listed as forty on the marriage certificate. My guess was Amos had caught Cherry's act in a second-rate club when her career was on the decline. The old goat probably flashed his money around and treated her like a queen. Voilà! One career ended and another begun. The sugar daddy and the gold digger—a match made in Heaven. Charlotte Mooney bought the Golden Pole shortly after their marriage—most likely a wedding gift from Amos.

According to his ad in the Yellow Pages, attorney Richard

Moats offered a free twenty-minute consultation to prospective new clients. I made an appointment. His law office was located on 4th Street near downtown Panama City, within easy walking distance of the Bay County Court House. I parked the Silverado in the shade of a big oak in the court house parking lot and hoofed the three-quarters of a block to his office. The first day of autumn dawned hot and muggy that morning, and I was grateful for the cool air that greeted me as I opened the door and stepped inside. A quick glance told me no one else was in the room other than a lady sitting behind a large desk.

The receptionist, a slender older woman dressed in a peach pantsuit, looked up from the desk and greeted me with a pleasant smile. "Good morning, sir. How may I help you?"

I glanced at my watch. Right on time. "I have a ten thirty appointment to see Mr. Moats."

She keyed something up on the computer sitting on a slide-out shelf to her left. "Mr. McClellan?"

"Yes, ma'am."

She picked up a desk phone and punched a number. "Mr. McClellan to see you, sir." She nodded and placed the receiver back in its cradle. "Right through that door, Mr. McClellan," she said, waving a hand toward a door to my left. "First room on the right."

Richard Moats, J.D., Attorney at Law was stenciled in fancy lettering on the door's opaque window. I knocked and a voice said, "Come in." Richard Moats got up from the plush high-back swivel chair and extended his hand across a fancy wooden desk that must've cost a bundle. He was dressed in another expensive suit, gray this time, and a blue dress shirt and a tie with blue and gray swirls. I couldn't see his shoes, but my guess was they didn't come from Wal-Mart.

"What can I do for you this fine morning, Mr. McClellan?" he said as we shook hands, his smile revealing almost perfect teeth. "Richard Moats. Have a seat, have a seat."

He waited until I'd chosen one of two matching leather

chairs in front of his desk before he sat. He was a good six inches taller than his old man, and there was a slight family resemblance around the eyes and nose. I leaned back in the comfortable chair and crossed one leg over the other. "I knew your father. I'm sorry for your loss."

He wiped the smile off his face and replaced it with a solemn look. "Thank you. Such a tragic accident. Dad and I were very close."

"What about Rascal?"

"I'm sorry?"

"Rascal, your father's dog. Is anybody taking care of him?"

"Oh. I'm afraid we had to have the poor thing put down. You said you knew my father?"

I wanted to deck the heartless bastard. Instead, I pulled a business card from my shirt pocket and handed it across the desk to the grief-stricken son and animal lover. Moats glanced at it a moment. He looked up, his forehead furrowed. "Private investigator. Why would Dad need a private investigator?"

"Suppose you tell me."

His eyes blinked rapidly. "I have no idea. Look, I don't know what you're driving at, Mr. McClellan, but I place a high value on my time. It appears you've come to waste twenty minutes of it."

I faked a smile. "The first time I met your father, he greeted me with a double-barrel shotgun. Seems he was a little worried that somebody was trying to force him to sell his place. Worried enough to walk around his own property carrying a loaded weapon."

Moats let out a big sigh. He sat back in his chair and formed a steeple with his fingers. "My father could be quite eccentric at times. And he was beginning to show signs of dementia. That might explain his paranoia."

"Hmm, he seemed sharp to me. Sharp enough to know you and Cherry were trying your damndest to get him to sell out to the Kreuzbergers."

Moats squirmed in his seat and his fingers laced together like he was about to pray. "Her name is Charlotte, and yes, we were trying to convince my father to sell the property. He could have had his choice of any high-end condos to live in instead of that concrete block shack that was falling down around him."

"Ever hear the saying that home is where the heart is?"

"My father had no business living way out there all by himself. The entire area is crawling with rattlesnakes and sand gnats and god knows what other vermin. I only wanted what was best for him."

I forced a sarcastic laugh. "Amos wouldn't have been by himself if his wife wasn't shacking up with you."

Moats's face flushed. "Leave Charlotte out of this."

"By the way, have you noticed any bruises on your stepmom's neck lately?"

His eyelids moved like a camera shutter set on burst. "What is that supposed to mean?

"Ask Cherry."

"Her name is Charlotte."

"Okay. Did you know Charlotte is engaging in hanky-panky with the bouncer at her club?"

His face screwed up like he'd eaten a spoonful of alum, but he kept his mouth shut.

"Tell me something, Moats. What kind of man lives in a big fancy house his father paid for, shares a bed with his stepmother, and then, to keep the money coming, sends her home a couple of times a month so Daddy can get a little?"

Moats turned deeper red. He picked up the phone and tapped a button. "Maggie, get me Detective Daffin's number, would you, please?"

Oops.

He grabbed a pen and jotted down the number. "Thank you, Maggie." A smirk spread across his face as he drummed the pen on the desktop. "Do you leave now, or do I make the call?"

I checked my watch. "I do believe I have another appointment." I stood and took a couple of steps toward the door, stopped and turned. "I'd be very careful if I was you, Moats. Oh, and you might want to call the Orkin Man."

He leaned forward and rested his forearms on the desk. His fingers were back in steeple-mode. "And why would I want to call an exterminator?"

"I hear black widows can be deadly."

Chapter 14

———◆———

THAT EVENING I WAS grilling burgers for me and Henry. Kate had gotten Saturday and Sunday off and left for Destin after work to spend the weekend with her folks. I slipped the spatula under Henry's big patty and flipped it over. He likes his cooked medium rare, the way I like my steak, but my hamburgers have to be well done.

I stuck a fork in one of the split potatoes coated with butter and my special seasoning. Not quite done to my liking, so I moved the spuds closer to the bed of coals. I opened a Michelob and tossed Henry's new baseball into the next campsite that happened to be unoccupied. Henry took off after it as my phone rang.

It was Angie Decker, and she sounded like she'd been drinking. "Hi, Angie. What's up?"

"My husband. Up to no good, is what."

She was drinking, all right. And from the way she was slurring words, she'd gotten an early start. "Sounds like you need to hit the rack."

"Yeah? Hey, Mac, you wanna come over an' join me? The girls are sleepin' over somewhere an' the boys are with Ron's sister and her brats. Ron's outta town workin' *again*." She almost spit the last word.

Henry dropped his baseball at my feet. I picked up the slimy thing and gave it another toss. "I don't think that would be such a—"

"Know what that no-good bastard did? He hocked our goddamn business so he could invest in that island thingy you were talkin' 'bout the other day, tha's what he did!"

"How'd you find out about it? You told me you didn't care about the business."

"Ha! I care 'bout *my* goddamn half."

"So, how'd you find out?"

I heard the sound of ice tinkling in a glass. "Letter from the bank was sittin' right on top of his desk. Two million goddamn dollars."

I flipped the other burgers. "What bank?"

"Same bank we went to that day. Know what else?"

I sent Henry chasing again. "What?"

"My darlin' husband is screwin' the bank president. Least he *was* screwin' her."

"What makes you think that?"

More ice tinkling, then the sound of breaking glass. "Shit, dropped my drink."

"What makes you think Ron's having a fling with the bank's president?"

"I foun' her number in his cellphone."

"If Ron borrowed money against the company that could be strictly about business."

"Nooo, no no! Her cell number. You 'member that girl I tol' you 'bout, the one I caught Ron with back in college?"

"Yeah. You started dating Jake Lofton after you found out."

"Tha's the one," Angie said, and started crying. "Poor Jake."

"What about the girl, Angie?"

"Poor, dear Jakey." She sniffled and coughed.

"The girl, Angie."

"Oh, her. She's the president. Her daddy owns the bank."

A light bulb flashed on in my head, and then I remembered something I should've thought of from the get-go. "Angie, where are you?"

"Home, I already tol' you that. Wanna come over?"

"I mean *where* at home?"

"In the kitchen, why?"

Damn. If Ron Decker's mini-recorder was still under the island top, my goose was cooked.

———

AFTER SUPPER I BOOTED the laptop and researched for a couple of hours before me and Henry hit the rack. After my conversation with Angie, Mr. Sandman wasn't cooperating, but being unable to sleep gave me time to sort out a few things. Despite Angie being sloshed and me making another rookie mistake, I'd come away from our conversation with valuable info.

Carla Esposito, old flame of Ron Decker, was now president of the First Community Bank of Destin, owned primarily by her father, Carl Esposito. There was at least sketchy evidence that the two might've rekindled their relationship—to wit, Carla's personal number showing up on Decker's phone. It might also explain how Jessie's safe deposit box had been rifled. It took no stretch of the imagination to assume Carla had easy access to the vault and boxes. The fact that Decker had used his construction business as collateral for ready cash to invest in the Dunes Bayside Resort, LLC, gave him plenty of motivation to do everything in his power to ensure the project was a success. Otherwise, he stood to lose his ass.

During her middle and high school years, Laurel O'Donnell Lofton had the reputation of being an easy lay, and wasn't particularly choosy who she shared her wares with. If Laurel had nailed anywhere near the number of guys Angie claimed she had, who's to say hot-blooded Ron Decker wasn't a notch on her bedpost? And who's to say Decker hadn't tapped Laurel's resources a few times through the ensuing years? Maybe it was an ego thing—payback for Jake dating Angie in school. He sure as hell worked out of town enough to have plenty of opportunity.

Also, somebody had turned the inside of my Grey Wolf upside down looking for the key I'd found in Jessie's house. And the next day Laurel had the locks changed at her house in Tallahassee. That suggested there was a connection and communication between Laurel and Decker.

But what was Laurel's motive in having her husband waxed, if she did? Was the half-million in insurance enough to knock off the man you once loved, the father of your children? Maybe she'd found her true soul mate in her coach boyfriend, Steve Vann. But even so, divorce was a damn sight better option than murder. Unless ....

Maybe Jake Lofton's demons finally caught up to him. The guilt over the accidental killing of his best friend, his wife leaving for another man, not having his boys around often enough to be the kind of dad to them he felt he should be, and knowing another man might slowly but surely be taking over his role ....

So he finds Laurel's meds lying around the house. With pills and pistol in hand, he heads south and pulls off onto the shoulder of the road. He downs the pills and waits until they take effect and bolster his courage. And then, depression riddling him and his judgment impaired, he raises the 9-millimeter to his temple and squeezes off the round. Problems solved.

The only thing wrong with that scenario was my gut didn't buy it.

———+———

THE MALTESE FALCON WAS playing at O'Malley's Theater in Parkersville Saturday night. Not the 1941 gem starring Humphrey Bogart that I'd seen several times, but the original version of Dashiell Hammett's classic mystery, made a decade earlier. It starred Ricardo Cortez as Sam Spade. I never knew the prior film existed, so I thought I'd give it a shot. The flick was okay, but Cortez was no Bogey, and Bogey *was* Sam Spade.

I was about halfway home, driving through a long straight stretch of 98 that runs through a planted pine forest, when a vehicle slowly gained on me, flashed its brights and passed. The dark pickup's tag light was burned out. Chief Tolliver was a stickler for such things. The driver would be lucky to make it through St. George without getting pulled over.

On the radio a talk show chicken hawk was droning on about how the U.S. must maintain troop levels in Afghanistan and not begin a drawdown the president had recently announced. I glanced at the radio to hit the preset button for the contemporary jazz station, and when I looked up a thin beam of red light caught my eye. A cold fist of adrenaline slammed my gut. I ducked a split second before the blast.

The rifle round punched through the windshield a few inches above my head and tore through the back of the cab. When I ducked I jerked the wheel hard right. The Silverado veered off the pavement, lurched and bounced and hit the standing water in the drainage ditch paralleling the highway. The right side tires dug into the soft earth and the truck rolled and slid on its top into the pine forest, leveling a couple of trees with a violent crash before spinning to a stop. Upside-down, it took forever before I located the ignition switch. I turned it off, fumbled for the switch and killed the lights.

My left wrist hurt like hell, but I managed to unbuckle the seatbelt and drop to the roof. For whatever reason, no air bags had deployed. The radiator was hissing steam. It had probably busted when I mowed down the trees. The good news was I didn't smell any raw gas. There was a three-quarter moon, and enough light shone through the passenger-side window that it wasn't pitch black. I wormed and squirmed and finally contorted myself upright. More good news—the .357 magnum had somehow made its way from under my seat and was within arm's reach. I grabbed the case and pulled out the weapon.

I needed to get out of the truck pronto. If the shooter decided to stop and check out his handiwork, I'd be dead meat. I fumbled for the ignition switch and turned the power on. Great. The damn windows wouldn't work. My best option was to kick out the passenger window and crawl out. Easier said than done. From my cramped position I couldn't get the leverage needed to do the job.

What the hell. I cocked the S&W's hammer, point-aimed at the window and squeezed the trigger. The pistol bucked and roared, damn near busting my eardrums. I kicked out the remaining splintered glass. Now I simply had to crawl out without cutting an artery.

It took a couple minutes of playing Houdini before I managed to exit the vehicle. I crawled away from the truck and hid behind a nearby bush. A quick triage of my body revealed a small gash on my forehead. The bleeding wasn't bad, and I didn't seem to be leaking from any other wounds that I could tell. My wrist felt like somebody had whacked it with a hammer, and my knee hurt—the same knee I'd banged up jumping the ditch at the Panama Motor Court. My ribs weren't feeling all that chipper, either. Deep breaths weren't my friend at the moment.

A few cars passed in either direction, but I was in no hurry to flag one down for help. I had my cellphone, but didn't want to risk making further noise until I was confident the coast was clear. If the shooter was around, I hoped the boom of the S&W might give him something to chew on. My main concern was making sure the shooter hadn't stopped and snuck back without my hearing him. That truck was dark, maybe black, and if it was parked in the shadow of the woods I might not see it. I decided my best course was to sit tight for a while, keep my eyes peeled, my ears open. Speaking of ears, mine were ringing like hell from the blast of the .357.

A half hour went by. I figured if anybody was going to make a move on me they would've done so by now. I leaned back against a tree, fished the phone out of my pocket, and punched in Dakota's personal cell number.

——————

"YOU OUGHT TO LET me drive you to the emergency room, McClellan."

Dakota was off duty when she got my call, but she dropped whatever she was doing and came to pick me up in her battered old Corolla, opting to leave the county car parked at her apartment. With her Glock in hand, she'd covered my butt as I limped from the woods to her car. "I'm fine. I've been banged up worse playing football."

She huffed and finished taping the bandage a couple of inches above my right eyebrow. "You can be an obstinate asshole sometimes, you know that?"

"You learn that big word in school?"

Dakota didn't answer. She frowned as she stepped back to look me over. "How's the wrist?"

I held up my left arm. The hand was beginning to swell a little, but the pressure from the Ace bandage Dakota had wrapped it with felt good. "It's okay. I don't think anything's broken … probably a sprain."

"Knee, ribs?"

"I'm all better, Nurse Ratched."

"Who?"

"Never mind."

Dakota handed me the jeans hanging on the bathroom doorknob. "Put your pants back on, McClellan. I'm starting to get all hot and bothered."

I laughed despite my sore ribs as I stepped into the jeans and pulled them up over my skivvies. We had a little history of being less than fully dressed in each other's presence. But that's another story.

We made our way into Dakota's kitchen. The coffee had finished dripping, and she poured us both a cup. She sat at the table with me and swept a lock of strawberry-blonde hair from her eyes. "I should call this in, you know."

"Yeah, but I wish you wouldn't."

She sighed. "If Pickron finds out, it'll be my ass."

I started to comment on what a nice body part it was, but stopped myself. Dakota didn't need any encouragement. "I won't breathe a word."

She wrapped a strand of hair around an index finger. "What about the bullet holes in your truck? How you going to explain that to the insurance company?"

"I think it was all glass. I'll bust the rest of the glass out in the morning before I call. If there is an exit hole through the cab, I'll say it was an accidental discharge and I haven't gotten around to reporting it yet."

"Did you get a make on the truck?"

My turn to sigh. "Full size, dark, tinted windows, no tag light. I wasn't paying much attention."

"Regular cab, king, crew?"

I felt like a kid in grammar school being grilled by the teacher. "I don't remember. I do know the shooter was in the bed and used a laser sight."

"Net tailgate?"

"Most likely. Either that or a port cut in the tailgate. It had a tonneau cover on the bed."

Dakota's upper lip curled into her Elvis snarl. "Jeez, McClellan, you're about as observant as an ostrich with his friggin' head stuck in the sand."

Dakota was half my age, but I deserved the chewing out. If I'd been this careless in the Marines I never would've survived. "I could use a ride in the morning."

Dakota's big browns gazed at me above the rim of her cup. "I go on duty at seven."

"I'll be up and ready to go by six. How about a ride home?"

She looked past me to the clock on the stove panel. "It's damn near midnight. You know where the sofa is. I'll get you a blanket."

I considered it, but then remembered Henry. "Can't. Henry's in the camper. Got any Scotch for the road?"

"In the cabinet above the stove. I'll get my keys."

"Thanks." Grabbing the bottle, I felt a hand on my shoulder. I turned and Dakota placed both hands around the back of my neck. She planted a kiss on my cheek."

"I'm glad you're okay, McClellan."

Chapter 15

———•———

THE SILVERADO WAS TOTALED. No surprise there. The agent bought my story about hitting the brakes and swerving to avoid nailing a deer that darted out in front of me. No questions asked about the splintered remains of the windshield and back window that I'd altered to hide where the bullet punched through. It would take up to a week for my check to arrive. Meanwhile the company provided me a loaner, a red Chevy Impala.

According to the paperwork, the Impala came equipped with anti-lock brakes, airbags galore, and rollover sensing. If the occasion arose, I hoped the airbags worked better than the ones in the Silverado.

A couple of days after my "accident," I got a call from Bonnie Youngblood. She'd confronted Ray with the photos I'd taken of him and Cherry at the Golden Pole and the Panama Motor Court. At first he'd tried the old "It's not what you think" routine, and then he flew into a rage and took his frustration and anger out on the apartment walls and furnishings. He finally cooled down enough and the two later appeared in court, filed the necessary paperwork, and were granted a simplified divorce.

By the time Bonnie returned from work the next day, Ray had packed his bags and blown town. He was headed somewhere near Birmingham, Alabama, according to Bonnie, where he had friends.

To say Bonnie was relieved to be rid of the guy might be the understatement of the year. The Army had accepted her reenlistment and she'd retained the rank of sergeant. In a month she would be reporting to her new duty station at Fort Lewis, Washington. Case closed, client satisfied. I wondered if it was time to hit Frank up for a raise.

Freed from playing peeping Tom, I turned my attention back to the Lofton case. One thing kept bugging me. I could accept the fact that Ray Youngblood had found work as a bouncer at Cherry Moats's club. A guy with multiple combat tours, a bad case of untreated PTSD, and a history of violence against his fellow soldiers, both men and women, might have a little trouble finding a more conventional job. Bouncer fit him like a Latex glove.

What I couldn't shake was the feeling it wasn't a coincidence that Youngblood shows up in Panama City, and a couple of months later his boss's husband winds up floating in St. George Bay. And then, when an airtight connection is established between boss and employee, said employee hightails it out of Dodge.

There were now three people dead connected to this little caper, and I'd come within a couple of inches of joining the dearly departed. I was convinced that the person who took out Jessie Lofton was the same shooter who'd tried to waste me. And he'd used the bed of a pickup as his ambush site, meaning there had to be a driver involved, at least in my case. My gut told me there were at least two killers involved—the one who helped Amos Moats to his final swim, and the one who'd blown out Jessie's tire with a well-aimed shot. Jake Lofton's death was a tossup.

Wednesday I was having lunch with Kate at Carl's Sandwich Shop when Frank called. "Mac, I heard back from my friend about the wheels from Jessie Lofton's car."

"And?"

"There were traces of lead in that gouge you showed me, but that doesn't prove it was a bullet. She might have run over a wheel weight or something else lying in the road."

"Wheel weight? Come on. How the hell could a wheel weight puncture a new tire like that? Besides, I thought they did away with using lead for those things."

"They're in the process, but not entirely yet. It could have been one that fell off an older car."

I took a gulp of my iced tea. "But it could've been a bullet."

"It's possible."

"Did I mention that somebody tried to kill me last Saturday?"

Kate's eyebrows arched and she put down her shrimp po'boy. *Oops.* Major slip of the tongue. I had fed Kate the same story I'd used on the insurance adjuster.

Frank cut loose a long sigh. "Let me think … no, you didn't. What the hell is going on, Mac?"

"Relax. I swerved to avoid hitting a deer and totaled my truck." A quick glance told me Kate wasn't buying it.

"Are you okay?"

"Yeah, a few bumps and bruises, but I'm fine." Not for long, from the look the Fabulous Moolah was giving me. "You got any more cheating spouses you want me to tail?"

"Not at the moment, but you'll be the first to know."

I slipped the phone back in my pocket. Kate glared at me. "Deer, my butt!"

It took a couple of days to get back in Kate's good graces after coming clean about the wreck. A weekend stay at the Gibson Inn in Apalachicola did the trick. The place was supposed to be haunted and Kate had gotten hooked lately on ghost-hunting

TV shows. I even managed to reserve room 309, supposedly haunted by an old seafarer named Captain Wood who died there. It cost me a bundle, but Kate was worth every penny. The old captain failed to show, but the Gibson had one hell of a bar and the spirits were flowing there.

———·———

FIRST THING MONDAY MORNING I drove to the Ford dealership in Parkersville to take delivery on the F-150 XLT I'd ordered. The rental agency arranged to pick up the Impala at the car lot. I drove my new blue chariot onto Highway 98 and gunned it, enjoying the growl of the big V-8 as I headed back toward St. George.

I eased off the accelerator when my phone rang. Just when you get a new toy to play with .... "This is Mac."

"Mr. McClellan?"

"Yeah." There was something vaguely familiar about the man's voice that irritated me.

"This is Richard Moats. Could you stop by my office sometime today?"

Ah, the dog lover. "What's this about, Moats?"

"There is a matter we need to discuss."

"What's this 'we' crap? You got a mouse in your pocket?"

"Please, this is serious. Something has come up."

I eased the truck over the center line to give a small convoy of bikers plenty of room as I passed. "You mind being a little more specific? I place a high value on my time."

Moats let out a long breath. "Point well taken, Mr. McClellan. Please, can we meet?"

"When?"

I heard what sounded like shifting papers. "My schedule is free the rest of the morning."

I checked my watch. "Half hour?"

"That will be fine. And thank you."

———·———

"I'M AFRAID YOU MAY be right about Charlotte being involved with that man."

Moats delivered that stunner as I took a seat in his swanky office. "Ray Youngblood? You know he left town?"

"I heard he did." Damned if he didn't look close to tears.

"Why the sudden change of heart?"

He sighed and cleared his throat. "She has been spending more time than usual at the club the past few months, and I was starting to get suspicious. And then when you came in and said what you did, well …."

I waited. His chin quivered. He leaned back in his plush chair and folded his hands like he was about to pray. It reminded me of the statue in Jessie's house where I'd found the key to Jake's place.

"I did some checking. There was nothing at home, but at the club I found an email on the computer in Charlotte's office."

"You have access to her email account at work?"

Moats slowly rocked his joined hands back and forth. "I do now. Charlotte is big on making lists. She can be forgetful at times, so she writes everything down. It was a simple matter of looking through a few of her purses."

Maybe Frank should consider hiring this guy. "What was in the email?"

His hands rocked a little faster. "It was about money."

"Money?" I shrugged. "Maybe she owes him a paycheck."

"No, he said he needed the rest of his money. I think he's trying to blackmail her."

"Or he'll spill the beans about their affair?"

He nodded. "I love her, Mr. McClellan. And deep down I know she loves me. What else could it be?"

A picture of Amos Moats floating in the bay flashed through my mind. "What do you want from me, Moats?"

———·———

A WEEK AGO, IF somebody told me I'd be working for Richard

Moats, I would've said they were certifiably nuts. But damned if he didn't hire me to track down Youngblood and deal with him. I had a good idea what this was about, but I didn't share my suspicions with my new client. I didn't want to blow his vision of true love out of the water—not yet, anyway. Moats mentioned he'd seen Ray Youngblood at the Golden Pole a couple of times, but claimed he'd never talked to him personally. I was banking on it.

A quick call to Bonnie provided me with her newest ex's cell number. If he was using the same phone it would make my job a whole lot easier. Next order of business was a noon meeting with Moats at the Osprey's Nest, a waterfront bar and grill located near downtown Panama City on Massalina Bayou.

A perky young waitress dressed in a pirate costume led me through the inside dining area to the deck on the bayou where Moats sat at a small table. Several docks stood nearby, most with sailing vessels of various sizes and degrees of snob appeal moored to them. Atop several pilings, brown pelicans perched like statues on pedestals. Laughing gulls wheeled overhead. I hoped our feathered friends had the decency to mind their manners. I ordered a fried oyster basket and then got down to business.

"You're sure you never talked to Youngblood, not even on the phone?"

Moats twirled a bite of seafood pasta onto his fork. "Never. As I told you, I only saw the man a couple of times. I don't visit the club often."

"And he never called your house?"

"Not to my knowledge."

The lady pirate brought me a tall glass of iced tea and refilled Moats's glass. "Here's the deal," I said when she was out of earshot. "I'm going to give Youngblood a call using your phone. I'll be you, and tell him Cherry—"

"Charlotte."

I took a gulp of tea and swallowed the words I was going to

say. "I'll tell him that Charlotte confessed about the affair and I've forgiven her. All I want to do is settle up with whatever arrangement they made and for him to stay out of our lives."

As Moats reached for his glass I noticed his hand shook a little. He lifted the glass and took a drink. "There is something I haven't told you."

That got my attention. "As in what?"

With a sigh, he rested his elbows on the table and did the prayer thing with his hands. "The money. He wants fifty thousand dollars."

I almost spit out a mouthful of tea. "Fifty grand? How much did she give him up front?"

"Another fifty thousand."

"That's one hell of an expensive fling. You going to pay it?"

Moats started to answer as the cute buccaneer sauntered up to the table with my order. I thanked her and watched as she pranced back inside. With a crew like that I might've considered a life on the high seas myself.

"If I have to," Moats said, snapping me back to reality. "But I want him out of our lives for good. It's your job to make certain he gets the message."

"What do you need me for? You could handle this yourself and save my fee."

He sat back and exhaled, whistling through his nose. "I probably have twenty years on Mr. Youngblood. Besides, I've never been a physical person. I prefer to do my fighting in the courtroom."

"So, if something goes wrong and things get physical, you want me to do your fighting for you."

He gave a hint of a smile and nodded. "I did my homework after our first meeting, Mr. McClellan. Career Marine, excellent combat record. I'm sure you can handle yourself should such a situation arise."

"How long will it take you to get the money?"

He rearranged the pasta on his plate. "I can have it by this afternoon."

Must be nice. "Have you discussed any of this with your … with Charlotte?"

Moats set the fork on the plate and moved it aside. "No, not yet. But I'm certain she ended the affair and convinced him to leave town."

"To the tune of a hundred Gs."

He frowned. "There are certain things you can't put a price on."

I remembered an old saying: There's a sucker born every minute.

"Hand me your phone, Moats."

Chapter 16

———•———

THE PHONE CALL TO Ray Youngblood went off without a hitch. Lucky for me, either Cherry Moats hadn't checked her email at work for a while, or she was taking her own sweet time replying to Youngblood's message. My act convinced him that I believed the payoff was to cover up the affair, and he played right along. Sweet Cherry had 'fessed up and asked my forgiveness. We were determined to work things out and repair our relationship. Another fifty grand, Ray said, and we'd never see his mug anywhere near Panama City again, Scouts' honor. Right.

Amos's property hadn't been sold to the Kreuzbergers yet. So I suggested to Youngblood that we meet at eight the following evening at Moats's place on Five Mile Island. At first he balked, but I fed him a line of bull about having to get the cash out of "my" father's hidden safe. We agreed to meet there alone.

———•———

AN EARLY OCTOBER COOL front blew through the panhandle the next morning, breaking the summer heat. I arrived at Amos's house around seven that evening and parked the truck around back. Good thing I was early, because fifteen minutes later I heard a vehicle rumbling down the sand-rut trail that had served as Amos's driveway. I reached behind my right hip and double-checked the .357 tucked inside the new pancake holster I'd ordered a few weeks before. Good to go. I made sure the light windbreaker I wore covered it.

I knelt behind a clump of saw palmetto and waited as a souped-up Firebird rolled past and stopped in front of the house. The headlights reflected off the faded concrete blocks, illuminating the immediate area and letting me know Youngblood was by himself, unless someone was crouched down in the backseat or hiding in the trunk. I felt a little more secure then, but knew I'd better watch my back. He switched off the engine and killed the lights. The pipes coughed out a dying roar and fell silent.

I stayed where I was, letting my eyes adjust to the darkness. A door opened and then closed. Youngblood lit a cigarette and leaned against the Firebird's front left fender. Crickets were doing their thing, and mosquitoes were humming. Now and again Youngblood slapped at one. I gritted my teeth and forced myself not to.

After a couple of minutes I could see well enough to make my move. I looked again for movement inside the car, then stood up and called, "Evening!"

Youngblood jerked and glanced around, not sure where the voice came from. He did have the good sense to cup the lit cigarette in his fist. He waited a few seconds, eyeballing the area. "Moats?"

I stepped out into the drive. "Over here."

He craned his neck and stared my way. "I'm not armed."

I took a couple of steps closer and held out my hands. "This isn't a holdup, Ray."

His eyes must have finally adjusted to the poor light. "What the hell? Who the fuck are you, man? Where's Moats?"

I stepped closer. "He couldn't make it. I'm his personal representative."

"Hey, I saw you in the club before. What the fuck's going on?"

"A hundred thousand dollars, Ray? For murder? You work cheap."

He took a couple of steps toward me. "Look, man, I don't know what you're talking about." He lifted his left hand and held it out to his side. I kept my eyes glued on his right.

"Why'd you kill Amos Moats, Ray? Is Cherry that good in the rack?"

"I didn't kill nobody." He kept walking toward me, closing the gap, extending the left. "Where's my money, dude?"

The big man lunged. I sidestepped and slugged him as hard as I could in the family jewels. The air whooshed from his lungs as he sank to his knees. I followed up with a swift knee to the chin and he tumbled backward. He groaned, and then quickly rolled and bounced to his knees, pistol in hand. I'd already drawn the S&W. Its big barrel stared Youngblood right between the eyes.

"Drop it!" Damn, that's what *I* was about to say. Dakota appeared from the bushes on the other side of the drive, her Glock centered on Youngblood's broad chest. *Ah, my backup, and just in the nick of time.*

Youngblood slowly lowered the pistol, cutting loose a barrage of less-than-flattering words, most aimed at the fairer sex.

"Shut your friggin' trap and put the weapon on the ground!" Dakota wasn't fooling around.

Youngblood got the message. His fingers loosened their grip and the military-issue M9 hit the sand.

Dakota shouted for Youngblood to lie prone and put his hands behind his neck. When he did, she approached cautiously and kicked the M9 toward me.

"Keep your weapon on him, McClellan." She forced his legs

apart with a foot and frisked him, spending a little extra time in the crotch area, I thought. When she was sure he was clean, she grabbed her cuffs and secured his big hands behind his back.

When she was done, Dakota backed away and announced to Youngblood that he was under arrest.

"On what charge, bitch?"

"Trespassing, blackmail, murder one, take your pick."

"Murder? I already said I didn't murder nobody."

Dakota started reading Youngblood his rights. I walked over and squatted where he could see me. Mustering up my best Sam Spade voice I said, "Tell me, Ray, why'd you coldcock Amos Moats and toss him in the drink?"

"I'm not telling you shit."

I grabbed the back of his neck and pushed his face in the sand. "I hear you like to slap around women and little kids, big man."

Dakota kicked my hand away. "Back off, McClellan!"

I glanced up and saw a side of Dakota Blaire Owens I'd never seen before. I got up and walked away, disgusted with the whole mess.

After reading him his rights, Dakota got on the horn and called for backup to haul Youngblood's butt to the county slammer.

———

I HAD ONE HIGHLY pissed-off client the next morning when I walked into Richard Moats's office and dropped the paper sack with the fifty grand on his desk.

"What's this?"

"Early Christmas present."

Moats peeked into the sack and his face flushed. "You were supposed to give this to Mr. Youngblood so he would disappear and leave Charlotte and me alone."

"Are you always so damn proper with guys you catch

screwing around with your woman? Mr. Youngblood this and Mr. Youngblood that. The guy's a royal asshole."

He turned redder. "I'll remind you that you are working for me. Why didn't you give him the money?"

"Because sweet Charlotte wasn't buying him off to keep quiet about an affair. Youngblood saw her whack your father upside the head with a board out on the dock. The hundred K was hush money. But I think you already knew that."

Moats bounced up from the chair. His face turned from deep red to almost purple. "That's a lie! Charlotte would never do such a thing," he said, his voice shaky. "She's not capable."

"Ray Youngblood's down at the sheriff's office right now airing out his dirty skivvies. Word is he's about to cut a deal with the state attorney. The song he's singing says you were involved, too."

The color drained from Moats's face. He slumped into the plush chair. "Kill my own father?" He barely squeaked out the words.

"Your father wouldn't sell out to the Kreuzbergers. You and Cherry wanted that land bad. You planned to use the money from the sale to invest in the project, only your old man showed no sign of kicking the bucket anytime soon, so you decide to speed things along.

"Then Youngblood shows up looking for work, almost a gift from heaven for you and Cherry. She hires him as a bouncer for the club, and then lays him a few times to sweeten the pot. When Cherry has Youngblood eating out of her hand, she springs the deal—half a million big ones to knock off the old man and make it look like an accident."

"You think you have it all figured out, don't you, Mr. McClellan?" Moats kicked back in his chair and steepled his fingers under his chin. His color had returned to almost normal, and a smirk spread across his face. "You're forgetting who the lawyer is here. Your wild theory will never stand up in a court of law. The word of a bum who was dishonorably kicked out of the Army against a respected officer of the court? Good luck with that."

"So Youngblood goes with Cherry one weekend when she's supposed to shack up with your father," I said, ignoring Moats's comments. It was Perry Mason time. I planted both hands on the edge of his desk and stared him down. "Only, when it's time to do the dirty deed, he gets cold feet. Youngblood might be a dishonorable bum, but he's no murderer. So Cherry decides to take care of things herself. Youngblood hides out to wait for the ride back to PC. Your father and Cherry take a little stroll down to the dock to have a drink and watch the sun set."

Moats's fingers clasped together and began to move back and forth like an upside-down pendulum.

"When the time was right, Cherry picked up one of the scrap boards lying on the dock and whacked your father upside the head. Then she pushed him into the bay to make it look like an accident. Youngblood saw her do it. On the ride back to PC, he convinced Cherry a hundred grand would be enough to keep his mouth shut."

"That's a clever theory, Mr. McClellan," Moats said, "but a theory is all it is." He opened his desk drawer and pulled out a big checkbook. "Your services are no longer required. How much do I owe you?"

"A hundred thousand seems to be the going rate."

Moats dropped a fancy pen onto the opened checkbook and looked up at me. "Let's be reasonable."

"All your problems would've been solved last night if Youngblood had decided to use the pistol he was packing. You knew my background and figured I'd be ready and beat him to the draw. With Youngblood out of the way, your troubles would be over. Or if it went the other way, he'd have to vamoose to avoid a murder rap. Either way, you and Cherry come out smelling like roses."

Moats shook his head and smirked. "Just more grandstanding speculation, Mr. McClellan. You should try your hand at mystery writing. You have a highly vivid imagination."

"And you should try acting. You're Oscar material. Keep your blood money, Moats. See you in court." I headed for the door.

"Thank you, but that's highly doubtful. A case built on hearsay will never make it to trial. Besides, the state attorney is a close friend of mine, and a very reasonable man."

I stopped at the door and turned. "Let's hope he's a little more honest."

Chapter 17

———•———

I WAS SURE MY scenario about what happened to Amos Moats was on target, or close enough for hand grenades. I couldn't know everything that was going down with Ray Youngblood's interrogation, but Dakota promised she'd find out what she could and keep me posted. I had no love for the guy, but I was convinced Youngblood was a patsy. So far Richard and Cherry Moats had dodged arrest, although Dakota said they'd both been brought in for questioning.

Friday evening I was grilling T-bones for Kate and me. She was a few minutes late, so I'd already fed Henry his big hamburger steak. He was snoozing by the steps of the Grey Wolf when Kate pulled in the drive. Henry got up and yawned wide enough to swallow a baseball. He ambled over to greet her, tail stub wagging.

Kate made a big fuss over Henry, talking baby talk and scratching his ears and rubbing his stomach. *Damn, maybe I should try walking on all fours.* She reached inside the CR-V and grabbed a grocery bag off the front passenger seat. She held up a bottle of red wine she pulled from the bag. "I got you a six-pack of Michelob. Want anything while I open this?"

I drained the Bud I was drinking and tossed the can into the wire container where I kept my aluminum recyclables. "Dewar's, little ice. Thanks."

Kate frowned as she disappeared through the door with Henry at her heels. She'd been getting on me lately about drinking too much booze. But what the hell, the weekend was here and I'd made a significant step in the case, at least where Amos Moats was concerned. He'd owned the prime property the Kreuzbergers needed for the Dunes, and I couldn't shake the feeling that this whole mess, from Jake Lofton's death to Amos's, was somehow connected. After a few minutes Kate came outside and handed me the Scotch.

"Guess what I saw this evening while I was locking up?"

I took a sip of Dewar's. "A UFO piloted by Bigfoot."

"Very funny. Remind me to laugh. Try heavy equipment being trucked in, with 'Decker Construction' painted on the doors."

———⊢———

THE WHOLE DAMN CITY and county councils were on hand for the groundbreaking ceremony the following Saturday, as well as the mayor of St. George and about every other local dignitary you could think of. Decker Construction had leveled selected dunes and graded roadways for the past week, but today was the day all the bigwigs in their shiny hardhats and new shovels declared that construction of the Dunes was officially underway. Media from as far away as Panama City and Tallahassee were covering the event. Vendors selling handcrafted items and other wares set up shop under portable canopies. There were free hotdogs, hamburgers, and drinks, and a couple of huge inflatable playthings to keep the kids in attendance out of their parents' hair. Realtors were pointing out lots and giving their sales spiel to prospective buyers—mostly retired couples or young dreamers. All in all, it looked like the Dunes Bayside Resort was the most exciting thing to hit this area of the Panhandle since Hurricane Opal and sliced bread.

Kate was working at the marina, Henry was staying in her shady backyard, and I was scoping out the crowd on my own. I left my Canon locked in the F-150 and was snapping random photos with my cellphone, a trick of the trade I'd picked up from one of the PI books Frank loaned me while I was studying for my license. Later I'd load the photos on my computer and see if I happened to capture anyone or anything of interest to the Lofton case. Never could tell who might turn up.

At eleven sharp a man climbed the few steps to a makeshift stage and announced over the PA system that the groundbreaking was about to commence. Introductions were followed by polite applause. When the intros were done, around twenty of the big wheels in attendance stood in a semicircle wearing hardhats and manning shovels, courtesy of Mayor Jim Crowley's Ace Hardware.

Two of the Kreuzberger brothers, Karl and Kurtis, and their wives were in the center of the loose arc. Both men were tall and blond with Nordic features and athletic builds. The wives were definitely keepers. Ron Decker was there, standing almost shoulder to shoulder with Carla Esposito, Senior VP of the First Community Bank of Destin. The mayor and council members were also among the dirt diggers—pun intended—and several other men and women I didn't recognize. I assumed they were investors.

Karl Kreuzberger spouted a few grandiose words, and then video cameras rolled and shutters shuttered as blades dug into the sandy soil. The Kreuzbergers and their wives were asked to dig another shovelful and hold it up so photographers could capture the moment for posterity.

When all the pomp and circumstance was completed, a country band took the stage. About half the crowd scattered to shop the vendors or take golf cart tours of the different sections of the planned community. I kept mingling and snapping, being as inconspicuous as I could.

After a while the smell of grilling burgers had my stomach growling. I was having a hamburger and unsweetened iced tea at one of several foldout tables when a tall slender blonde caught my eye. She was a looker, her straight hair cut short with the ends tapering along her jaw line. It was warm for mid October, and she was decked out in tight white jeans and a sky-blue blouse with the tails tied around her tanned midriff. There was something vaguely familiar about her. I stopped chewing and watched her stroll past, heading in the general direction of a group who'd gathered near a large table supporting an architectural scale model of the Dunes.

I shoved the rest of the burger in my mouth, tossed the wrapper and cup into a nearby trash can, and tailed her. It was only about fifty yards to the table, so I lagged behind, being careful to keep people between us at all times. Occasionally I stopped and pretended to be reading a text or talking on the phone. Using my peripheral vision I saw she was heading for the small group by the scale model.

Detouring left, I put on the brakes beside a huge inflatable castle. Inside kids were bouncing on a giant trampoline or sliding from one level to another. I was only fifteen or twenty yards from the target group. If any of them happened to look my way, I was a dad eyeballing his kid.

Sure enough, Blondie walked right up to the gathering, casually greeted a few people, and gave one man a warm hug. When she backed away I saw who she'd been wrapped around and the light bulb lit up. It was Ron Decker, and he didn't exactly look thrilled with Blondie's affection. Maybe he was worried what Angie would think if a photo wound up in the papers. And Blondie? None other than Laurel Lofton, in the flesh.

———

KATE AND I DROVE to Tallahassee that evening and boarded a flight to North Carolina. The last thing I wanted to do, given the recent developments in the case, was to watch my ex marry her Naval officer boyfriend. Especially since they were getting hitched on the deck of what should've been our retirement home overlooking the New River. I wanted to back out, but Kate was right—I owed it to Mike and Megan to be there.

It was great seeing the kids again. Mike had bulked up and was looking forward to his junior year as catcher for the UNC Wilmington Seahawks. His goal was to be taken somewhere inside the tenth round in next year's Major League draft. Fatherly prejudice aside, my son had the necessary skills at the position, and a decent shot at the top ten. *Baseball America* backed up the projection.

Megan introduced me to her soul-mate squeeze, Trey, or rather Albert Louis Conner, III. No wonder he went by Trey. Turns out he wasn't such a bad guy after all. In fact I liked the kid. Well, sort of.

I even managed to be civil and politely hug Jill and congratulate the newlyweds—at Kate's urging, of course. Live long and prosper, and enjoy life in your beautiful riverside home. Not that I'm bitter or anything.

WE GOT BACK TO St. George late Monday afternoon. Kate had to work the next morning so I dropped her off at her place, picked up Henry, and headed for Gulf Pines Campground. Home sweet home. A note was taped to the door knob. I peeled it loose and unlocked the door. Henry damn near knocked me off the steps rushing inside.

I grabbed a beer from the fridge and opened the note: *Call me. D.* I took a swig of beer and punched Dakota's number. "It's Mac. What's up?

"Jeez McClellan, where you been? I've been trying to get hold of you since last night."

"North Carolina, marrying off my ex-wife. My phone was turned off most of the time."

Dakota snickered. "I bet that was a blast."

"Yeah, a real bomb. What's up?"

"Ray Youngblood cut a deal with the state attorney. I don't know the details, but warrants are out for Richard and Charlotte Moats. Evidently they both skipped town."

"What's the charge?"

"Murder one and criminal solicitation is what I heard. You can probably throw in flight, unless they turn up soon. Guess what else I heard?"

"I give up."

Dakota snickered louder this time. "Old man Moats stiffed that wife and son of his. He changed his will and left everything he owned to the St. George Church of God."

———

AFTER DAKOTA'S UPDATE, I uploaded the cellphone photos I'd taken at the groundbreaking ceremony to my laptop. I now had visual proof that Laurel Lofton and Ron Decker had a relationship, even if they were only good friends. My guess was it went deeper than that, or used to. The bug in Decker's house, my trailer being ransacked, and Laurel changing the locks all made a lot more sense now. It had to be Decker who'd tipped her off about the key. Was there anything I'd missed during my excursion to Laurel's house? Too late to worry about it now. There had to be something else, something I'd overlooked, or maybe in the lines of code that Mark hadn't been able to crack yet.

Then it dawned on me. Jake had loved Laurel, so much that he was willing to forgive the affair she was having and work to put their marriage back together. He must've confided in her about his work, probably even told her about his discovery on Five Mile Island. Jessie had mentioned that the find on the island could be a career-builder for Jake. It stood to reason that he would've wanted to share that news with Laurel.

Another trip to Tallahassee was in order.

It was a little past three when Laurel Lofton crossed the school parking lot and climbed into a light metallic blue Honda Odyssey. It was a nice vehicle, and practical too, but a far cry from the Corvette Grand Sport Jessie told me Laurel had bought with Jake's insurance money. I followed her as she turned right onto West Tharpe and hung a left on North Monroe. I trailed along, using the usual PI trick of keeping vehicles between us.

After five or six miles she took a right into a swanky apartment complex. I followed her past a big swimming pool to the second of six large four-story buildings. Landscapers were busy trimming bushes and edging sidewalks, trying to get in as much work as they could before cold weather put things to rest until spring. Laurel parked in front of a ground floor apartment, exited the Odyssey, and disappeared inside.

I parked in a visitor's slot, waited about ten minutes, and then rang the doorbell. She opened the door, looking good in faded jeans and a loose gray sweatshirt. "Mrs. Lofton?"

Her brows arched a little. "Yes."

I handed her my card. "I'm Mac McClellan. Could I have a few minutes of your time?"

She glanced at the card and then back at me. She seemed hesitant. "What's this about? I have to pick up my boys from daycare in a little while."

"I was hired by your late sister-in-law to look into your husband's death. May I come in?"

Her gaze drifted past me for a moment. "I'd rather you didn't. My husband committed suicide as you know, Mr. McClellan. That's in the past, and I'd really prefer not to discuss it."

"Jessie believed Jake might've been murdered."

Laurel let out a long sigh. "Jessie believed a lot of things."

I wasn't sure where she was going with that statement. "She

said the first thing you did with your husband's insurance money was buy a new Corvette."

Laurel placed a hand on her forehead for a couple of seconds, like she had a headache. "Jessie was mistaken, or lying. My boyfriend bought the Corvette, with his own money, by the way. I believe you know what I'm driving. I need the van for my kids."

"Jessie also said your husband loved you and the kids, and wanted nothing more than to make your marriage work."

She looked down at her feet and shook her head. "I loved my husband, Mr. McClellan, but he changed. He had problems, mental problems. Did Jessie mention that Jake got violent sometimes, with both me and the children?"

That was news I hadn't expected. "No, she didn't."

"Well, it's true. And it was getting worse. Jake was bipolar. Do you know what that is?"

"I've heard of it."

"My husband was like Jekyll and Hyde. He'd be kind and loving one minute, and then the next thing you knew he'd fly into a rage for no good reason. His doctor prescribed Symbyax, but Jake wouldn't give it a chance to work. I begged him over and over to get help, but he wouldn't."

It was time to play hardball. "Maybe your affair with the coach had something to do with it."

Her blue eyes burned into mine. "Yes, I was having an affair, but Jake practically drove me to it. There was no love left in that house, for me or our boys. I finally took them and moved in with my boyfriend before something terrible happened."

"What about your boys? Jessie said you allowed your husband to see them often."

Another shake of the head. "Only when I was with them. And only in public places."

"They never spent the night alone with him?"

"Never. He couldn't be trusted."

"You ever think about getting a restraining order?"

"I considered it," Laurel said, "but Jake seemed to calm down after I left him. I think he realized if he pushed the issue, things wouldn't go his way."

"What about the drugs found in your husband's system? They were prescribed for you."

Another sigh. "Yes, they were. I've discussed this at length with the authorities. I told you that Jake wouldn't go for help. I'm a nurse, and I encouraged him to take a Xanax daily to calm him down. And the sleeping meds so we could all rest without worrying about him having one of his episodes and keeping the boys and me up all night."

I couldn't argue with that, if she was telling the truth. I slipped the photo of Laurel and Decker embracing out of my shirt pocket and handed it to her. "How well do you know Ron Decker?"

She glanced at the photo and her cheeks flushed. "I see you've been busy, Mr. McClellan." She handed the photo back and leaned against the doorframe. "Let's talk inside."

"We were lovers for a while," Laurel said, when we were seated in her comfortable living room, "a long time ago." She tucked her legs under her in a plush La-Z-Boy recliner. "I was a senior in high school and Ron was in college. He'd broken up with his girlfriend because she cheated on him, and well, I'd always thought he was attractive. He asked me out one day, and we dated for a couple of months. Then he and his girlfriend got back together."

"By 'girlfriend,' you mean Angie, his wife?"

Laurel nodded. "Have you met her?"

"Yeah. She said some less-than-flattering things about you."

Her eyes narrowed and she sat up straighter. "Like what?"

"I'm only the messenger here. She said you were rather promiscuous, as far back as middle school. That you'd slept with half the guys at Niceville High."

Laurel's face reddened, and from her expression I figured it was from anger instead of embarrassment. "That bitch was describing herself. I was no virgin, but Angie was about the biggest whore you could imagine. She even fooled around with one of the PE teachers."

Laurel brushed a wayward blonde lock from her eyes. "Ron's big weakness is that he's always been crazy in love with Angie. And she's always used sex as a weapon to control him. No matter what she does or how many men she sleeps with, he always goes crawling back to her. It's pathetic."

This was one hell of a development. Who was I supposed to believe? "How do you explain the photo of you and Ron Decker?"

"Simple. We've remained friends over the years. Not lovers, friends. I never cheated on Jake until he became unbearable and Steve and I fell in love."

"Steve Vann, the coach."

"Yes. He's at football practice right now. About the other day. Ron, Steve, and I are business partners. We've all invested heavily in the Dunes Bayside Resort on Five Mile Island. What you saw was simply me greeting an old and dear friend."

"Does Steve know about you and Decker?"

"Only that we've been good friends since school. And I'd prefer to keep it that way. The past is the past, Mr. McClellan." She glanced at her wristwatch. "I need to get going."

"A couple of more questions?"

She sighed. "Make it quick."

"How much did you know about Jake's work, Five Mile Island in particular?"

"He told me he'd found evidence of a possible site from the de Soto expedition. That's all."

"What about artifacts or old documents?"

She shook her head. "He never mentioned that, and I never saw any. I do have to run or I'll be late."

"Who tipped you off about the key?"

Laurel tilted her head, looking puzzled. "What key?"

"The key that prompted you to change the locks on your house."

"I don't know what you're talking about. There have been several break-ins in the neighborhood. It's an older house, the locks barely worked, and there were no deadbolts. I had them changed to prevent a burglary or vandalism until the house sells. Now, I have to pick up my boys."

"Just one more. Why'd you kick Jessie out of your house the day you found her there?"

"Because she was rummaging through Jake's office, looking through his desk and files for things that had to do with his work at the university—things she had no business touching."

"Jessie told me she and Jake were close, and that she was there looking for photos and items from their childhood."

Laurel cut loose a sarcastic laugh. "Are you kidding? The last few years those two could hardly stand the sight of each other."

Another shocker. "Why's that?"

"They were fighting like cats and dogs over their parents' will."

Chapter 18

———•———

I THOUGHT I'D BEEN flying blind before my little powwow with Laurel. Now I felt like a man with cataracts walking through pea soup fog on a moonless night while crossing eight lanes of heavy traffic. Somebody was lying, big time, but who?

Laurel seemed sincere, and came across as a nice person who'd made a few bad choices in life but wanted to move on and put the past behind her. But if Laurel had been upfront with me, what the hell was Jessie's game before her so-called accident? And what about Angie Decker? I'd spent twenty-four years in the Marine Corps surrounded by guys I could always trust to watch my back. Right now I wouldn't want to turn my back on anyone involved in this case. I decided to focus on Angie for now. If I pushed her enough, maybe she'd slip up and spit out something worthwhile.

When I got home that evening Henry bolted out the door and lifted his leg to christen the nearest pine tree beside the gravel drive. I grabbed a beer and joined him outside, taking a seat on top of the picnic table. I was about to call Angie when Dakota drove up in her old Corolla.

She looked nothing like a deputy sheriff as she unlimbered

herself from the compact car and strolled toward me. She wore skintight jeans with a low-cut blouse and a button-up sweater that wasn't buttoned-up. As she leaned over to greet Henry, her cleavage got in the way of my eyes. I averted my line of vision elsewhere. The last thing I needed was another distraction, and Dakota sure as hell qualified in that department.

"Hey, McClellan," she said when she'd finished loving up Henry. For my next life I'm putting in a request to be an adorable dog.

"Hey, yourself."

She pointed to the Michelob. "How about a beer?"

"Thanks, but I got one."

"Jeez, you're a real friggin' comedian tonight."

"I take it you're off-duty."

Dakota struck her trademark model pose—hand on hip, hip thrust out, head cocked to one side, coy smile. "You think?"

I pointed to the camper door. "In the fridge, and bring me another one while you're at it."

She lost the pose and scowled. "I'm not your friggin' barmaid. How about a 'please'?"

"Pretty please."

Dakota was back in a flash and hopped up on the table beside me. Henry made a couple of circles and plopped down directly in front of her. So much for loyalty. She handed me the unopened beer and took a swig of her own.

"Thanks," I said, setting the spare Mich on the table beside me.

Dakota scooted over until our hips were touching and leaned into me. "Anything for you, McClellan."

Dakota gets a kick out of making me uncomfortable. I scooted the other way, putting a couple of feet between us. "How're things on the island?"

"Busy. Those dudes are doing a super awesome job, though. They're being careful to spare most of the dunes. Did you see the model? It's gonna be awesome when they're done."

"You should buy yourself an awesome house out there when they're finished." I hate the "A" word. One of my pet peeves.

Dakota snickered. "On my salary? Yeah, right."

I took another swig. "You need to find yourself an awesome rich husband."

She tapped my thigh with the back of her hand. "How much money you got, McClellan?"

I laughed. "Not enough."

Dakota took a sip of beer. "Speaking of husbands, isn't that Decker dude married to the woman you went to see in Destin after Jessie Lofton got killed?"

I'd brought Dakota up to speed on the case when she'd agreed to help me nail Ray Youngblood. "Yep. What about it?"

"I think she was at the site this afternoon, chewing his ass out about something."

"Dark hair, stacked, mid-thirties?"

"Jeez, McClellan, no wonder Kate stays pissed at you. Yeah, that sounds like her."

"Did you happen to see what she was driving?"

"Hard to miss a black Jag."

I CHECKED AROUND THE better motels and the few bed and breakfasts in St. George before I turned east on 98 headed for Five Mile Island. If Angie was in the area, so much the better. My best guess was that Ron Decker and most of his crew were staying at the Trade Winds Lodge on the island. And the restaurant would be serving dinner for a couple more hours.

There was no sign of the Jaguar, but I did recognize Ron Decker's Toyota Tundra dually parked in the restaurant lot. I pulled into an empty space and turned off the lights and engine, debating whether to wait in the lot or take my chances inside the dining room. *What the hell.* This case had dragged on for over two months now. Time to stir up the hornet's nest.

As the hostess was showing me to my table for one, I spotted the Deckers sitting side by side in a booth on the opposite side of the room. Angie sat nearest the wall. They were talking and seemed to be getting along peachy. I took my seat and a minute later, a smiling young waitress welcomed me and handed me a menu. I ordered a double Dewar's on the rocks and a Caesar salad. She returned in a couple of minutes with my drink.

Showtime. I grabbed my drink and strolled across the polished hardwood floor to the Deckers' booth. "Mrs. Decker, fancy meeting you here," I said, offering up a friendly smile.

Angie's eyes grew wide above the rim of the highball glass she was sipping from. There was no reaction from Mr. Decker, who was chewing a bite of food. Angie recovered quickly. "There's no need for formalities, Mac," she said with a smile of her own. "I don't believe you've met my husband, Ron."

I offered my hand. "No, haven't had the pleasure, but I do recognize you from the groundbreaking ceremony the other day."

The big man cracked a half smile. "The pleasure is mine, Mr. McClellan." He motioned with an open palm to the empty bench seat. "Will you join us?"

"If you'll call me Mac."

"Sure, Mac."

I slid onto the padded bench and took a sip of Scotch. Decker was wearing a black polo shirt with his company logo above the breast pocket. His full head of hair was as black as the shirt. "Angie mentioned you spend a lot of time working out of town."

Decker nodded as he chewed and swallowed half a french fry. "Which is why I'm here now, of course. In the construction business you have to stay on top of things, Mac."

I almost spit out the sip I'd taken. "I bet you do."

Decker glanced at Angie. "So, how do you two happen to know each other?"

Angie patted her husband's hand resting on the table. "We're having a torrid affair, dear," she said, and laughed. I joined in. Decker didn't, but he did manage a weak smile.

"Mac's a private investigator," Angie said. She took another sip of her drink—vodka with a twist was my guess. "He called and we met for lunch not long after Jessie's accident."

Decker nodded and took a drink from his glass of iced tea. "Were you investigating for the insurance company?"

"No. Miss Lofton hired me to look into her brother's death. She believed he might not have committed suicide."

Decker's brow arched. "She believed Jake was murdered?"

I nodded. "But I haven't been able to turn up anything that points that way."

He stabbed a fried shrimp with his fork. "Jake Lofton was a troubled man."

"Oh? How so?"

The fork made it halfway to his mouth before he set it back on the platter. "His wife had recently left him for another man."

"Laurel? I had a little chat with her this afternoon in Tallahassee." Angie's eyes narrowed, and Decker's jaw clenched. "I needed to ask her a few questions about Jake. And wouldn't you know, it turns out I'd seen her at the groundbreaking, too. Sure is a small world sometimes."

Angie looked like she was about to spit nails. Her husband frowned and his cheeks flushed. "Come to find out, she and that new boyfriend of hers are investors in the Dunes. She said you tipped 'em off about it, Ron, but hey, what are friends for, right?"

Angie bit her lower lip and turned her face toward the wall. Decker squirmed, his nostrils flared. I saw the waitress heading for my table with a tray. "There's my order. Nice seeing you again, Angie, and sure nice meeting you, Ron." I extended my hand. His was clammy.

I hurried across the room as the waitress glanced around for me. "Something's come up," I said. "Could I get that to go, please?"

She smiled, probably relieved I hadn't stiffed her for the double Scotch. "Sure. I'll meet you up front."

———|———

WHEN MY PHONE RANG at two in the morning I would've bet my retirement check on who the caller was.

"What in hell did you think you were proving coming over to our table like that?"

"Good morning to you, too, Angie. By the way, it was a booth, not a table."

"That wasn't wise, Mac. Ron's asking all kinds of questions. And why did you bring up that slut?"

"Laurel? She seemed rather nice to me."

"Nice? That bitch would bed anything that breathes."

"Hmm, a few weeks ago you tried to get me to come over and fool around. We got a double standard going here, Angie?"

"I was drinking, damn it."

"So was I, but I don't think that matters."

"Screw you!" she yelled, putting a serious dent in my eardrum.

"No thanks. What would Ron say?"

The call went dead. Henry whined, hopped off the bed, and headed for the door. I followed to let him out.

———|———

I CALLED AND MADE an appointment to see Carla Esposito at ten-thirty Thursday morning under the guise of discussing a two-million dollar loan. I didn't mention it was Ron Decker's loan I was talking about. Her office in the First Community Bank of Destin was as swanky as they come. Huge half-round oak desk, plush furniture, what looked to be original paintings hanging on the walls—first class, all the way.

Carla was decked out in a black business suit with a ruffled ivory blouse. Her dark brown hair was parted to one side and neatly styled in a French braid. She was tall and slender and damn near as good-looking as she was rich.

"What can I do for you, Mr. McClellan?" she said, after all the formalities had been dispensed with and we'd settled in our chairs. "My secretary mentioned something about a loan of two million dollars."

I pulled out a business card and handed it across the desk to her. "I work for Hightower Investigations. We've been looking into the death of Jake Lofton. I believe you went to high school together."

She gave the card a quick glance and began tapping it against the desktop. "Yes, Jake was a year or two behind me, but I do remember him. He was a nice boy, as I recall. What does this have to do with me?"

"Your bank recently made a two-million dollar loan to Ron Decker."

Carla frowned. "Two and a half, actually, but what business is that of yours? Decker Construction has more than ample collateral for that amount."

"Ron Decker and Jake Lofton had a history of bad blood between them, and there's reason to believe Ron could have something to do with Jake's death. Jake dated Ron's girlfriend for a while after she caught him cheating with you."

Carla took a deep breath, leaned back in the chair and exhaled. "Mr. McClellan, this is a waste of time. Yes, Ron and I dated briefly, but he was seeing another girl, too. And for your information, Angie was the one who cheated on Ron, not the other way around."

"This other girl you mentioned, would that be Laurel O'Donnell?"

"Yes. She and Ron were almost inseparable for a while. Then he suddenly broke it off and went back to Angie. God only knows why. Angie was ... well, let's be kind and say she got around."

"Did you know Jake and Laurel were married at the time of Jake's death?"

"I was aware of it, yes."

"So, Ron Decker and Laurel were lovers back in the day." I handed Carla the photo from the groundbreaking. "Looks to me like they've stayed rather friendly through the years."

She stared at the photo a few seconds and handed it back. "This doesn't prove that Ron had anything to do with Jake's death."

"Doesn't disprove it, either," I said, slipping the photo back in my shirt pocket. "How well did you know Jake's sister, Jessie?"

"Hardly at all. She was several years behind us in school. It's such a tragic shame about her accident. Her poor daughter."

"Did you know Jessie lived with Ron and Angie Decker after she got knocked up and her father kicked her out of the house?"

Carla had a good poker face. "No, not that I recall."

"You do know Sydni is living with the Deckers since her mother died."

"Yes, Ron told me."

"Ms. Esposito, do you believe Ron Decker is capable of murder?"

She sat up, crisscrossed her arms across her breasts, and shot me a dirty look. "Absolutely not. Why would you think that?"

I stared into her big brown eyes. "Because Jessie Lofton was pregnant with Ron's baby when she was killed, and there's good reason to believe he's Sydni's father, too."

Chapter 19

———•———

THE HORNETS WERE BUZZING. Friday morning I got a call from Ron Decker. He was in Destin visiting his family, but would be back on the island that afternoon and wanted to meet with me after work. We agreed on six thirty.

Decker's truck and a silver Nissan Xterra were parked in the small gravel lot in front of the singlewide trailer that served as his on-site office. I climbed the three steps and knocked on the door. Decker called for me to come in. He was seated behind a gray metal desk, talking to a twenty-something brunette standing beside the desk. She wore a light-blue Decker Construction polo and black jeans. Behind thick-lensed tortoiseshell glasses lurked a pretty face.

Decker stood, shook my hand, and introduced me to Rebecca, his secretary. Before leaving for the night she disappeared into another room and brought the boss and me steaming mugs of fresh coffee. He motioned to a chair in front of the desk. I set my Decker Construction mug on the edge of his desk and positioned the chair to my liking. The Xterra's engine fired and gravel crunched as Rebecca pulled out of the drive and turned east on Island Drive, probably headed for the Trade Winds Lodge.

"What's going on between you and my wife?" he said, losing the friendly demeanor he'd put on for Rebecca's sake.

"We're not having an affair, if that's what you're thinking."

He leaned back in the leather office chair and took a sip of coffee. "I don't like repeating myself, McClellan. I want to know what's going on between you and Angie."

"Jessie Lofton hired me to look into her brother's death. She was convinced Jake didn't commit suicide like the authorities ruled. Your wife and Jessie were close friends. I met with your wife to see if she might have any useful information."

"I see," Decker said, sliding open a desk drawer. I started to reach for the S&W, but held back. He tossed a small black rectangular object onto the desktop. "What's the meaning of this?"

Damned if it wasn't the mini recorder Angie had found planted under the island countertop in her kitchen. "You tell me."

"Angie said you must have put this in our home to eavesdrop. Private eye or not, that's illegal."

I took another sip of coffee. It suddenly tasted bitter. "Well now, the plot thickens. Looks like we've got ourselves a little dilemma here, Decker."

"How's that?"

"Angie told me *you* planted it, either to keep tabs on her or to find out how much we knew about Jake and Jessie Lofton's deaths."

"You're a damn liar, McClellan."

I felt the heat rise to my face, but kept my cool. "There may be a liar in this room, Decker, but it's not me."

His jaw tightened. "Why were you talking with Carla Esposito about me?"

"It's called doing the job I was hired to do."

"Spreading lies about me. Is that your job?"

"And exactly what lies would that be?"

"Jessie being pregnant with my child, for one."

I smirked. "Oh, that. And Sydni, for another?"

Decker leaned forward, his hands balled into tight fists. "I should have my lawyer sue you for slander."

I grinned. "If my math is correct, Jessie was a minor when you two started your fling. Maybe your lawyer will be interested in that little fact. Tell you what, Decker. You agree to a paternity test, and if Sydni's not your child, I'll make a public apology."

The veins in Decker's neck stood out. "I ought to crush you like a bug."

"I'm right in front of you."

He stood up. I followed his lead, ready to rumble. "Get the hell out of my office, McClellan," he said, pointing at the door, "and don't let me catch you on this property again."

I stopped at the door and turned. "Last I heard, you were the contractor, not the majority owner. I'll stay away from your office. Otherwise, I'll go where I damn well please."

———

HENRY GROWLED AT THE pounding on the door. I grabbed my watch off the nightstand and pushed the light button. Three twenty. Who the hell would be knocking on my door this damn early? I pulled shorts over my skivvies and grabbed the .357 in case it wasn't Kate or the Avon lady. You never know.

I parted the curtain enough to peek outside. It was Sheriff Bocephus Pickron and a couple of deputies I didn't recognize. Now I was worried. I hoped to hell nothing was wrong with Kate. I opened the door and was welcomed by the barrel of Pickron's nine-millimeter Beretta staring me in the face.

"Drop the weapon, McClellan!"

I'd forgotten I was holding the S&W. I tossed it onto the nearest chair. Henry was by my side, hackles raised, teeth bared, and growling up a storm at the sheriff. I always knew he was a good judge of character. "Henry, sit!"

He backed up a couple of steps and sat, low growls still rumbling from his throat. "What the hell is this about, Pickron?"

"You're under arrest for the murder of Ronald Decker."

———

"JUST HOW DID I commit this dastardly deed, Sheriff? Did I shoot him, poison his coffee, or what?" I was sitting in the interrogation room at the sheriff's office in Parkersville with Pickron and a plainclothes detective who so far hadn't said a word.

"Clam up, McClellan. We ask the questions, you give the answers. Got it?" Pickron planted his fists on the table in front of me and leaned in. "Funny you should mention coffee. We found your prints all over a cup sitting on the victim's desk."

I let out a deep sigh. "I already told you I was there. I got a call from Decker yesterday morning. He was at home in Destin, said he wanted to meet me at his office later that day. We agreed on six thirty. Check the phone records, or ask his secretary. Name's Rebecca. She was in the office when I got there."

"Don't tell the sheriff how to conduct his investigation, wise guy," Plainclothes said. He'd been leaning against the wall and shooting me dirty looks. He was mid-thirties, with curly red hair and freckles splattered across a round face.

"Hey, Howdy Doody can speak, and you didn't even pull his string, Pickron. Who would've thought?"

Detective Doody took a step toward me, but Pickron stopped him with a hard look. "Insulting department personnel isn't helping your case, McClellan. I suggest you keep your smart mouth shut and answer the questions you're asked."

"You got no good reason to hold me, Sheriff. Fingerprints on a cup? Purely circumstantial, and weak at that. Unless I used the cup to kill Decker."

Detective Doody piped up, "Mrs. Decker said you threatened

her husband at the Trade Winds Restaurant Tuesday night."

"Then Mrs. Decker is a liar. The three of us had a friendly talk, that's all. No threats. And you haven't told me how Decker was killed."

Sheriff Pickron turned to Detective Doody and motioned toward the door with his head. "Hill."

In a minute Howdy Hill was back carrying a large plastic bag by the top edge. Pickron took it from him and set it on the table where I could get a good look at it. "I believe this belongs to you, McClellan."

Oops. It was the KA-BAR combat knife given to me by my last command during my retirement ceremony. The Marine Corps emblem and my name and dates of service were engraved on the blade, along with dried blood. I'd kept it stored in my bedroom closet inside its case and hadn't noticed it was missing when my Grey Wolf was ransacked.

I glanced up at Pickron. "Yeah, it's mine. Where'd you find it?"

"In the parking lot outside Decker's office, where you dropped it."

"Somebody turned my camper inside out a couple of months ago. Whoever did it must've stolen it then."

Pickron wore a big smirk. "And of course you reported the break-in to the St. George Police."

"No, I didn't think anything was missing so I didn't bother. I thought he, she, or they were looking for something that had to do with a case I'm working on."

I stared at the knife again, and then back at Pickron. "You really think I'd be careless enough to drop a knife I'd used to kill somebody at the scene?"

"You were careless enough to lose your pocketknife when you found Maddie's body."

Touché. "Fingerprints?"

"Mostly smeared, but we found a couple of yours. You should learn to wipe better."

This wasn't going well. "Can I talk to you in private, Sheriff?"

Pickron and Hill looked at each other. Pickron nodded. Hill shut the door behind him. Bocephus slid a chair over and sat directly across the table from me, still smirking. "You ready to confess?"

My eyes burned into his. "You know damn well I didn't kill Decker."

"Do I?"

"Where's the motive?"

He lost the smirk and ran a hand over his high and tight hair. "You tell me."

"Somebody set me up, and I think I know who."

He looked away for a few seconds and then back at me. "Okay, I'm listening."

I spent the next half hour telling Pickron every detail I could remember about the Lofton case, from Jessie's phone call to my meeting last night with Ron Decker. For good measure I also filled him in on what I knew about Cherry and Richard Moats.

"Those two have a real surprise waiting when they turn up," Pickron said when I'd finished.

"So I heard."

"What?"

"Nothing." I realized the info Dakota had leaked must be confidential. I didn't want to land her in hot water.

"McClellan, you been a royal boil on my butt ever since you showed up in St. George. But for whatever insane reason, I believe you. I'll talk to the judge and see if we can rush a hearing and get you released on your own recognizance."

"For a murder rap?"

Pickron cracked a rare half-smile. "I do have pull around these parts."

———

PICKRON PULLED IT OFF. I appeared before Judge Stanley Winters Tuesday morning at ten, and was a free man fifteen minutes later. Well, not exactly free, and not on my own recognizance. I couldn't leave the state and had to report in weekly to Sheriff Pickron. It also cost me ten Gs in bail money—about as cheap as you could hope for under the circumstances. My military record and the fact that Winters spent twenty years in the Army as a judge advocate probably didn't hurt matters any. I'd done my share of head butting with Bo Pickron, but he'd put his ass on the line with the judge for me, and I damn sure owed him a big favor now.

The sheriff did his best to keep the incident low key, but it was a matter of public record, and I caught more than a few of my campground neighbors staring and whispering to one another as I passed by. At least Kate and Henry were on my side ... for now, anyway.

Work on the Dunes was halted Wednesday for Ron Decker's funeral. I figured it wouldn't be appropriate for the deceased's accused murderer to attend, but I sure as hell wanted to know what Decker's grieving widow was up to. Kate had the day off, and jumped at the chance to play PI in my stead. I was grilling shrimp kabobs and Henry was chasing a pair of squirrels that live in the big oak in Kate's backyard when she returned late that afternoon.

Henry was first in line for Kate's attention, but she did save a warm hug and kiss for me. "Get any good shots?" I said, turning one of the wooden skewers.

Kate fished a Michelob from the cooler I'd brought. "A bunch. The crowd was huge." She grabbed a kabob off the warming rack, tossed Henry a shrimp, and helped herself to one. "Those poor kids were a mess, but Angie didn't seem all that heartbroken. Stoic's a good word."

"Those shrimp were eight bucks a pound," I said, watching Henry swallow the large shrimp without chewing. I pulled one off Kate's skewer and popped it in my mouth. "Maybe she's in shock."

"Maybe." Kate took a sip of beer. "But I doubt it. A certain guy could hardly take his eyes off her at the graveside service. He stood outside the awning where the family sat during the entire service, right near Angie's chair."

"What'd he look like?"

Kate smiled. "Hunky, like a tall Tom Cruise."

"Angie was an only child. Maybe the guy's her cousin."

"I doubt it."

"I'm betting you got a couple of good shots of the guy," I said, reaching in the cooler for another beer.

She batted her eyes like a flirt. "Now *that* would be a safe bet."

———

AFTER DINNER KATE LOADED the photos from her phone to her computer. Mark had installed a photo enhancement program for her a while back, and with a few tweaks, any photos that were questionable were transformed into much sharper images.

Kate had managed to sneak a few photos of the family members as they'd filed out a side door of the funeral home chapel. A couple of women with children led the way, most likely Ron Decker's sisters, nieces, and nephews, according to the Destin newspaper obit. Tom the Hunk was standing by the door as Angie exited the chapel. He escorted her to the black limousine that would transport the family to the cemetery, and then climbed behind the wheel of a new Lexus, the first car in line following the hearse and family. Damned if he didn't look a lot like Tom the actor, except a few years younger and several inches taller.

Kate had discreetly shot most of her pics at the graveside service. Laurel Lofton and a tall, athletic-looking man I assumed was Steve Vann showed up in one photo, standing well back in the crowd. There were about a dozen photos of the Hunk, or him and Angie. Judging from Angie's height in the low heels she had on, I'd say the guy was around six-two, and it looked like he hit the gym on a regular basis. The short beard and moustache he sported was right out of Cruise's *The Last Samurai.* Kate and I studied the photos and picked out the best straight-on and profile shots of Mr. Hunk. She enlarged them and printed out a few copies.

Kate sent copies to Frank's email address with a note from me asking him to run a check on the guy. Tomorrow I planned to give copies to JD and Dakota and ask them to be on the lookout for Tom the Hunk. I hoped JD might also be able to run a check on him.

We were about to hit the rack when Kate's phone rang. Her eyes lit up and she turned to me. "It's Mark. Grab something to write with. He thinks he's figured out the other code."

Chapter 20

————•————

Mark had cracked the code all right, but none of it made much sense or added any useful info about de Soto's men and the winter spent on Five Mile Island. Long story short: Mark finally figured out that Jake Lofton used the same code as before, but instead of translating the words into English, he'd translated them into Spanish. With the help of Mark's college Spanish teacher, the two concluded the last few lines on the flash drive were Spanish quotes or sayings. Kate had scribbled down the sayings and Mark's best interpretation of their meaning:

> *Los trapos sucios se lavan en casa.* "Dirty clothes are washed at home." If you have issues with your spouse or family, it's best to work them out in the privacy of your own home.
> *Lo prometido es deuda.* "What has been promised, is debt." People should regard their words as oaths.
> *Más vale solo que mal acompañadi.* "Being alone is preferable to being in bad company." Even I could figure that one out.

La venganza es un plato que se sirve frio. "Revenge is a dish which is served cold." Acts of revenge usually don't occur in the heat of the moment. The offended person often waits for exactly the right opportunity before striking.

La verdad es hija del tiempo. "Truth is time's daughter." Things may be unclear right now, but the truth will come out in time.

El más terrible de todos los sentimientos es el sentimiento de tener la esperanza muerta. "The most terrible of all feelings is the feeling of one's hope having died."

The last was a quote from Federico García Lorca, a Spanish poet and playwright who was executed by Franco supporters in 1936 during the Spanish Civil War.

"What on earth do you think it means?" Kate said after we'd gone over them a second time.

"I think it means Ron Decker was right the other night when he said Jake Lofton was a troubled man. That last quote sold me. I think Jake was at the end of his rope and committed suicide, like the medical examiner ruled."

———•———

Around noon the next day I met Dakota for lunch at the 7-Eleven on the island. This time her meal was a foot-long hotdog, corn chips, and a Snickers bar. She washed it all down with a thirty-two ounce Diet Coke. After all, a girl *does* have to watch her figure.

"Never seen him before, but I sure wouldn't mind making his acquaintance," Dakota said, studying the photos of Hunky.

"You sure?"

She snorted. "Am I friggin' sure? Of course I'm sure. What girl wouldn't remember a hot dude like that?"

"And I thought you only had eyes for me."

Dakota pursed her lips around the straw and took a sip of Coke. "Jeez, McClellan, get real. I don't date murderers."

I ignored the dig. "Seen any dark pickups with a tailgate net?"

"Nope. I'll let you know if I do."

I tapped the photos. "Will you *please* keep a lookout for this guy?"

She smiled. "Wow, McClellan, I'm impressed. You're finally starting to learn some manners."

———

JD AGREED TO PASS the word around the department to be on the lookout for Angie's friend/cousin/whatever. He also said he'd check databases for any possible info on the guy when he had the time.

I packed a duffle bag and dropped Henry off at Kate's, and then drove to Gillman's Marina, where I swapped vehicles with Kate. I planned to shadow Angie Decker for a couple of days and didn't want to risk having her recognize my truck. Kate had borrowed her dad's Honda Accord to attend Ron Decker's funeral, so I figured I was on safe ground driving her CR-V.

After driving through a pounding thunderstorm—one of many we'd been having the past several days—I arrived in Destin around five that afternoon. I checked into the downtown Motel 6. I had no plans to pull an overnighter unless things got real interesting. The motel was also within easy walking distance of Frank's office and a couple of good restaurants. I tossed my bag onto the bed of my second-story room and made use of the bathroom. Then I headed downstairs to where I'd parked Kate's SUV.

Approaching the open gate leading to the Decker home on Indian Mound Trail, I slowed to a crawl. There was no sign of Angie's Jaguar, but a sporty Mazda Miata convertible, red with a black top, was parked in front of a garage door. My guess is it was the wheels of the Deckers' daughter, Riley.

I drove on past and turned around on a side street. There was a vacant lot between two swanky homes where I parked on the shoulder of the road. I'd thought to buy a local newspaper at the motel. I folded it to the want ads and circled a few properties in the real estate section with a red pen. If any civilians questioned my presence in the next couple of hours, I was out looking at houses or land for sale. If cops came snooping and push came to shove, I'd flash my PI license and claim I was on a stakeout for a client. That wasn't a total lie. Jessie *had* hired me to look into her brother's death—my reason for being here in the first place.

I'd been there a good hour and it was getting dark when I noticed a black car approaching from behind. I lifted the newspaper, turned my head a little and pretended I was reading as the car passed. It was the Jag, and Angie was alone. I watched as she made the turn into her driveway.

I decided to sit tight for a while in case someone was following her home or planning to visit. No such luck. After another hour I called it a night and drove back to the motel.

———

ON THE WAY I picked up a six-pack of Bud at a convenience store, and then bought a burger and fries at the nearby Whataburger. I was finishing the last bite when my cellphone rang. Dakota got right to the point.

"Hey, McClellan, could that truck you're looking for have been a real dark blue?"

"It was dark. It's possible. What you got?"

"Late model GMC Sierra."

"Regular cab?"

"Yep. It was on the causeway coming from the island. I noticed the tailgate net in my side-view, so I turned around and passed the guy. Only problem is, the driver was a blond dude, maybe forty. Looked sort of like you, but no beard. Not as hot, either. I only got a quick look at him when I passed. I didn't want to spook him in case it was your guy."

"I never said that Angie's hunk and the pickup were connected."

"No, but wouldn't that be convenient?"

I popped the top on a second beer. "Any Decker Construction sign or decal?"

"Nope."

"What about the tag?"

Dakota sighed. "That's another problem. It was a North Carolina plate, but the truck was so friggin' muddy I couldn't read the whole thing."

"What *did* you get?"

"LWS-6 or 8, I couldn't tell which. The rest was caked with mud."

"There's no mud on Five Mile, is there?"

"Only what they haul in for foundations and stuff. That GMC looked like it had been to a friggin' bog-in."

IN THE MORNING I called Frank and made a beeline for his office.

"Yeah, I know, any PI worth his salt will always have access to the Internet," I said as Frank did a search for Decker Construction on his desktop computer. "I didn't feel like lugging my laptop around while tailing Angie."

"That's why they make smartphones, or iPads," Frank said. "You should join the twenty-first century and get one."

"You don't pay me enough."

"Here we go." Frank straightened in his chair and leaned closer to the big flat-screen monitor. "The Dunes Bayside Resort," he read quietly, "and ... aha! Athletic area upgrade on Eglin Air Force Base." He glanced at me. "Decker's Construction is a big outfit, Mac. With all the military facilities in the area, they bid a lot of government contracts. I knew they had another project going somewhere."

———

Eglin Air Force Base is the largest military facility in the country, over 724 square miles of land, taking up a good chunk of the Florida Panhandle. I followed the directions on the map Frank Googled for me, and showed the young SP guarding the East Gate my military ID. It didn't take long to find the athletic complex located behind the shoppette. I stopped near the ball field complex and parked. From the info I'd found on the base website, there were several ball fields clustered together getting a major overhaul, with new dugouts, fences, and the works.

Yesterday's rain system had passed, and the sound of heavy equipment rumbled nearby. The smell of diesel fumes was heavy in the cool air. I could've closed my eyes and tracked the earth-moving machines with my ears or nose. I walked around to the back of the track and field house building, and there they were. Dozers and backhoes and heavy dump trucks were spread out across the complex. Several Decker Construction Company signs on four-by-four posts spanned the work site. The place was a mess. Mud from the recent rains was everywhere, and hardly any Decker or workers' personal vehicles parked nearby had escaped without a good coating.

I walked around eyeballing the area for a while, hoping to spot a dark pickup with a tailgate net, especially the dark blue GMC Sierra Dakota had mentioned. No such luck, but the odds of that truck being involved with Decker Construction had shot up.

Unless the blue Sierra *had* participated in a bog-in.

———

I was on the road heading back to Destin when Frank called. "Good news, Mac. The guys in the department came through again. We've got a make on the guy Katie saw at Decker's funeral." Frank was retired from the Okaloosa County Sheriff's Department and had friends in high places.

"I'm all ears."

"Kenneth Alderman, Junior. Thirty-eight years old. He owns a horse ranch a few miles north of Crestview. Breeds thoroughbreds."

"Married?"

"Divorced, no children. And get this: Ken Senior used to be the partner of Ron Decker's father when they started the business back in the sixties. Decker bought him out in the early eighties, but part of the deal was that Alderman maintain a ten percent interest in the company, in perpetuity."

"In what?"

Frank cut loose a heavy sigh. "In perpetuity. It means 'forever,' unless Alderman decided to sell, which he didn't. Junior inherited the ten percent when Senior died a few years ago."

"I know what the word means, Frank. You sound like you got a mouthful of marbles."

"It's that cheap phone of yours."

"I'm guessing Junior's ten percent is enough to keep his horses in hay and oats for a while," I said, ignoring Frank's jab.

"That's putting it mildly."

"So, Angie and Junior are business partners."

"Her ninety percent to his ten, at least on paper. It also gives Alderman a sound reason for attending the funeral."

I snorted. "Come on, Frank. You don't buy he was there to comfort and console his new business partner, do you? Kate said they looked *real* friendly together."

"You're cutting out again, Mac. Get rid of that dinosaur and buy a real phone."

"Later."

IF KENNETH ALDERMAN WAS thirty-eight, there was a good chance he'd gone to high school with Angie, Ron, and Jake Lofton. That is, if he'd also attended Niceville High, like the others. I figured the chances were fair. If their fathers started a business together, they might well have lived in the same area at the time.

I'd grabbed another six-pack and a Whataburger meal to go since this was going to be a working night, at least for a couple of hours. I let myself into Frank's office with my key and woke up the computer. I'd eaten half the burger and fries and polished off two Buds and still hadn't turned up anything worthwhile with my searches.

Then I came across Classmates.com. What the hell. I whipped out my Visa, bought a year's full membership, and went to work. It was money well spent. It didn't take long to find the correct edition of *Aquila,* the Niceville High Yearbook. Kenneth Alderman was a senior and a jock on the Eagles' football and baseball teams. Ron Decker was in his junior year; Angie and Jake were sophomores. Connection made. I wondered how long this streak of good luck would hold up.

———

Kate was working Saturday so there was no good reason for me not to stay in Destin in case Angie or Kenneth Alderman made a move. I'd noticed another vacant lot on Indian Mound Trail where I would have a decent view of anyone coming or leaving the Decker house. I arrived around nine that morning and took up where I'd left off a couple of nights ago. My trusty newspaper ads were close at hand, and I'd even picked up a couple of free real estate magazines from a rack at the motel.

At ten thirty sharp the red Miata squealed its tires as it whipped out of the Deckers' concrete drive, making a left onto Indian Mound Trail. The two-seater sped by me, top down, two brunette ponytails threaded through white ball caps flying in the breeze. Both girls wore sunglasses so I didn't get a real good look at them, but I had no doubt it was Riley and Sydni heading somewhere fast. Riley was talking on her cellphone and it looked like Sydni was punching up a text message or phone number, so neither girl paid me any mind.

About forty minutes later the black Jaguar turned right onto Indian Mound. I cranked the CR-V, gave the Jag a good head start, then followed, keeping well back. Once the Jaguar turned east on 98, I closed the gap some, making sure traffic stayed between us. It appeared that Angie was alone. I figured her boys must have spent the night elsewhere, maybe with their aunt.

Angie continued east and cut north across the Mid-Bay Bridge. She followed State Road 20 into Niceville, and then turned north on 85 toward Crestview. By then I had a good idea of her destination. Traffic thinned. I stayed on my toes to make sure she didn't suspect I was tailing her.

A few miles north of Crestview near a little place called Four Lakes, Angie turned left onto Big Buck Road. I backed off. A couple of minutes later a lake appeared in the distance. I must have passed by a good half mile of fancy white fencing by the time the Jag slowed, turned right through a stone gateway, and disappeared around a bend. I eased off the gas, and as I passed by the entrance I noticed the wrought-iron gate had swung closed. A horseshoe-shaped sign above the gate read *Alderhaven*. So this was Junior's thoroughbred ranch. Looked like that ten percent of Decker Construction had served him well.

I continued on for another quarter mile before the fence right-angled back to the north. The lake was visible through the trees. Pulling off the road, I parked in the shade of sprawling live oaks. I got out, slung the Canon around my neck, and secured the holstered S&W behind my right hip. I backtracked to the fence corner. Inside the fence the area was mostly wooded. Glancing around to make sure nobody was eyeballing me, I climbed over.

I eased my way a couple of hundred yards until the woods gave way to foot-high grass. Less than a quarter mile away the house came into view. It was two stories, with a stone foundation, fireplace, and what looked to be natural cedar or cypress planking. A scattering of big oaks and pines stood between my location and the house. There was no sign of horses. Maybe Junior kept them in the lower forty. Even with the zoom lens, I needed to get closer. What the hell. I was already trespassing; might as well go for broke.

I eased out into the grass, doing my best to keep a tree between the house and me. I made it to a thick pine, took a deep breath and headed for another. I hoped to hell no dogs were roaming the place. Stepping carefully, I worked my way from tree to tree until I was within fifty yards of the house. It was sided with native cypress. The house wasn't all that big or fancy, but it was built to last.

Hearing voices coming from the back of the house, I crept diagonally in that direction. A large swimming pool came into view. Two people were laughing and splashing water at each other. It was a cool day, so the pool must have been heated. I snuck forward another ten yards and took refuge in the shade of a big live oak. I was only about thirty yards away now and could make out the voices of a man and woman. Keeping my cheek close to the tree trunk, I took a gander.

Damned if it wasn't Junior the Hunk and Angie the grieving widow, frolicking in the pool as butt naked as the day they were born.

Chapter 21

———•———

"How on earth did you get an angle like this?" Kate said after she'd uploaded the photos I'd shot of Angie and Junior to her computer.

"Playing squirrel."

Kate shot me a look like I'd lost my last marble.

"I climbed the big oak I was hiding behind."

She glanced at my arms. "I guess that explains the scratches."

A German shepherd had made an appearance at the pool and I'd decided getting off ground level would be my best bet to escape detection by Rin Tin Tin's super nose. I'd almost fallen out of the tree while literally going out on a limb to get a good vantage point to shoot the photos. I managed to hang on and right myself, but it cost me several deep scratches on my inner forearms and wrists.

"That's the guy I saw at the funeral, all right," Kate said, after she'd worked her magic with the photo-enhancing software. She clicked up another photo, took a closer look and frowned. "What on earth? Did you have to take pictures of them doing *that?*"

"Well, it proves they're more than business partners."

Kate fired off a dirty look. "Pervert."

"I don't see you averting your eyes," I shot back.

She pinched my arm and got back to business. "Most of these should enhance nicely."

I couldn't resist. "From what I see of Junior, he doesn't need much enhancing."

If looks could kill .... "Does your mind ever crawl out of the gutter?"

"Hey, I was in that tree until dark. Give me a break." It was true. I'd waited until nightfall before climbing down and making good my escape under the cover of darkness. The two lovebirds had gone inside the house a little after four, but didn't call Rinny inside until nearly dark. I figured a little more tree-time couldn't hurt, especially with that four-legged schnoz on the loose.

"The Marines' Hymn" sounded from my pants pocket. I checked the caller's number and wasn't overjoyed with what I saw.

"Mac here," I said.

"McClellan, you need to come to my office right away." Bocephus has such a charming decorum.

"On Sunday? I thought I was supposed to check in with you on Tuesdays, Sheriff."

"You thought right. This concerns another matter."

Things were getting more interesting by the moment. "When?"

"As soon as you can get here."

"I'm on my way."

———◆———

DAKOTA WAS SITTING IN Pickron's office when I walked in. Obviously off-duty, she was decked out in jeans and a garnet FSU sweatshirt. Pickron didn't bother to stand and shake my hand, but waved at a chair near the one Dakota occupied.

"I believe you two know each other," the sheriff said, wagging a finger in our direction.

Dakota shot me a quick glance with a come-hither look, one eyebrow raised. "Oh, now I remember. You're that dude we rescued at the casino."

I tried to keep a straight face. "Yeah, Deputy Owens and I have met a few times."

The sheriff shuffled through a stack of papers lying on his desk. "Owens got the plate number from that GMC pickup you're interested in."

Dakota shifted in the chair and folded one leg under her. "I was patrolling the island last night and noticed it parked outside the Trade Winds Restaurant. It was raining friggin' cats and dogs, so I stopped behind the truck and shined my flashlight on it. Enough mud had washed off that I could read the whole plate."

"I think I know where that mud came from." I spent the next few minutes recounting my little excursion to Destin, but I left out a few delicate details. "I think whoever belongs to that truck is somehow connected to Decker Construction."

"You should find this interesting," Pickron said, pushing a sheet of paper across the desk to me. It was a photo of a man with dark blond hair, strong jaw, rugged looks. "Owens says this is the man she saw driving the pickup the other day. We ran the tag and put his name through the system. His name is Zackary Dean, age forty-two. Born in Clayton, Georgia, joined the Army in 1989, and saw combat duty in the First Gulf War.

"He served twelve years and then left the Army and joined a little outfit you might have heard about, McClellan."

Pickron paused, waiting for me to say something, I guess. "What outfit?"

"Blackwater."

"I hear they pay better than the military." Blackwater will always leave a dirty taste in my mouth. Billed as a private security firm, they were employed by our government to 'assist' our armed forces in their various duties. What they are is a private army for hire, better known as mercenaries.

The Blackwater bunch earned themselves several deserving black eyes while performing their Punch and Judy show in Iraq. Four of their operatives managed to get themselves killed and hung from a bridge. That incident wound up leading to the battles in Fallujah. In an effort to reinvent themselves after the Iraq fiasco, they've undergone name changes to bolster their image.

"Dean was evidently one of Blackwater's bad eggs," Pickron continued. "He got himself in a big stink over some dead Iraqi civilians. He left Blackwater in 2005 and has worked construction since, mostly in North Carolina."

"So how'd he wind up down here working for Decker Construction?"

Pickron grunted. "Word of mouth, maybe? Or he saw an ad in a trade paper? There's something else that should interest you."

Another pause. "I'm waiting."

The sheriff leaned back in his chair and folded his hands behind his head. "While he was in the Army, Zackary Dean trained as a sniper at Fort Benning."

———

THE NEXT DAY WAS Halloween. What better day to confront a witch? I was waiting in my truck outside Laurel Lofton's apartment when she drove up. We exited our vehicles at the same time. She stopped in her tracks and frowned when she noticed me.

"What are you doing here?"

"Looking for the truth."

Laurel tried to brush by me to her front door. I sidestepped and blocked her.

"Look, Mr. McClellan, I've told you everything I know. Now please leave me alone or I'll call the police."

I pulled my phone out of my pocket. "Would you like me to make the call? I'm sure the cops would be real interested in hearing how you blackmailed Ron Decker."

"You're crazy."

"I did my homework again, Mrs. Lofton. You recently bought a foreclosed house on Lake Jackson to the tune of a quarter-million bucks. And you're having renovations done. But hey, it's worth every penny. I drove out there earlier this afternoon. Looks like you made a honey of a deal."

Laurel's mouth dropped open. "How could—"

"That little tidbit was courtesy of the Leon County Tax Assessor's Office. The Corvette Grand Sport was a little harder to track down."

Laurel recovered enough to find her house key on the ring in her hand. Her big blues burned through me like lasers. "Let's take this inside."

I followed her through the door and into the living room. She collapsed in the La-Z-Boy and dropped her purse on the floor. "Just what is it you think you know?" she said after staring me down a few seconds.

"Math was never my favorite subject in school, but I can do a little figuring without using my fingers and toes. A quarter-mil for the house, over sixty grand for the 'Vette, paid in full with your check, I might add. Over thirty for the Odyssey, let's see … that comes to more than three-hundred and fifteen thousand. Now, if we subtract that from the five hundred Jake's insurance paid, hmm, you're down to a hundred-eighty grand at best. And I know it takes a million minimum to buy into that island project LLC."

Laurel lowered her head and massaged the bridge of her nose. "You're fishing in an empty pond, Mr. McClellan. My boyfriend happens to be—"

"Up to his ears in debt," I said. "It's amazing what you can learn from the Internet these days, especially if you're willing to shell out a few bucks to the right sites. Steve Vann is paying alimony and child support to two ex-wives. Plus, he filed for bankruptcy last year. You sure picked yourself a winner. But hey, Vann's a jock. Maybe he's worth it in the rack."

Laurel's face turned red and her jaw quivered. "Just what do you plan to do with this information?"

"That depends."

"On what?"

Leaning forward, I rested my forearms on my thighs and stared her in the eye. "How truthful I think you've been after I ask you a few questions."

———

"A million dollars?" Kate took another sip of red wine. "Why on earth would Ron Decker pay Laurel that much money to keep quiet about Jake's discovery?"

"Elementary, my dear Kate." I moved the grilled potatoes away from the coals and took a swig of beer. "Decker put his business, or at least a big chunk of it, up for collateral against the loan. He stood to lose his shirt if word about the Spanish fort got out and the state put a stop to the project. Even a long delay would've put him in a serious bind."

Kate tossed Henry's chewed tennis ball toward the back of the fence. We'd switched from baseballs to tennis balls because Henry had developed quite a taste for leather hides. "So Jake told Laurel about the evidence he found on the island, and Laurel told Ron Decker?"

"Yeah," I said, turning the thick sirloin over. "Laurel knew Decker had a bid in on the project. If he got the contract, she wanted a piece of the pie."

"But I thought she and Decker were good friends."

"They were. Friends with benefits every now and then, as it turns out. And Decker stood to benefit nicely from the Dunes, both from the contract and by investing in the project. The Dunes was a surefire winner, and Laurel wanted in on it."

"Or else she would take the news of Jake's discovery to the department head at FSU."

Henry hustled up the steps and dropped the ball at my feet. I kicked the slimy thing back into the yard. "It wasn't exactly a threat, but yeah. Decker talked Laurel into a private partnership and fronted her the money to buy into the Dunes."

Kate opened another beer for me and topped off her wine glass. "But how did Jessie Lofton get dragged into this mess?"

"Decker must've told Angie what he knew about Jake's find, and then Angie persuaded Jessie to get in on the act. She and Jake had had a falling out over their parents' will, remember? My guess is Angie offered her BFF a slice of the pie, too. Jessie used her key to Jake's house and swiped the artifacts and map she showed me before Laurel caught her in the house and made her leave."

"Dang. And then Angie double-crossed her. Some best friend."

"Yeah, but don't forget that Angie knew Jessie and Ron had been lovers ever since Jessie moved in with them after her dad kicked her out. I'd bet my retirement check that Decker was the sperm donor for both Sydni *and* Jessie's unborn kid."

Kate let out a deep sigh. "Why in the world did Jessie hire you in the first place? If they didn't want Jake's discovery to leak out, why tell you?"

"I think that was Angie's idea. She wanted to throw suspicion about Jake's death on Laurel and Ron. Angie knew those two had a thing going. Her main goal all along was to get rid of Ron one way or another and take over the business herself."

"But what was to stop you from going public with the news about the winter fort?"

"Client confidentiality, for one thing. Angie and Jessie knew from Frank that I'm a career Marine. Semper Fi and all that. Plus the fact that I'm a nobody when it comes to archaeology stuff. Who would stop a multimillion-dollar project like the Dunes on the basis of my expertise? Besides that, I would've implicated myself for trespassing and stealing artifacts on private property."

"So, you believe Angie is responsible for killing Jessie and her own husband?"

"I don't think she pulled the trigger or used my KA-BAR, but yeah, I think she hired somebody to do her dirty work."

"Who, her boyfriend?"

"Nope. There's a guy working for Decker Construction who trained as a sniper in the Army. He also served in Iraq with that scumbag outfit, Blackwater. He drives a dark pickup with a tailgate net. He's got a tonneau cover stashed somewhere that he uses whenever he has a sniping gig. My gut tells me he's our man. Now I have to prove it."

"How?"

"Simple. I'll ask Angie."

Chapter 22

————•————

I HAD MY FIRST court-ordered meeting with Bocephus at eight sharp the next morning, and then set out for Destin. I pulled into Angie's driveway around ten thirty and parked with the truck headed back toward Indian Mound Trail.

No cars were in sight. All the kids should have been in school, so that explained the Miata being gone. I hoped Angie's Jag had spent the night inside the garage. It took three tries with the doorbell before Angie answered. She looked like fifty miles of bad road, with puffy dark circles under her bloodshot eyes. She pulled the robe she was wearing tighter around her throat.

"What the hell are you doing here, Mac? I thought you were in jail."

"You must not read the papers, Angie. I promised to be a good little boy and they let me out."

"You bastard. Why did you kill my husband? Ron never did anything to you."

I put on the best smirk I could muster. "I was about to ask you the same question. Why did you kill your husband? His only crime was falling in love with a bitch like you."

I caught her wrist before the open palm reached my face. "Bastard," she hissed again, "let go of me."

I gave the arm a little twist. "Would I like to come in? Why, yes, thank you very much. You lead the way."

"I'll have your goddamn ass arrested for this!" she spat as I tightened the grip on her arm and forced her inside. I kicked the door shut behind us and pushed her along until we reached the kitchen where I forced her to sit on a barstool at the island. I let go of Angie's arm and joined her.

"This is assault and battery and trespassing, you son of a bitch," Angie said, rubbing her arm where I'd gripped it.

"So what? I'm already a murderer, or don't you remember setting me up?"

"I don't know what the hell you're talking about."

"You're lying, Angie. Better watch that tongue of yours or your nose'll start growing."

She spit in my face. "Screw you."

"Not today," I said, wiping my left eye and cheek, "I'm all booked up. Tell me something, did you hire the same goon to kill Ron that you used to kill Jessie?"

"You're crazy, Mac. I didn't kill anybody."

"You knew all about what Jake discovered on Five Mile Island, didn't you? And you knew if they stopped the project, Ron stood to lose the company. You couldn't take the chance of having somebody spill the beans about it, so you had Jessie killed, tried to take me out, and then had Ron snuffed. You wanted it all. You are one greedy woman, Angie Decker."

And then my running lights went out.

I DON'T KNOW HOW long I was out, but when I woke up the back of my head hurt like holy hell. I tried to lift a hand to check for blood, but realized my hands were tied behind my back. My vision was blurry. Everything was spinning. There was a constant humming running through my head.

"He's coming to."

It was a female voice, but I couldn't place it.

"Keep the gun on him. He's not going anywhere."

Male this time, unfamiliar.

It took a few minutes, but my head finally began to clear. It hurt like crazy, but the world had stopped spinning. In another couple of minutes I realized the humming sound was tires against pavement. I was inside a car. I groaned and struggled until I was upright. Angie was sitting next to me in the backseat.

"Wow, nice car. Never rode in a Jag before."

At the sound of my voice, the driver glanced in the rearview mirror. It was Junior. "May as well let your last ride be in style," he said, and grinned.

I didn't like the sound of that *last ride* bit. I glanced out the window and noticed a few landmarks from a couple of days ago. We were headed north on 85. I looked at Angie and saw the barrel of my .357 magnum staring me in the face. I mustered up a grin. "Careful, that thing might go off. I wouldn't want you to hurt yourself."

"Shut up, Mac."

"Hey, Junior, can we go swimming when we get to your place? You got a real nice pool."

Angie's mouth flew open and her eyes widened. "What pool?"

"The one you and Junior were frolicking around in butt naked a couple of days ago."

His eyes filled the mirror again.

"Oh, by the way, since you said this is my last ride, you might be interested to know I took several nice photos of you two. Telephoto lenses sure come in handy. I gave copies to people who'll go right to the cops if something unfortunate should befall me."

Junior glanced over his shoulder and shot me a dirty look. "Don't worry, hon, he's bluffing."

Angie's faced relaxed a little. I decided to up the stakes. "Junior's wrong, hon, I'm not bluffing. That's a real nice tramp stamp you got. I couldn't quite make out what it was, but it sure is colorful."

Her jaw clenched.

"And Junior, well, let's concede Mother Nature was very generous to you in the nether region. Not that I'm jealous. Okay, maybe a little."

Angie leaned forward, her face and neck flushed. "Ken?"

"So what?" Junior said. "Even if he has photos, that doesn't prove he's given copies to anyone. I say he's bluffing."

"Yeah, hon," I said, "maybe I'm bluffing. Or, maybe not."

I'd been working at the rope around my wrists since coming to my senses and was making headway. Whoever did the tie job could stand more practice. "Hey, Junior, if you won't let me go swimming, could we take a horseback ride? I've never ridden a thoroughbred, either."

Angie pointed the revolver back at me. Her hands were shaking like she had the palsy. "Will you please shut the fuck up?"

I took a sharp breath. "Angie! Shame, shame, shame! What would your kids think if they heard you speak that way? And speaking of your kids, how do you think they're going to feel when they find out what their dear sweet mother's been up to?"

"Shut up, Mac."

"And what will they think if they see the photos of their mom screwing around with another man so soon after their poor dad's untimely death?"

Her jaw went slack.

I grinned. "Yeah, I got you two doing the big nasty in living color."

Angie sighed and slumped in the seat. Things were quiet for a while, so I figured I had them both thinking. Meanwhile I kept working at the rope, hoping to get it loose enough so

I could free myself quickly, but not so loose that it would be obvious to Angie and Junior.

By the time the gate swung open and we entered *Alderhaven* I had the rope where I wanted it. As we drove toward the house I tucked the loosened rope in my fist to make it appear tight. Lucky for me, Angie had been staring down at her feet or out the window most of the way and hadn't noticed my fidgeting.

Junior pulled the Jag up to the garage and turned off the engine. He got out while Angie kept the S&W trained on me. He opened my door, grabbed my upper right arm and jerked me out of the car. I strained to keep my wrists tight together.

He reached in a pocket of his sports coat and produced a snub-nosed revolver, probably a .38. "In the house," he said, pushing me forward with the barrel in my back. I climbed the steps to the covered front porch and obediently stood aside as Junior unlocked the door and swung it open. He nodded toward the doorway and followed me inside. Angie closed the door behind her.

"Nice place you got here, Junior," I said, glancing around the open great room. The walls were paneled in rustic cedar, and a rough cedar beam spanned the high-pitched ceiling from stem to stern. On the mantel above a stone fireplace stood several trophies, most topped with a rifleman aiming at an imaginary target. I moved closer to read the inscription on the largest trophy centered on the mantel:

> 1994 NCAA National Rifle Championships
> Men's Gold Medalist
> Kenneth Alderman, Jr.

Alderman waved me away from the fireplace with the pistol before I could read the name of the college. "I see you're handy with a rifle, Junior," I said, light bulbs flashing in my head. "Gold medalist. Wow, I'm impressed."

He prodded me with the pistol barrel toward the kitchen/

dining area. "I did all right for myself. All-conference three years in a row. Now shut your mouth and sit in that chair."

Angie stood behind a chair she'd pulled away from the table. "Thanks for the hospitality," I said as I sat.

Junior grabbed a key ring from a hook on the wall. "I'll be back in a minute," he said. "Keep that gun on him. If he tries anything funny, shoot him."

He exited the kitchen through a back door. Angie stepped closer, waving my heavy revolver in my face. I loosened the grip on the rope and eased it from around my wrists, hoping my legs would block Angie's view as I let it slip to the floor behind me.

"You disappoint me, Angie. How could you let Junior kill your best friend like that?"

Angie's arms drooped with the weight of the big piece. "Best friend? A best friend doesn't screw the other's husband in their own bed while she's out working to put food on the table."

Angie turned loose of the S&W with her left hand. She shook the freed hand while clenching and unclenching her fingers to restore circulation.

"From what I've heard you did your share of screwing around in those days, too."

"Shut up, Mac! I've had about enough of your—"

I lunged out of the chair and karate-chopped Angie's right wrist. A bone snapped and she screamed in pain as my revolver skidded across the kitchen floor. The back door flew open and Junior dashed in. I dove behind the table as the snub-nose barked. My right thigh felt like it had been slammed with a hammer. He fired again, nailing the leg of a chair inches from my head. Damn, he wasn't too bad with a pistol, either.

I reached out and grabbed my revolver, executed a half roll, and got off two quick shots. As the big slug slammed into his right shoulder, Junior spun and dropped to his knees. I scrambled to my knees as he turned and raised the pistol. No time for niceties. The S&W roared again and Junior dropped like a rock.

Chapter 23

———•———

KATE TURNED HER BACK to the cold gust of wind coming off St. George Bay. The auburn tresses not anchored by the wool toboggan cap she wore whipped around and covered her face. It was the first official day of winter, but we'd had unseasonably cold weather for the past two weeks. Not exactly perfect conditions for lot-looking at the Dunes, but I'd promised Kate we'd go on her next day off. She blew hair away from her mouth.

"I almost forgot. Uncle Frank called this morning. He wanted to know why you're not returning his calls."

I pulled my Braves cap tighter on my head and tried to turtle into the sweater and light jacket I wore. "Probably because I still haven't learned how to use that stupid smartphone I bought."

"Dang, Mac, it's not rocket science."

"I guess I'm smartphone challenged." Junior's first shot had smashed into my cellphone in my pants pocket. The phone deflected the round, but bought the farm for its efforts. I missed it like an old friend. Besides, it was a retirement gift from Mike and Megan.

Kate snickered. "No, you're smartphone stubborn and lazy."

I ignored the remark. We stopped along the boardwalk at an overlook between two high dunes. The bay was choppy. Whitecaps danced on the dark water. "What do you think of this one?" I said, noticing Kate gazing at the scenery with a smile on her face.

"I like it. It's a big lot. And wow, look at that view! But can we afford it?"

"What's this 'we' stuff? You got a mouse in your pocket? I'm buying."

Kate poked my chest with a gloved index finger. "I've told you before: I won't be a kept woman. If we do this, it's fifty-fifty all the way."

Never argue with the Fabulous Moolah. We backtracked to the front lot markers where my truck was parked on a paved access road that wound through the dunes on our right. Even here the view was beautiful. Sugar-white sand and tall dunes stretched as far as you could see. Sea oats topping the dunes bent horizontal with the wind.

We decided to walk the perimeter of the lot, Kate heading one way and me the other. My thigh was still a little sore from the deep bruise I suffered when my phone gave up the ghost while saving me from a big-time injury. My mind drifted as I limped along. Only last week had Angie Decker finally given in and plea bargained to two charges of accessory to murder, and one attempted murder—yours truly. A sizeable rifle collection was found in Alderman's house, along with a black Chevy pickup in the garage fitted with a tonneau cover and tailgate net. Angie swore up and down for the month and a half she'd been in jail that the dearly departed Kenneth Alderman Jr was the instigator of the entire plan to kill her husband and take over the company together. I guess Angie's lawyer finally talked some sense into that thick skull of hers.

One of Ron Decker's sisters and her husband assumed responsibility for the kids, Sydni included. The brother-in-law had worked for several years as a foreman for Decker

Construction, and he'd assumed oversight of everyday operations. With Angie most likely spending the next couple of decades in the slammer, the judge ruled as part of the plea bargain that the company be kept in trust and co-owned equally by the children—all four of them. A court-ordered paternity test proved that Ron Decker was indeed Sydni's father.

I kept my word with Laurel Lofton about her involvement with Decker. I hoped she would keep hers, and Jake's boys would someday benefit nicely from the Dunes investment. They'd lost their dad to suicide and didn't need more disruption in their young lives.

As for Zackary Dean, former Army sniper and Blackwater mercenary, he was simply a troubled man attempting to put his life back together through hard, honest work. I wished him well.

The safe deposit box at the First Community Bank of Destin was opened by court order, and the artifacts and map Jessie had stolen were turned over to the FSU Department of Anthropology's Archaeology Division. I was a good boy and added my finds to the collection Jake discovered, claiming I'd found them while walking the beach near the Stumps. I also turned over the flash drive and the decoded message it contained. I told the authorities that Jessie had given the flash drive to me when she hired me—hey, that's my story and I'm sticking to it.

Probably the saddest thing about the entire case was that Jessie Lofton and Ron Decker died for nothing. The area overlooking the Stumps was graciously donated to the state by the Kreuzbergers. They decided the winter fort site would be a windfall for the Dunes, drawing visitors and prospective buyers to the new bayside community.

A preliminary site examination was already underway. I kept my word to Ed Duncan. He and the Emerald Shores Archaeology Society were part of the team of qualified volunteers for the upcoming dig. Once the excavation was completed, the area would become a state historic site. The head honcho of Florida State's anthropology department assured me that Jacob Devon Lofton's name would appear on the historical marker as discoverer of the winter fort site.

The St. George Church of God was constructing a new and bigger facility from the sale of the property Amos Moats had bequeathed to the church. Cherry and Richard were still on the lam.

I snapped back to the present when I bumped head on into Kate standing midway on the northern lot line enjoying the view.

"Dang, Mac, watch where you're going."

"Sorry," I offered. "Well, what do you think?"

Kate smiled, the tip of her tongue showing through the tiny gap between her front teeth. "I love it." She wrapped her arms around me in a bear hug. "How about we go to the sales office?"

I pressed closer. "How about I spend the night?"

Kate pulled my head down, blew her warm breath softly in my ear, and whispered, "*Yo deseo tu cuerpo.*"

I pushed her away to arm's length. "What the hell does that mean?"

She grinned. "You'll find out."

E. MICHAEL HELMS GREW up in Panama City, Florida. Turning down a baseball scholarship offer from the local junior college, he joined the Marines after high school graduation. He served as a rifleman during some of the heaviest fighting of the Vietnam War until wounded three times in one day. He discounts it as "waking up on the wrong side of the foxhole."

Helms's memoir of the war, *The Proud Bastards*, has been called "As powerful and compelling a battlefield memoir as any ever written .... a modern military classic," and remains in print after twenty-five years.

A longtime Civil War buff, Helms is the author of the two-volume historical saga, *Of Blood and Brothers*. Seeking a change from writing about war, he decided to give mysteries a try. The first novel of his Mac McClellan Mystery series, *Deadly Catch*, was published in November 2013, and named Library Journal's "Debut Mystery of the Month." The second Mac McClellan Mystery, *Deadly Ruse*, followed in 2014.

While concentrating on his mystery series, Helms dusted off a manuscript dealing with Post Traumatic Stress Disorder which had sat in his desk drawer for over two decades. *The Private War of Corporal Henson*, an autobiographical fictional sequel to *The Proud Bastards*, was published in August 2014.

With his wife, Karen, Helms lives in the Upstate region of South Carolina in the foothills of the beautiful Blue Ridge Mountains. He enjoys hiking, camping, canoeing, and playing finger-style guitar. He continues to listen as Mac McClellan dictates his latest adventures in his mystery series.

For more information, go to emichaelhelms.com.